THE STRAW MAN

THE STRAW MAN

A NOVEL BY

DANIEL POLIQUIN

TRANSLATED BY

WAYNE GRADY

DOUGLAS & McINTYRE

TORONTO VANCOUVER

99 00 01 02 03   5 4 3 2 1

Douglas & McIntyre Ltd.
2323 Quebec Street, Suite 201
Vancouver, British Columbia
V5T 4S7

Canadian Cataloguing in Publication Data
Poliquin, Daniel
[Homme de paille. English]
The straw man
Translation of: L'homme de paille.
ISBN 1-55054-269-9
I. Grady, Wayne. II. Title. III. Title: Homme de paille. English.
PS8581.O285H6513 1999   C843'.54   C99-932285-0
PQ3919.2.P577H6513 1999

The publisher gratefully acknowledges the support of the Canada Council for
the Arts and of the British Columbia Ministry of Tourism, Small Business and
Culture. The publisher also acknowledges the financial support of the
Government of Canada through the Book Publishing Industry
Development Program.

Canadä

Book design by Michael Solomon
Printed and bound in Canda by Métrolitho
Printed on acid-free paper

To Roger Le Moine, and all the scholars who, without knowing it, made this book.

BOOK ONE
THE STRAW MAN

1

From a distance, he looks like a pale winter sun, a sun rimed with hoarfrost.

He is the troupe's playwright. Voluminously clad in a Pierrot costume surmounted by a huge, wide-brimmed hat, the face beneath it pale and lanthorn-jawed for want of food, he is exhorting passersby with an exuberance that seems to me forced.

"Come one, come all! This way, ladies and gentlemen! Tonight's play, entitled *The Double Inconstancy*, is to be performed at the residence of the Viceroy of New France himself!"

His name is Barnaby. Although he cannot, in truth, set down three words without committing four errors, he hath styled himself an author since he bought an old escrítoíre, three goose quills and a nearly full bottle of ink from an itinerant notary public. The other players humour him, but he maintains, with some celerity, that a theatre without its own playwright is no theatre at all, and that if the war had not brought such shortage of paper, he would be an author of no small moment. He would be a second Molly Air, he says, had he enough paper.

Writing is not his only talent: he is a tumbler, a singer, a player of comedies and pantomimes. He would do tragedies, he avows, if only his colleagues were up to them. And it is he who plays Pierrot in the Italian farces that the troupe performs on slow days, which is to say, every day. Most of all he likes to play the come-hither:

"Ladies and gentlemen!"

I confess I find him wonderful, but perhaps that is because I am the most recent arrival here. The war blew open the doors of the seminary, and out of it I skipped. Now I live to become the troupe's prompter.

No one is listening to Barnaby. The character known to the public as Colombine, who is known to her fellow actors as Jericho, is painting her face for the fourth time today. The troupe's director, Auguste, who plays the Doctor of Bologne and who should be practising at swallowing swords, is washing out his last remaining shirt. Bernard the Bear-Tamer is roasting a cat on a spit, which delicacy he will later share with Telemachus, his bear. At the moment, Telemachus is sleeping in his chains, contentedly dreaming of a full stomach. Ignatius is playing at dice on a tambour with Blaise Corolère, the Public Executioner. Ignatius wants to perform in *The Imaginary Invalid*, but for now he must be content as Pantaloon, receiver of innumerable kicks to the backside. Blaise dreams of one day placing his talent for drawing at the disposal of the troupe, in the hope that he would be less despised as an artist than he is as a hangman.

"Don't wear thyself out, Barnaby," says Auguste. "You know no one is going to come. The bombardments have caused everyone to flee the city. Everyone with money, at any rate."

Barnaby continues as though he hath not heard. It is his belief that if he performs his duties conscientiously, every day, then his inmost desires will be gratified: the English army will decamp, food will flow into the city, the public will be generous again, and the company will finally make enough money to go to Europe, the largest of the continents, where princes compete extravagantly with one another to procure for their courts such talents as he possesses. Mistaking such ideas for reality is the mark of the true writer, he hath confided to me.

"This way, mesdames et messieurs!"

The others leave him to it. What purpose would it serve to remind him that the author of the play he is so enthusiastically proclaiming, a certain Marie Vaux, is unknown even to the governor-general, an old, rich marquis who once lived in Paris? Or to tell him that the copy of the play, purchased by Auguste from an officer in the Guyenne Regiment, is missing half its pages, and that no one therefore knows whether it is a comedy or a tragedy? If only they could do Molière's *Scapin* again, they might have a chance to fill their stomachs. But to do *Scapin* they must needs find a new Capitan.

No one knew his real name. They called him the Captain even though he preferred to be known as Scapin, an honour they refused him on the grounds that he was ever an unremittingly loathsome human being. Granted, they malign him slightly less now since, several nights ago, while the troupe was playing *Scapin*, as it happened, he received an English six-pounder in the head just as he was taking his curtain call before the few people in the audience. He had contrived to be alone on the stage, having performed his role so well, at least in his own estimation, that he disdained to share the glory with the rest of the players. His colleagues grumbled at his fatuousness – he was, at best, a mediocre actor whose most challenging role was arriving at the theatre sober and in time to dress, and thence to remember more than a quarter of his lines without prompting. But when they beheld his bloodied corpse, quite decapitated by the force of the shot, they forgave him a great many sins.

It was not an inconsiderable loss. They had been putting on the play since spring, long before the English fleet had sailed up the river and anchored just below the town. The cannon bullet destroyed not only Le Capitan but also much of the stage, and the audience, furious at having their fine vestments splattered with the Captain's brains, had been the only paying personnages left in the capital. Others arrive carrying a bag of nuts or a crust of bread, or more often nothing at all, but are admitted anyway to create the illusion of a full house. Acting is marginally less depressing that way.

And as if that were not enough, the troupe could find no suitable replacement for the Captain in the pantomimes, either, where he had been the swashbuckler of young demoiselles in distress. He was, of course, even more wretched as this fine character than he was as Scapin, the role of swashbuckler requiring little more than a certain hauteur and a well-cut cloak, but in this country, where any theatre at all is something of a novelty, the Captain could not help but stand out. In an hundred years the students at the seminary have put on Corneille's *El Cid* two or three times, and someone attempted a version of *Tartuffe* once before it was proscribed by the bishop, the Catholic faith having gained in acerbity what it hath lost in proximity to Rome, so much so that Auguste fears he will not be able to bury the Captain in the cemetery, the Church having withdrawn the right to a Christian burial from actors, as is well known.

While discussing these and such like matters, which have the unfortunate effect of evoking the Captain's final bloody exit from the stage, the players, to their surprise, find themselves admitting merits in the old rogue that are no less creditable for their being posthumous. And, it must be said, no less fleeting.

Barnaby briefly interrupts his exhortations to say that all the troupe need do is find another actor whose figure pleases the ladies as well as the gentlemen, dress him up in the Captain's old clothes, feed him his lines as they had been obliged to feed them to the Captain, and the thing is done. Whoever they find for the part will of necessity be a less pretentious braggadocio than his predecessor was, will certainly not regale them with tales of how he once played at Versailles, and how his dear friend the great Farinelli, and so on, than which nothing could be more welcome. The others find the idea attractive, and if I had not set my heart on being their prompter, I would try out for the role myself.

Ignatius, or Pantaloon as he is known, misses the Captain somewhat less than the others. "When we played *The Marriage of Pierrot*," he says, "the bastard would verily smite me with his stick. He very nearly caused me to reconsider my choice of avocation. The audience loved it, of course, but his colleagues, most especially I, bore the bruises of his popularity for weeks afterwards. Once, in Montreal, after a particularly long bout of smiting, I began returning the favour blow for blow, and very soon we were having it out in earnest." He neglects to mention that upon that occasion, the audience laughed so heartily at their antics that the troupe took in the highest receipts of the season.

Bernard the Bear-Tamer, who normally says little about anything, offers the opinion that the Captain's rough-housing usually cost the troupe more in the replacement of damaged properties than it earned them in entrance fees. And that when he was not destroying the set with his ranting, he was doing nothing at all but sleeping the day and getting as drunk as David's sow at night.

Jericho, who plays Colombine, misses him the least of all. None in the company know her real name, but she hath a tale or two about the Captain, the which she hath laid often enough at his door when he was alive but which the others pretended not to hear, the Captain being too useful to them. Now, however, they listen. The Captain, she says, was a brute.

"He ever preferred his pint of jackey to tupping a dearee. Never a kind word, never a flower or a thank-you. He took his women as he found them, whether from behind, standing up, lying down, in their sleep, whenever and however the fancy struck him, without so much as a by your leave." He liked nothing better, she continues hotly, than to rob them of their second maidenhead. "Once he even wagered my virtue in a game of cards with an officer," she says. "Luckily, he won that night. At least he knew how to cheat at cards. Like most of us, playing the whole game was something he learned at his old mother's dairies. Which is why we never play amongst ourselves."

As they listen to her, the other players heave great sighs, chew at their nails, swat at imaginary flies or affix their attention on the smallest mote – in short, do anything to prevent themselves from laughing aloud. Jericho's virtue is the one subject they never discuss openly, because she will sulk for weeks afterwards. There is some truth in what she says, but there is also much that is mere gossip and much more that is unadulterated spite, very little of it being founded on fact. The Captain was never one to be discreet in his liaisons, it is true, but he showed not the slightest interest in Jericho. She is not exactly ugly. She hath a firm body and easily passes for a man when wearing breeches, but her face is badly pocked, for which reason she never goes abroad unpainted. She is fair only on the stage.

When the troupe first arrived in Quebec, it was Jericho who went to the intendant's residence to procure the necessary permission to perform plays within the town's walls. Auguste calculated that she would have better luck with the intendant, who is himself as ugly as sin, smells as evilly as he looks, and whose very name, Bigot, is a disheartenment, than would have been the case with, let us say, the Captain. Bigot heard her out agreeably and then signed the authorization without making a single demand of her, whereupon she marched triumphantly back to the troupe, waving the permit in the company's face and braying loud asides as to how wrongly they had gainsaid Monsieur Bigot, a gentleman who exhibits the proper degree of respect for women of quality. Or at least for actresses who portray them.

Bernard the Bear-Tamer was the only one of the troupe who could tolerate the Captain, whose bravery, like Jericho's beauty, was reserved entirely for the stage. He greatly feared angering Bernard. Bernard is a veritable Hercules, albeit a quiet and gentle one, and is without equal in his ability to teach any trick imaginable to a variety of beasts. He hath placed cats in little harnesses and taught them to pull miniature carts, and trained crows to sing operatic arias. Even monkeys have, at his instigation, become adepts of the violin. Or so he claims. The company hath seen him at his work only with Telemachus, his bear. But the conceit among them is to accept what anyone says without scruple, to refrain from questioning one another about their alleged country of origin, or of the feats they claim to have performed. They guard any doubts they may entertain on certain matters until such time as the informant's back is turned. Or until he is dead.

But they never speak badly of Bernard. They all like him, even Jericho, whose tongue is usually as sharp as an adder's. They rejoice in seeing him dancing with his bear, or watching Telemachus claw at his guitar or turn somersaults, as he hath been taught to do. Auguste would never admit to it aloud, attentive as he is to the sensitivities of his colleagues, but in his opinion Telemachus is the most accomplished tumbler in the troupe. For a price, Bernard will wrestle with his bear upon the stage, and he always wins. Audiences pay well to see these spectacles, especially the men, although there are some who express their doubts as to the authenticity of the performance, often aloud, at which times Bernard invites the doubter onto the stage to wrestle Telemachus himself, if he wishes to ascertain whether or not the bear is shamming. The challenge is never taken up, and the audience is twice pleased to see the hector swallow his own words in humiliation. Sometimes, if the audience is a particularly dull one, Auguste sits in the stalls disguised as a shopkeeper and plays the hector himself. No, the Captain left the bear-tamer alone, excepting when he ate Telemachus's food, which neither Bernard nor the bear appreciated.

None of these malicious calumnies, however, whether they be true or false, fill the void created by the Captain's death; neither could the company put his memory to rest by vilifying it. Ignatius, having gone into town to seek a more literal means of laying the Captain's ghost, hath returned with the information that not a priest in town is acquainted with the papal bull prohibiting burial to actors, so that there need be no trouble on that score. It appears that what faith gains in distance, it also loses through ignorance, fortunately for them. The rub, however, is the dearth of room in the cemeteries. Many are being turned away. Every night new ground must be broken for citizens killed by stray cannon shot, or for soldiers fallen during skirmishes with the English, and their number is daily augmented by an alarming increase in the number of English prisoners dying of disease. Then, too, there are the deserters and thieves, who are nightly hanged from the lynch posts of the town's gates. Even with the Church's blessing, where are they to bury the Captain?

Meanwhile, they have stored the Captain's body in a wooden box that once contained molasses. As its lid cannot be properly closed, it has begun to emit a repellant odour. "Captain smells worse now than he did when he wert alive," observes Ignatius, to which Jericho adds, "How truly it is said, that a dirty dog can shake off fleas, even in death."

Something must be done. In a town weakened by famine, the Captain will soon infect the entire populace. Blaise the Public Executioner has an idea. The next time a bombardment starts a fire in town, he says, they must toss the Captain into it. He will burn thoroughly, and it is a much cleaner method of disposal than the throwing of his body into the river, to wash up who knows where. This way they will be rid of him forever. But even although it is judged a good idea, yet do they hesitate to act upon it, each contemplating the same fate befalling them. It is, they conclude, too like being consigned to the eternal flames of hell. The Captain was a foul-mouthed poltroon, an intemperate swaggerer, but all the same, could they not make some small effort on his behalf? Suddenly the entire troupe finds itself pitying the man, dead though he is.

Ignatius, or Pantaloon, if you will, wins at another game of dice. Corolère is now penniless, and as a means of recouping his losses he offers to take it upon himself to dispose of the corpse. The others are quick to reply: "Thank you all the same, we will take care of him ourselves, you may leave him to us. Trust a hangman to come up with such a solution! And to ask us for money to boot, well..." They have never been overly friendly towards the Executioner, which doth pain him a great deal, they being his dearest and indeed his only friends.

Barnaby is still exhorting non-existent crowds: "Come one,

come all." Nothing, it seems, will induce him to give o'er his infernal refrain. But then, with a sudden start, Telemachus, who hath been sleeping all this while, rises up on his hind legs and claps his great paws together, a trick that his trainer rewards with a morsel of roasted cat. Whereupon Barnaby takes a deep bow and, at long last, exits the stage.

2

AUGUSTE silently applauds Barnaby's long-overdue exit, for the latter's ineffectual barking was gravely interfering with his ability to think.

Though he joined in the general plaint about the Captain, who is now so happily deceased and likely to become an even more appealing topic of discussion when he is finally six feet under ground, it hath been only as a relief from having to contemplate the real difficulties occasioned by the rogue's precipitate death. There is, for example, the undeniable fact that without him the troupe's continued existence is in some doubt. Ham-fisted though he was as an actor, with gestures that ever seemed out of keeping with the action they were meant to convey, his huge frame and wooden sword impressed the vulgar sort. Soldiers saluted him in the street, mistaking him for an officer in his costumed finery, and they kept their distance from the troupe's wagons. Even pious citizens, ordinarily opposed to the theatre, treated the Captain with a measure of respect. However legion were his faults, he attracted audiences, and that was sufficient cause to regret his demise. The troupe must find another Captain, concludes its impresario, and that soon.

But where to find such a one? Auguste's colleagues leave such matters to him, as he is the director. The troupe, in fact, is entirely his creation. None of them had even been a player before they met him, not even Auguste himself. They had, one and all, been either outlaws or on the point of starvation, if not both, for the company came into being just when the famine struck, three years before, at the outbreak of the war.

It started one night in Montreal, when, for the amusement of a group of officers of the Royal-Roussillon Regiment, who seemed at a loss to know the quickest method of spending their pay, an unemployed notary clerk known as Blow-Me-Down, recently discharged from a French regiment, had stood up and begun reciting love poems in any accent requested by his audience, whereupon he passed around his cup and collected a few pennies. His reputation quickly spread, and soon he was invited to other regimental officers' messes. Eventually he took to calling himself Auguste, which name he chose as being more reflective of his recently exalted status than had been his previous *nom de guerre*, which had not served him particularly well.

Shortly thereafter, Auguste chanced to make the acquaintance of a farm labourer who was employed at hawking turnips in rue Saint-Paul. This rusticated young man, dubbed Drunk-as-a-Skunk by his employer, confessed that he would happily sell his sister for a chance to escape from farm work, which he characterized as unrelieved drudgery rewarded by long hours and short wages. Auguste easily persuaded the man to join him and baptized him Ignatius, a Jesuitical name that implied a certain amount of learning.

Ignatius did not immediately take up the role of Pantaloon, but rather made his debut singing coarse ditties in the several taverns frequented by farmers who came into town with the purpose to sell their produce, and stayed when the markets closed with the purpose to drink up their profits. Nor were Auguste and Ignatius above singing psalms in churches, the burden of the matter being that to make ends meet in such times and in such a country one must needs have the widest possible repertoire.

Sometimes they worked separately, as when Ignatius, dressed as a beggar and taking the name Carnaval, sang lewd ballads on street corners to his own rude accompaniment on a Barbary organ. The money rolled in.

Auguste, wishing to emulate his friend's success but judging it too noticeably coincidental for two mendicant musicians to take up their trade in the same street, donned a different disguise and, under the name John of Lent, intoned sacred canticles at the other end of Montreal. If he had hopes of profiting from the religious sentiment that was reportedly rife throughout the country, those hopes were soon dashed. He was accorded alms, yes, but most often they took the form of something to eat rather than that with which to acquire drink, and even such victuals as were tendered were shoved at him with lowered or averted gaze, as though the donors had been shamed into their show of generosity, and knew it. Before long, Auguste began to consider that his poor returns were the result of his poor voice, and his spirits darkened. He became consumed by jealousy, and continuously picked quarrels with poor Ignatius, who was genuinely pained by his companion's lack of success.

Ignatius suggested they change places, insisting that to a good actor there were no bad roles. They would see whether an empty alms can was the result of a want of talent on Auguste's part, or of taste on the part of the public. The idea pleased Auguste: he turned himself into a salacious songman while Ignatius was reborn as a squawking apostle of repentance, whereupon it was Auguste who was offered drinks, and who returned at night with money in his cup, whilst Ignatius had little to show for his labours but a few crusts of hard bread. Thus did our confederates learn that the public will spend more copiously for the well-being of their bodies than for the health of their souls, and for the attainment of the latter they would, in any case, far rather pray than pay.

Carnaval and John of Lent, satisfied that their talents would stand them in good stead through fortune or misery, decided to remain together. They alternated their roles, shared their takings equally, and expanded their repertoire, to the great delight of their auditors. It was a superb beginning.

One day, however, there appeared in Montreal a tamer of

bears, who came up from New York, or perhaps Boston, I forget which, except that he had travelled a great distance and his name was Bernard. Very soon the entire town was in his thrall, and his was the only act anyone wanted to see. His alms can filled up faster than an ale-house chamber pot, and John of Lent and Carnaval perceived that a change of air was called for.

On the road to Trois-Rivières, they were accosted by what they at first thought to be a man with the voice of a woman. "Take me with you, I pray thee!" exclaimed the apparition. "I have put my life at risk to follow you! I can be of use to you, you will see. I can sing, I can commit an extraordinary number of perfectly useless things to heart, and with a little paint I can be quite pretty. Ever since I heard you singing from my bedroom window, it hath been my ardent desire to follow in your noble profession. I beg of you, take me with you. You are my last straw!"

Auguste was the first to apprehend that the ragged figure standing before them was that of a woman and, recovering from the astonishment into which the contrast between her voice and appearance had plunged him, though still at a loss to know quite what to say, asked her whether she knew how to sew and cook, to which she responded haughtily that she held such housewifely occupations in the lowest possible regard, that she had been born to be an actress, or a countess, or possibly both, since they often amounted to the same thing.

Ignatius did himself then respond in a manner that precipitated its own chain of reactions. Assuming an idiotic smile, he endeavoured to assure himself that their new acquaintance was indeed of the female sex, by insinuating his hands into the folds of her garment. The woman knocked him to the ground with a single blow. He regained his senses in time to hear Auguste engaging her on the spot, having reasoned that a woman of such a fiery temperament would prove useful in their travels, though she knew nothing of acting.

There are those who maintain, myself among them, that

women exert a civilizing influence, and that it is not well for men to be left too long without female companionship, and here is certainly a case in point, since it is true that John of Lent and Carnaval underwent a profound improvement of their characters as a consequence of their acquaintance with this pugnacious woman.

By seeking atonement for the unseemliness of his initial exploratory contact with the woman, Ignatius discovered in her company a flare for gallantry and even a modicum of courage that had hitherto escaped his notice. He would often push away from her the importunate foot-soldiers, or farmers reeking of garlic and manure, that a woman of her station tends to attract. Auguste, for his part, and in like wise, lost some of his soldierly ways. Before the woman entered their lives, the two men would open their flies to piss wherever the urge came upon them. Now, they desported themselves as modestly as did she, and when nature called, they excused themselves politely, turned to one side, and resumed the conversation without remarking upon the circumstances of their withdrawal from it, just as they imagined the better sort might do. And they took barely two years to learn such refined behaviour.

Auguste, moreover, knew that it was to the woman that he owed his position as director, for under normal circumstances he would have been as precipitous in his amorous advances as Ignatius had been, and indeed would have pressed his investigation even farther had not the latter beaten him to it. The woman, however, mistook his hesitation for gallantry, it being well and truly said that the sins we commit often lower us in the eyes of those who see us punished for them, while those that fail to occur to us may infer upon us an unexpected advantage. Thus did the newcomer take it into her head that Auguste must needs be a good and wise gentleman, loath to affront a lady's modesty, and quick to help a fallen companion to his feet without reproaching the lady who had knocked him down. Her introduction to the troupe thus elevated Auguste, while it demoted Ignatius forever in her estimation.

She, it must be said, underwent a similar improvement. From nothing, she rose to the exalted title of comedienne, and discovered in herself a true genius for the stage. There hath, moreover, been a notable change in her comportment *vis-à-vis* the opposite sex: now, when she passes wind she merely laughs, and when a drunken admirer presses his case too insistently she is more likely to swear at him than to tear off his head.

Before she took the name Colombine, she had been called Jericho. When she joined the troupe, her head had been shaved, a common punishment accorded to cut-purses and prostitutes. Jericho was a wing of the General Hospital of Our Mother of Youville, in Montreal — a dozen rooms under the eaves of the hospital set aside for the confinement of former whores, thieves and other miscreants. Before that, they had been housed in a building surrounded by a high stone wall that recalled to the minds of the district's more pious inhabitants the crumbling walls of Jericho, and the name had been transferred to their new quarters in the hospital.

To be kept by the Grey Nuns was not necessarily a commendation. The hospitallers had taken their popular name from the circumstance of their founder, Madame d'Youville, who had been married to a man who sold brandy to the Indians. In the early days of their order, stories circulated that these Sisters of Charity, as they were properly called, celebrated the sabbath by drinking like *coureurs de bois*. It is not known what misdemeanour caused Jericho to be taken into their custody. She never spoke about it, nor, as I have indicated, do the members of the company press her on the matter. Of one thing I am certain, however: she was not confined for peddling her virtue in the streets like a common squirrel, since hardly a day goes by that she doth not remind her companions that her maidenhead is intact, and that she would never join giblets with a man who is not prepared to marry and take her out of New France. She may have been a canter, or she may have used the Lord's name in vain, since it did not require a grave crime to end up with the Grey Nuns. She doth not object to being called Jericho – by her fellow actors, it must be said, for she will not abide being so appellated by strangers – perchance because it reminds her that on at least one occasion in her life she had the courage to run away.

The three did not yet know that they would become a troupe of strolling players. For one thing, they did not have a play to perform. They soon found one, however, and in this wise. It was in Trois-Rivières, as it happened, on the eleventh day of June. Had they met the man the day before, they would have called him Guy, but since they made his acquaintance on the eleventh, the feast-day of Saint Barnaby, that was the name he gave them when he presented himself. He was the scion of a noble French family whose indiscretions in that country had caused him to be exiled to Canada. For a length of time he had turned his hand to teaching in schools up and down the St. Lawrence River, but having been dismissed from that occupation after repeated charges of intemperance, not to say debauchery, he prevailed upon the few contacts that remained to him to have himself appointed secretary at Fort Frontenac. That position, alas, suited him all too well, since he was a genius at figures: on the day he chanced upon our three adventurers he had just been released from prison.

It was seeing the three of them strolling along the quayside that first gave him the idea of forming a troupe of Elsibeth players in search of an audience. Instinctively recognizing leadership qualities in Auguste, and taking advantage of the fact that the latter had turned his back to scratch his private parts, Barnaby saluted Auguste with a low bow. "Good master," he said. The others, impressed by a man who possessed such good manners and a flare for servility, judged that he must needs be learned. Anyone, they reasoned, who behaved in such a way must have a great many of books in him.

He was skilled at talking, at least. He asked questions and provided answers with the enthusiasm of one who hath determined to pull his chair up to the table of society and eat his fill.

"You are players, are you not? I could see it immediately. What do you play? Italian pantomimes? Exactly as I thought. Do you perhaps need a Pierrot, then? If so, I am your man. I know every line of Pierrot's by heart. You, sir, must play the Doctor? You have the physique for it, no doubt about that. And you must be Pantaloon. I trust that I do not deceive myself: your ears appear to have been made for being boxed. And thou, my dear lady, thou art the very soul of Colombine. Oh, yes, I know it, I am never wrong about such things. Oh, I prithee, may I not be your Pierrot?"

Auguste, who was taken completely by surprise, cleared his throat as a means of hiding his delight.

"Yes, yes, we are well and truly actors. We have just this day formed our little troupe, and are indeed in search of a man of letters. We need, sir, someone who can write. I hasten to add, although I hardly think it necessary to do so, that the position is not well remunerated. It requires devotion. It demands character. Art thou absolutely certain that thou hast it within thee to live such a life, to suffer such hardship and privation for the sake of the theatre?"

The newcomer was inwardly anxious that the troupe wanted none of him, whereas Auguste feared that in his appeal he had laid on with too thick a brush, and that his words had had the opposite effect of discouraging this handsome youth, whose sudden appearance seemed too fortunate to be credited. The two men fell into a deliberating silence, each attempting to regain his countenance.

Without forethought, as usual, Ignatius broke the spell by inquiring of the newcomer whether he knew any plays. Upon a twinkling the future Barnaby rattled off a list of scribblers' names with such alacrity that the hearts of his listeners fluttered with excitement. On his fingers he counted Molière, Aristophanes, Racine, Euripides, Shakespeare, Corneille, Sophocles — names the troupe had never heard in their lives but which they thought must be very important if their reputations were known to Barnaby. He also mentioned Harlequin and Scaramouche.

Again Ignatius demonstrated his talent for frankly owning to an ignorance that the others were concerned to hide.

"Who, pray, are they?" he asked. At which Barnaby recounted to them the story of Pierrot's love for Colombine, of Harlequin's antics, of the Captain's courage and the asinine brayings of Pantaloon. The three auditors were captivated on the spot, especially Jericho, who promptly dropped to her knees before Auguste and begged him to engage this veritable fountain of knowledge with which Providence had so thoughtfully provided them. And since, as I have noticed before now, a play in which all is well that ends well is most pleasing to those for whom things are not well at all and will probably end worse, Auguste complied with a great show of benificence.

A few days later, the players presented their first pantomime on the quayside of Trois-Rivières. It was very well received: they took in three louies, two bent piastres and twenty sous, enough to keep them in food for four days, or in drink for one.

That, at least, is how I heard the story, I who want nothing more than to be the troupe's prompter, and who asks nothing more than that you, benevolent readers, believe in my tale from the beginning.

3

WE seldom thought about the war in those days. Skirmishes were frequent, we heard, but were conducted without anything like real passion. We were apprised that a certain ensign by the name of Jumonville had been killed in a cowardly fashion by a certain major named Washington, but the incident took place at so far a remove from us that we simply received the news, observed that the major in question was indeed a pig, and thought no more about it. In like manner we learned that the Acadians had been uprooted from their farms and transported a great distance from their homeland, so great a distance in fact that no one knew what had become of them. Acadian refugees occasionally turned up in Montreal, in Trois-Rivières, and in Quebec; they looked as though they carried a great burden of misery, and we felt pity towards them, but that was all. The war was an abstraction, a word with an assortment of meanings, none of which had very much to do with us.

Certain among us were even of the opinion that, if war indeed there were, it were folly in us to complain about it. War is a good enterprise for those who do not happen to be caught up in it, and countless merchants have enriched themselves by provisioning the troops, and ask nothing more from us than that we entertain them with amusing spectacles. Added to their number are the French officers, who will spend any sum to dispel the boredom of their routine. And there are others, as well, persons of high social rank, who would laugh at a post and pay handsomely for the privilege.

Auguste's strolling players profited from each case. Following their first performance on the quayside, the governor of Trois-Rivières retained their services to amuse a visiting count-colonel who was pining for Versailles. They were then invited to the residence of the governor of Montreal, but for that they had to wait until Jericho's hair grew longer, since she was afraid of being recognized by the Grey Nuns and forced to earn her assumed name a second time.

Their success at the governor's residence was resounding – His Excellency was seen to fall asleep only once, during the recitation of a scene from *Phaedra* – and the players were honoured to receive an invitation to join forces with none other than Bernard the Bear-Tamer, the same who had earlier eclipsed John of Lent and Carnaval in that town. Bernard's fortunes had declined; he had lost his companion, a bear from the Pyrenees that had taken him years to train, and with whom he had travelled the length and breadth of Europe, from Aragon to Navarre. The ungrateful wretch, thinking only of his own interest and not in the least mindful of his master's, had run off into the woods with a Canadian she-bear. Bernard was busily training a new one, a native species this time, a less talented but more obedient pupil than his predecessor had been. In the meantime, he had to live. The strollers took him on: there were now five players in the company, not counting the bear.

Bernard was something of a magician into the bargain. He could make a thief's face appear in a mirror by the employment of certain alchemical powders and a crucifix. He also knew how to fashion a shoulder-knot, a device to rob bridegrooms of their potency. Such arcane sorcerer's tricks, however, could send one to the galleys in Canada or the gallows in Europe, and so Bernard disclosed only his more harmless accomplishments to the troupe. How to swallow a sword, or nails, or fire, or rum bottles; how to make coins or pigeons appear from behind an ear or under a skirt; how to make birds and puppets seem to talk; in brief, how to marvel a rude audience without either inducing pain in them or arousing their desire to induce pain in the players.

The players were quick at learning new roles. Jericho acquired the art of ventriloquy, and now plays the part of a wizened singer of carnavalesques. Ignatius, who assumed the role of Pantaloon in Trois-Rivières, now also juggles balls, hen's eggs and even kittens. Barnaby has honed his skill as a barker and has learned to somersault. Auguste can swallow an officer's rapier as though he hath been at it all his life.

Their fame spread all the way to Quebec, and thither did they follow it. They perhaps ought not to have, for it was in Quebec that they made the acquaintance of the infamous Captain.

They were invited to perform at the Château-Richer, the residence of Intendant Bigot, who was desirous of amusing the governor-general, the Marquis de Vaudreuil, and the commander-in-chief of the army, also a marquis, by the name of Montcalm, in celebration of the taking of Fort William Henry. The players chose an extract from a tragedy by Corneille, a bit of a comedy of Molière's, followed by a brief pantaloonade. Barnaby had not yet styled himself an Author, and so the troupe could perform only what plays he could find ready to hand. Sometimes they made up little parlour-comedies, which the future playwright would later exantlate from his increasingly fertile memory.

They were nonetheless loudly applauded at the intendant's residence, and the purse was a handsome one. After the performance, Ignatius, disguised in the uniform of a naval officer, fell in among a group of card players which the intendant never failed to keep at hand. With the aid of Jericho, who, newly painted, made outrageously flirtatious innuendoes at all the prominent personages seated around the card table, Ignatius raked in a cool five hundred pounds before the night was out, a sum he divided equally amongst the other members of the troupe, players being honest amongst themselves, at least.

The following day, they repeated their soliloquys and tumbling acts on the streets of Quebec, after which their profit was again such that, as calculated by Auguste, if they continued in likewise manner they would be able to return to France in a mere eight years. One member of the crowd, however, had not applauded with the others. He followed the actors with his eyes, but refrained from laughing at their antics or puzzling over their magic tricks. He seemed to like the bear, but that was all.

The players could not have been aware that the man in question was a former secretary in the king's navy who, having set sail for Martinique, and having met with extremely contrary winds during his crossing, had fetched up in Quebec with neither a job nor the prospects of finding one. His secretarial post had been revoked when he was discovered to have lost at the gaming tables the ship's entire purse, which had been confided into his trust. The only reason he had not been arrested was that everyone else in the ship's company had spent nearly as much of the king's money as had he. He was thus looking for a new employment, and living on the occasional charity of strangers in the meanwhile.

Having remarked the odd behaviour of this singular specta-
tor, Jericho, something disquieted in mind, set out after the performance to find him. An hour later the troupe was sitting at his
feet. Unlike Barnaby, who had secured his engagement by inces-
sant blandishments, this new addition seemed about to obtain
his through misprision.

From the start, they took the man's fluidity of diction for
genius, and accepted his disdain for humanity as a pardonable
idiosyncrasy. He told them that he, too, had been a player in his
time, in Paris and Venice, that he enjoyed the acquaintance of
the Duke of Such-and-Such and the Marquis of So-and-So. At
last, thought Jericho, a man of enlightenment.

"How," she asked him aloud, "did you find our performance
today?"

"Very bad, sir, very bad indeed! Pardon me, madame. You
make up the better part of your lines, none of you knows the
first thing about acting, you mumble and mutter, and your acro-
batics are such as would amuse none but the most abjectly
dispirited. Your only salvation lies in the utter and irremediable
stupidity of your audience, which, by my troth, would be slack-
jawed at the spectacle of a cow lifting its tail."

Upon delivering himself of this contumely, the man was
besieged by the troupe, who begged him to join them. They
gave him supper. They offered him the driest corner of their
new wagon in which to sleep. They fitted him for a fine costume.
The tumblers throve on the viciousness of the man's criticisms.
It might almost be said that the players were so insufficiently
confident of their talent that they asked nothing better than to
be punished as imposters and mountebanks. Bernard alone
among them attached not the slightest significance to the man's
vituperations.

And so it was that, after several such days, the worthy gentleman who was so knowledgeable in the ways of the world
deigned to accommodate his hosts by allowing himself to be
selected for the role of the Capitan. It would not be inaccurate

of me to say that the man had not so much been engaged by the company, as that he himself had taken the company under his wing. Among the first of his changes was to reconstruct every piece that poor Barnaby had painstakingly composed from memory. He changed lines to conform to his own fancy, and when a certain scene sounded clumsy or lame, it was of course Barnaby who was blamed for it. Jericho, more than any of the others, hung on each of the Captain's criticisms as though they had been carved on the tablets on Mount Sinai. Auguste, for his part, was less enamoured of the newcomer, but he kept his own counsel, not merely because he, like the others, had at least partially fallen under the spell of the Captain's caustic manner, but also because he knew that audiences prize bombast above all else. Especially in the matter of costumes. It was only after his death that the others felt able to dwell on the extent of his shortcomings. This in itself is worthy of remark, as an instance of a truth once observed by the English poet who said that

The evil that men do lives after them,
But the good is oft interrèd with their bones...

There is another way in which the Captain was of use to the troupe, for by listening to accounts of his numerous exploits in the great metropolis, the players were able to imagine their future lives, by the projection of his past life onto their dreams of travelling to Paris. At first it was to please the Captain that they strove to uplift themselves to his exalted level. Then it was from a desire to shock the public, a favourite pastime of the false evangel who had come to them from such a distance. Finally, it was to out-do the Captain himself, and perchance thereby to shut him up.

Thus it is that Auguste became a former officer and a member of the lesser nobility, who participates in theatrical performances for his own amusement and directs this his small troupe out of charity for those less fortunate or talented than himself.

Barnaby is a well-known author of plays, whose self-imposed exile from Versailles is daily remarked upon. Ignatius hath arrived in New France fresh from a leading role in *The Imaginary Invalid*. Jericho was the Captain's prize protégée: it is very heaven to hear her, surrounded by admirers, describe how she was born to a troupe of strolling players in Spain and accompanied them to the New World, since when she hath played *Andromaque* in command performances before the Governor of Montevideo, the Alcade of Buenos Aires and the Viceroy of Brazil in Rio de Janeiro. The more she inflates her list of accomplishments, the more she is adored. She is intimate with Mexico, knows Louisiana like the back of her hand, frequently visits the West Indies and New England. Wherever she performs she is extravagantly celebrated; only in New France do her prodigious talents remain underappreciated.

Lately the players speak more and more about returning to Europe now that the war hath reached the walls of Quebec. Indeed, they talk of little else. Auguste and Barnaby long to return because they were born there; Ignatius and Jericho long to go there because they were born here. Everyone dreams of success in a land where people pay in hard currency to enter a theatre; they also understand that nostalgia for the Mother Country is an undeniable sign of nobility in a colony.

It was the Captain whose happy thought it was to mount plays for the edification of the pious members of the public. In Montreal, his idea took the form of a Passion-play to be staged, at Easter, before the Fathers of Saint-Sulpice. A real Mystery play, complete with Jesus, Roman soldiers, wicked Pharisees and weeping saints.

The Passion was instantly popular, and soon occupied a privileged and profitable place in the troupe's repertoire. Barnaby played Pontius Pilate and all the Romans, which accorded him a certain amount of respect; Ignatius was Barabbas and the rest of the Jews, for which he was roundly pelted with stones and dead rats during each performance, a reception to which he was well accustomed, having played Pantaloon in the Italian farces; Auguste took advantage of his position as director to give himself all the dignified roles, such as Simon of Cyrene and the apostle John; the female roles fell, naturally, to Jericho, who loved to play the Virgin Mary and Saint Veronica because, she felt, she was more beautiful when she suffered. Even Bernard the Bear-Tamer had his parts, mostly those with no lines, such as those of the Executioner and the Roman soldier, and he also assisted by holding the cross steady while the others nailed the Messiah to it. The Captain made a passable Christ.

The Passion, as I've said, took Montreal and Trois-Rivières by storm, but it was a complete flop here in Quebec. It opened on the morning of Good Friday last, and I intend no exaggeration when I say it was a dismal failure. In order to ingratiate the company with the clergy, Auguste had offered free admission to all Jesuits and students of the seminary, at which I was then a student. It was the first time I saw them play, and I never went back.

The Captain had drunk too much the night before, as usual, and forgotten all his lines. Before allowing himself to be hoisted onto the cross, he dealt Barnaby, dressed as a Roman centurion, a ringing blow to the head for having laid on the whip too heavily, in his befuddled estimation, during the ascent to Calvary. Only the other players noticed this vicious rebuff on the part of He who preached the turning of the other cheek. But when He was crucified, His arms bound along the cross-trees, He sobered up quickly enough when he saw how poorly constructed was the seating for the heavy post in the stage floor, and trussed as He was, He was unable to protect Himself when the whole construction fell, face forward, onto the stage.

Christ swore like a trooper, and this time the audience heard Him. The others tried their best to stand Him up again, His face covered in blood, but the faulty seating would obviously not hold a second time, and the Black Robes in the nearer seats began to shift about in a decidedly nervous fashion. Especially when the Pharisee, Ignatius, whispered loudly to Our Saviour, "Oh, Christ, we do require a miracle to save our play!" At a slightly less audible prompt from Saint Veronica, Bernard, who is as strong as his bear, left off gaping and grabbed at the swaying cross, and held it upright for the remainder of the play. During the applause that followed, however, he released his hold to take his bow, whereupon Christ descended again, still affixed to the Cross, but this time backwards and off the stage entirely. He stayed down for the next three days.

Upon the third day, Easter Sunday, he rose from the bed and fetched Jericho's ears a mighty box for having laughed at his double fall. (In truth he fell three times, the third when he was being placed in his tomb, still unconscious from his second fall: Ignatius and Auguste had been laughing so hard themselves that they had let Christ's body slip through their hands.) Then he berated Bernard for not properly holding onto the cross, though he did not press this matter, being mindful of the bear.

The students had also laughed loud and long at Christ's Passion, and the Jesuits chased the players from the seminary like so many money-changers from the temple. Their misfortune dates from that Easter. Their misery is truly pitiful to behold, and I have vowed never to leave them.

4

THAT spring, the company returned to Quebec with money jingling in their pockets after a triumphal tour of the villages along the St. Lawrence, from Baie Saint-Paul on the north shore to Rimouski on the south. They felt almost rich. Back in town, however, they found that they had become objects of scorn.

The townspeople muttered about them, calling them beggars in fancy dress. The war was their fault; it was they who brought famine to the town. The Recollets preached from their pulpits that the players committed a sacrilege by performing their mock Passion for the amusement of the Jesuits. Street urchins followed at their heels, hurling abuse. Shopkeepers bruited it about that Jericho was Intendant Bigot's mistress, a slander she found flattering until, upon betaking herself to Hotel Dieu to have a canker in her mouth lanced, she was turned away by the Augustinian Sisters and told not to come back until she had mended her ways. She imagined herself to be the victim of an organized religious persecution, of which she was as proud as she had been of being the grist in the shopkeepers' rumour mill.

The situation worsened when General Wolfe chose that time, around the middle of June, to show up at Quebec with two hundred ships of the line, one thousand of cannons and thirty thousand of foot soldiers and marines. The players, having so recently basked in the public esteem and admiration, are sunk into a despondency by this new campaign against them. Pantaloon, it is put out, is a mere drunkard; Pierrot a seducer of young boys; the Doctor of Bologne is not a real doctor but a charlatan; Telemachus the bear devours little children; and Colombine, when viewed at close range, clearly hath the pox.

Since they cannot leave the town, it having virtually been placed under siege by the English, the company hath reluctantly accepted the hospitality of the Public Executioner, Blaise Corolère, who is the only personage in town more universally despised than themselves. Reviling the hangman is an ancient tradition, having crossed the Atlantic along with another fine European tradition, that of swift and blind justice. Corolère hath no need to inquire into the sufferings of the outcast artists, as he already knows what such misery is.

Although none do admire a hangman, a more admirable fellow than Blaise there could not be, for there is not another executioner in the world of a pleasanter disposition. With a full head of blond hair, ringlets fairly tumbling over his temples, he is the very image of John the Baptist's lamb. His beardless face, his ruddy cheeks, his eyes of such a pure blue that, looking into them, one can easily imagine that one is reading in them his very thoughts. He is loathsome only when he dons his hood of office, and even then he is the only hangman of anyone's experience to have taken up his hateful profession out of love for a woman.

Before the war, he was a drummer in the grenadier and gunner company, and as such was much favoured by his comrades at arms, being one of the unluckiest card players in the colonial army. His favourite tavern was the Golden Dog, whose landlord had a daughter who was as comely a wench as could be found, and who made mongrel eyes at Blaise, promising to give him that as would make his drumsticks hop the next time he was off duty. Not long thereafter, however, Blaise had words with a corporal of the guard who boasted, I doubt not with good cause, that he had already lain with her, and that she was a light-heeled hoyden, whereupon the next day, Blaise was arrested for insulting a superior and was sentenced to a year in prison and two hundred strokes of the paddle.

In gaol, he met Marie Laurent, an orphan of thirty years of age who had taken up the profession of midwifery since, with her family, she had been deported from Grand Pré. Her only crime appears to have been that of being Acadian. The good people of Quebec do not welcome Acadian refugees, since Acadians can lay legitimate claim to having suffered more outrageously at the hands of the English than have the good people of Quebec. By enduring the Great Derangement, Acadians have ascended to occupy the highest moral ground, which occupation is deeply resented in Quebec, itself having merely been dragged down by hunger and war. Administrator Hébert, who was allotted funds to facilitate the establishment of Acadian refugees in New France, spent the money to pay his gambling debts to Intendant Bigot. Too bad, then, if the Acadians are dying of hunger and cold, according to the general sentiment in Quebec; they will find no pity from this quarter. We have had our own share of misery.

Upon her arrival in Quebec, Marie performed abortions for the wives and daughters of the bourgeoisie, and had from time to time trysted with soldiers to procure for herself a meal or a night out of the cold. Few there are in this town who can blame her for that, but when she took to thieving, she was sentenced to hang. At the time Blaise made her acquaintance in the prison, the authorities were waiting to find a new hangman, the previous executioner, a Negro from Martinique, having recently died of cold and loneliness. Marie knew several things to her advantage, one being that the governor would grant a pardon to any prisoner who took up the post of hangman. She also knew that no woman worthy of the name would take a hangman for a husband. For the unfortunate Negro, the authorities had had to fetch hither a woman of Louisiana, a tall and beautiful Negress named Angélique, who arrived at Quebec only to discover herself a widow before she had become a wife, and who had subsequently been sold to his worship Master Hébert as a house slave. But Marie also knew that it was permitted for a hangman to marry a condemned woman, which woman would then also be granted a pardon.

His first night in prison, Marie asked the obliging young drummer if he would be kind enough to hold a sheet around her while she changed into her nightshirt, not omitting, if it please him, to avert his gaze. The next morning, Blaise applied for the post of Public Executioner of Canada, and the morning after that, he and Marie Laurent were married.

He had talked himself into it, but by means of an argument unanticipated by Marie, who naturally did not know his true nature at so early a stage in their acquaintance. Certainly he desired his freedom, but he knew that once he took up the post of executioner, his first duty would be to whip Marie Laurent, stripped naked and in full view in the public square, and then to hang her by the neck until she was dead. This he scrupled to do. He would never admit it to himself, but he would do almost anything to be loved, or even liked, a weakness very nearly universal in men, though the least admitted.

Alas, there was no grand passion between Marie and the hangman. Indeed, before the marriage knot was long tied, she told him forthwith that she had wedded for no reason other than to effect her release from prison, and that that end having then been attained, she knew no more pressing desire than to expand the horizon of her liberty to include the very borders of the colony. She would lie with him, she said, when there was no one else to lie withal, but she would not compromise her freedom to such an extent as to lie with him exclusively. She demonstrated her sincerity in this by taking up with her former paramour, a sergeant in the regular army who, quite naturally, prefers not to be seen going out with her; nonetheless, Blaise spends a considerable amount of time alone, consoling himself as best he can. It hath come to this, then: a kind man, a good man, despised of his neighbours and hornified by his wife.

And that is by no means the end of it, for the truth is that Blaise Corolère is the worst executioner that New France, or indeed any other country, for aught I know, could have. Though he is quite skilled, none more so in the colony, at erecting a scaffold, and is punctilious in his other duties, such as announcing that a hanging is to take place on such-and-such a day at such-and-such an hour, his military training having instilled in him a conscientiousness, not to say a fastidiousness, that is useful in a public functionary, yet when it comes to the actual execution of his office, if my readers will pardon the expression, his finer capabilities desert him and his performance is, to set it down as charitably as I can, unlaudable.

To hang a man well is not an easy task. It is first necessary that your client proceed you up the ladder to the staging, a thing not easily accomplished, since a condemned man is rarely of sufficiently repentant a frame of mind that he will leap to his doom in a spritely and obliging manner. Once the platform is achieved, however, it is then essential to knot the cord tightly about your man's neck, and Blaise is not a proficient knotsman. He is, moreover, frequently seized with convulsions, to such an extent that on two occasions his clients have inadvertently slipped through the noose and tumbled to the ground, their would-be executioner in close attendance, to the great amusement of the onlookers. Once the noose is tied properly, the hangman, accustomed to embracing only persons of the opposite sex, must then push his client off the scaffold and, in order to hasten strangulation, either deal him a succession of stout kicks to the chest or, such dealings proving ineffectual, hang with his client by the method of clasping him about the shoulders or by the knees and jumping off the platform with him. As it commonly requires thirty or more minutes to strangle a man depended by the neck in this fashion, it can rightly be said that a hangman's job can weigh heavily on his conscience. Blaise lies awake in his bed for nights before an execution, for fear of dreaming, and for weeks afterwards is unable to leave his lodgings, and, when he doth go abroad, is wounded deeply by every sharp word flung at him in the street. It need hardly be added that he further detests his obligation to pierce the tongues of clients convicted of blasphemy.

With a view to becoming more proficient in his occupation, by which I mean to give his executions a more humanitarian flavour, Blaise has taken up the study of human anatomy. And though, enthralled as he is by his venturesome forays into the realm of pure science, yet will he baulk at the application of it in real life. And so it is that, unbeknownst to the good burghers of Quebec, the greater part of the executions in the colony are now performed by Marie, dressed in Blaise's cowl and leather accoutrements, a charade that began on a day when Blaise was required to hang a young girl of twelve years of age for the crime of having stolen a loaf of bread from the Recollets, which the prelates had intended for the preparation of hosts for Holy Communion. The very thought of fulfilling this obligation turned Blaise's hair white overnight.

Marie took pity on him and offered to replace him on condition that their subterfuge remain a secret. She hath a facility with sufferers, born of long familiarity with suffering herself. Thus, spurned as an Acadian under ordinary circumstances and despised as a hangman while performing in the role of her husband, Marie Laurent perfectly demonstrates the low regard in which both immigrants and artists are held in this province.

She attends to almost all the hangings now. If the condemned is very heavy, or makes much difficulty, Blaise will come back into service and do the best he can, but only after his wife has administered some drug or other to calm the patient and relieve his suffering.

The same for torturings. One day, Blaise fell down in a dead faint while attempting to brand the letter G on a man condemned to the galleys for having raped two young girls in Cap-Rouge. Marie took his place once again. After that, Blaise was barely able to maintain his composure unless the matter involved monstrous criminals who deserved their punishment a thousand times over; in cases where the punishment was out of all proportion to the crime, he remained entirely useless. Especially when it came to women.

Only once was he obliged to make an exception. The client in this case was none other than the beautiful Angélique, the Negress who had been sold to his worship Master Hébert at the death of the former executioner. She was to be branded for theft; she had stolen from her master a packet of sugared almonds and a bottle of Port, with which she desired to make a present to her lover, a sailor who had, by the time of her arrest, already fled the country after having relieved her of all that remained of her virtue. The hangman was required by law to place a branded fleur-de-lys on the woman's cheek, as a signal of her crime.

Marie Laurent, still mindful of the evil that Master Hébert had visited upon the Acadians, refused to take her husband's place. Giving satisfaction to that vile man, she declared, would be like unto allowing her own sister to be violated. No, this time she would not come to her husband's aid. He was therefore obliged to overcome his repugnance and enfloriate the beautiful Negress's cheek himself, and was violently ill for two days thereafter. This episode was not, however, without its consequences.

As it is the executioner's duty to dress the wounds of his victims, Blaise visited Angélique daily in prison for that purpose, and it was inevitable that he should fall in love with her and she with him, he being prostrate with anguish at the blemish he was compelled to inflict on her otherwise flawless features. He is thus her stigmatum; she is his remorse. An executioner falling for his victim, and the victim falling in return, is not as unusual, innocent reader, as you may suppose.

The Negress had not been condemned to the gallows for her crime because she was a slave and was therefore of some marketable value, and the intention was to resell her to the plantation in Louisiana from which she had been transported. To prevent this, Blaise gathered all his savings and Marie contributed the money she had earned by performing abortions, and the two together purchased Angélique and promptly bestowed upon her her freedom.

Since then the three have formed a proper unholy trinity. The Negress hath taken the name of Fleurdelysse and taught Marie the black art of making African potions that have the power either to kill the living or revive the dead. Marie, who knows the secret of making the beast with two backs without running the risk of conception, imparted this knowledge to Fleurdelysse, to the great delight of Blaise. The women have yet, however, to discover a means whereby to render Blaise a competent hangman, and since he must needs fulfil his own duties on occasion, he continues to shame them publicly.

Just the other day, for an instance, Blaise was ordered to burn in the public square a seditious document proclaiming the Freedom and Equality of Man. Before burning it, he quite naturally read the paper to ascertain what scurrilities had been written upon it, and in the perusal was so overcome by an access of emotion, so filled with admiration for the author's generosity of spirit, felicitousness of phrasing, even for the very quality of the paper on which the document had been printed that, unable to bring himself to consign the folio to the fire, he burned instead a sheaf of pages torn from a missal.

Such was the house to which the players repaired, though they were not destined to remain long under its roof, the house itself not being long destined to have a roof. One day an English cannon ball, an errant practice shot, as we later learned, shattered the house wall completely. Only the Captain was at home, and though for a brief, happy moment we thought him dead, he crawled from under the rubble unharmed except in the matter of his frock coat, which was only slightly more filthy than usual. The next day a second cannon ball, also errant, struck the Captain in the head and killed him, this time permanently. The poor devil must have had his name inscribed on at least a half dozen of English balls.

Rendered desperate by the destruction of their house, if not of the Captain, the outcasts took refuge in the Lower Town, in a building in rue Sault-au-Matelot consigned to the Executioner by the king's lieutenant as a replacement. The new house hath a pleasant prospect, if a somewhat coquettish mien, and best of all is almost without neighbours, the majority of the residents of Lower Town having moved inside the town walls above the escarpment for their protection. Rumours have been circulated to the effect that the harbourfront will be the first to go when the English fleet begins bombarding in earnest, which it is daily anticipated they will do.

"A mere will-o'-the-wisp," Blaise hath assured the players. "A truce will be signed long before it comes to that, I vow. Meanwhile, there are none to bother us down here. We will be left in peace."

He spoke true. No one ventures down here into Lower Town, with the singular exception of an Ursuline, who comes to treat Jericho's cankered mouth. A good, brave soul, in the opinion of everyone but Jericho, who detests her on principle, not only because she feels herself to be less justified in inveighing against nunnery in general, but also because the Ursuline's act of charity detracts from the force of her grievance against the Grey Nuns in particular. Thus we see that, in seeking only to give, we run the risk of giving only offence.

And now here is the hangman, home from a hard day's work. He forgets that when he comes home early he puts everyone in a dejected frame of mind. And he has brought with him Marie Laurent and Fleurdelysse. Just what we needed: now the cast of characters is complete.

5

COROLÈRE produces five small loaves and two smoked eels from his sack. Bernard, having already a mouthful of cat, politely declines the offer, but the other famished players throw themselves upon the food, scarcely glancing at their benefactor as they mutter their thanks. The Executioner well knows that puppy gratitude is the only sentiment he can expect from them, of a kind that lasts only as long as the bread and eels, which is not long at all. But he is content enough, having become accustomed to the expectation of being liked only when he hath done some service, and judges such utilitarian love to be better than no love at all.

Corolère also brings news. By way of apology for the cannon bullet that put so peremptory a period to the career of the late Captain, by the killing of him, the English General Wolfe hath sent to Intendant Bigot a case of Amontillado, whereupon the intendant, not wishing himself to be in the general's debt, returned the messenger with a case of best Pacaret claret. He hath, moreover, promised to release a prisoner, a certain Lieutenant Tristram Stillborne, who was captured by militiamen on the Ile aux Coudres. This Stillborne and several of his companions had taken two horses from one of the abandoned farms on the island and were larking about in a very clownish manner when the militiamen came upon them; all the others were killed but Stillborne, who was made a prisoner on account of his nobility of bearing.

Blaise pauses in his relation to judge of the effect of his discourse on those whom he counts as his only friends. They say nothing, however, although they appear to be in close attendance. He therefore continues in a different vein, by offering the curious observation that the weather this year seems colder than usual.

"In faith," he avers, "it is already July, and yet we had snow again last week. And there is rain every day and frost every night. But at least we are not suffering from the heat, as we usually do at this time of the year. What is more, the early frost seems to have killed off all the gnats and mosquitoes, with which we are normally so abysmally plagued. Thank God for small mercies, I say."

The company answer nothing to this, either, which prompts the hangman to admit that there are, of course, still flies in Quebec, "only not the same kind as before, as you will no doubt have remarked, the kind we have now being quite fat and without stingers, and of a different hue, that is to say, mostly bluish-green. They are, I believe, what the learned call carrion flies, and are attracted hither by the many corpses we have strewn about. Hanged men left at the gates, deserters that have been shot or had their heads cracked open to save powder. These flies seem able to smell Death from an hundred leagues distant, and should be very welcome in our town, since they do us a great service by ridding us of carcasses that would otherwise breed and spread pestilence. They are thus public benefactors. There are indeed a greater many this year, but peradventure next year there will be fewer. They may go somewhere else, do you see. One never knows, does one?"

Blaise would feign stop this tapering speech, but does not know how to go about it. He wants so much to comfort his friends, to help them to see the brighter side of their situation, but he hath the impression that they are awaiting only such time as he will misuse a word or phrase, whereupon they will chase him away like a cur and erase the memory of his presence from their minds. Having exhausted the subject of flies, then, he searches his brain for another topic. Not even Marie and

Fleurdelysse are listening to him now. They are making a fire, upon which they intend to boil the water they have fetched from without the walls of the town, in plain view of the English, whom they observed to be leisurely installing their great cannons across the river at Pointe-Lévy. The women busy themselves with faggots. Telemachus turns a somersault and Blaise laughs, but he is the only one who is amused. The players seem to want him to continue talking, and so he does.

"The war will not last forever, you know. The English have thirty thousand of foot and the French barely fifteen, from which must be subtracted the twelve hundred of Indians, who will take orders from no one, and the two thousand of Canadian militiamen, who think of nothing but their planting and reaping. I say two thousand, but that is counting runaways and deserters. No, the war will soon be over, the English will win, for they are very strong. Why, on their flagship alone, the *Neptune*, they have ninety cannons, while we are so short of powder and ball that our artillery units are told they may fire upon the enemy for only one hour out of the day. Very well, let us say we can in such manner hold them off until winter comes, at which time the English ships must depart. In either case, we will have peace before Christmas, and peace is all that matters. That is what everyone is saying, at least."

Since no one either aids or hinders him, he flails on.

"I was present when they questioned Lieutenant Stillborne. They thought they would have need of me in my capacity as interrogator, which is a part of my duties as Executioner, but happily the Englishman burbled away without hindrance, as though under orders to do so by his own general. He even dropped the name of Captain James Cook, master of the *Pembroke* and a much celebrated sailor who I think will go far: it was he who personally piloted the English fleet up the St. Lawrence to Quebec. There was nothing for me to do but listen, since Monsieur Stillborne's command of the French language is remarkable, whereby you can tell he has received a good education, and indeed he indicated that he has been to school in England. He is a distinguished gentleman. From his father, who is a wealthy merchant, he hath inherited the right of salvages in Newfoundland; he was taken prisoner by the Esquimeaux in Labrador and held by them for three years, during which time he learned to speak their language fluently. He is now in command of a detachment of Newfoundland Volunteers. General Wolfe also speaks French, and so he, too, must be high born, and therefore in my opinion we have little to fear from the troops under their command. The New England Rangers, however, are a different matter. They are commanded by a Captain Rogers, they most certainly do not speak French, and they are at the present time engaged in sacking farms along the north shore. We are not soldiers, and as for Canada, the English can have it. Nor are they otherwise than of that mind at Versailles, according to our own officers: even those born here detest this place. All they want is peace, to go about their business and be left alone. That is not to be wondered at, is it?"

Corolère does not wish to leave the impression that he favours the English cause. "No, no, not in the least," he assures them hastily. "There are some Canadians, merchants here in Quebec, who want to hasten us into battle, to which end they have made the war council the generous offer of financing an expeditionary force to raid the English battery positions on Pointe-Lévy, and have even proposed, as commander of such a battalion, none other than Major-General Jean-Daniel Dumas, the distinguished officer who engineered the defeat of Braddock at Monongahela.

"At first the war council declined the offer. The council, as you know, is simply another way of saying Montcalm, Bigot and Vaudreuil, and Montcalm hates the way the Canadians make war, by fighting in the forests like Indians instead of lining up on a proper battlefield in orderly rank and file, as is the custom in Europe. But the merchants having persisted in their entreaties, Montcalm hath acceded to their plan, and is in the process even now of organizing a detachment of sixteen hundred volunteers, to be made up of all sorts: children, old men, family men, young men who dream of dying a glorious death, even pardoned deserters. They will take anyone. Students from the seminary are forming a small regiment, which for a laugh they are calling the Royal Syntax."

To make an end of this prattle, Pantaloon asks of Blaise whether it is his intention to sign up for this raiding party. The players scoff at this – all but Auguste, who merely smiles to conceal his thoughts, and Bernard, who affects not to have been attending to anything save the antics of his bear.

Blaise is spared from answering by the sound, which comes suddenly from behind him, of a column of soldiers being drummed into Lower Town. They are Lieutenant Stillborne's escort. A barque awaits them at the quay. There is a white scarf tied over the lieutenant's eyes, which neatly offsets the brilliant red of his uniform. He makes a handsome prisoner.

Just as the barque sets off, he removes the scarf, and the first person he sees is Jericho, standing on a small stage attached to the side of the church of Notre-Dame-des-Victoires. The Englishman removes his hat, bows deeply towards her and tosses a word in her direction upon the wind, which fails, alas, to reach our ears. Jericho is stunned into silence and manages but a slight curtsy before he is gone, returned to freedom.

"What did he say?" the others ask feverishly, but Jericho pretends that it is of no consequence, a word, nothing more, perhaps a small gallantry. She did not hear it, either, she says, but then is betrayed by the blood that drains from her cheeks. She hath never felt so beautiful in her life. More radiant, even, than when she is suffering.

"I heard him," says Barnaby. The players turn to him, Jericho standing a little off, a curious smile playing on her lips, as though she would have this moment last forever.

"What did he say? Pray tell us, what was it?"

"It was an English word – "

"Yes, we guessed that, you idiot, anyone could see that it was an Englishman who spoke and that therefore what he said must have been in that language. But what did he say?"

"He said, 'O Colombine, I have watched you from the window of my prison, and by my troth you are the most beautiful creature that ever I have seen. E'en from such a distance your beauty dazzled my eyes: your madonna-like face, your angelic hair, your breasts rippling beneath your blouse, the fullness of your thighs. You have the voice of a great tragedienne, and yet you have the power to make me laugh. It was of you I dreamed as a prisoner of the Esquimeaux, and here, on the walls of my lonely cell, I have inscribed a poem to you in invisible ink, using an admixture of water and lemon juice, so that none but the sun and I might read it. One day, when this accursed war is over, I will return for you, I will seek you wherever you are, and I will beg for your hand in marriage.'"

"He said all that?" the players ask him. "He's a fast talker, that one." No one dares to suggest that Barnaby is inventing it all to please Jericho, whose eyes have drifted off into the clouds, and who evidently has had no difficulty in persuading herself of the truth of Barnaby's words. She knows well enough that Barnaby is a great, if unrecognized, translator; that languages, whether alive or dead, hold no secrets from him. For the company, he has translated plays by Euripides, Virgil and Shakespeare; he also translates from French into French, for example he hath done *Sganarelle* and *The Impromptu of Versailles*, and brilliantly, too, if the French officers, who have seen the same plays performed in Paris, are to be believed. He can even translate from languages he doth not know, believing, along with Monsieur Diderot of the *Encyclopedia*, that it is unnecessary to know the language of an author if the public is incapable of reading the author for itself. All translation is invention, and Barnaby is a better inventor than ever the late Captain was.

As my readers will have guessed, Barnaby is in love with Jericho. She, however, will have nothing to do with him. In life, as on the stage, they are ever Colombine and Pierrot, she haughty and disdainful, he lonely and broken-hearted. He pledges his troth an hundred times or more, albeit on the stage, and she ever declines it, both in and out of her character. Barnaby's only consolation is that none of the other players have tupped her, either, not even Auguste, who always reserves the best roles for himself, and would easily qualify as a suitable suitor to the fair Colombine.

Barnaby continues his translation as he walks towards her, and whispers much more to her in like vein. Then he offers her his hand. He hath never played Pierrot so well, and she hath never been more Colombine as on this day. Well may Colombine wish to accept the hand of her Pierrot, but it is not in the text for her to do so, and so she turns her face in the direction of Pointe-Lévy, where the English are preparing their bombardment. The others rest their eyes on the pair, transfixed, enraptured; even Marie Laurent is holding her breath, so fully hath she entered the drama, a thing that does not often happen. All this from a single English word, thinks Auguste; of all the arts, translation is truly the most wondrous, and Barnaby is a master of the genre.

Fleurdelysse chooses this interlude to announce that the pea soup is ready, and the spell is broken, which I deem to be a pity, since it hath been a moment of such passing beauty and truth as hath never been before among them. The players gather at the steaming cauldron, all but Pierrot, who stands alone, his translated love as it were remaining in his hands, having once more been handed back to him by Colombine.

No sooner doth the company begin to eat than Blaise recommences his prattling. It appears he hath been only temporarily diverted from his aimless path. The troupe is unanimously of the opinion that he should shut up, but reason that the more he talks the less he will eat, and therefore the more will be left for them.

"If properly regarded, famine may be seen to be a blessing," says he. "Have you not remarked what good fettle the people appear to be in these days? It used to be that, what with their custom of chewing garlic all day and eating thick slices of onions and bread, you could smell them coming around a corner. But not any more, do you not note it? Their breath is clearer, now they have nothing with which to pollute it. And that, as I warrant, is a blessing. Myself, I have not tasted of wheatloaf since 1756, to be precise, since the fall of Fort William Henry, but you will not hear me complain of it. Pierce me if I even speak of it. And consider this: the Indians do hold that starvation favours the visionary, by helping him to see more clearly. I conclude from this that famine is a positive boon to humanity, and we should pity those poor souls who suffer from obesity, were it not that they must needs be suffering much less from that condition of late.

"Sieges I hold to be even more beneficial than famines! Have you not remarked that no one hurls insults at us in the streets since we have moved down here to Lower Town? It is not simply that this part of town will be the first to be struck by the English bombardment, but rather that people are more charitable in their relations with one another during difficult times. Do you not agree? See, as an instance, how this young Ursuline comes to visit us so often, she has almost become friendly with our bear. She is proof that God loves us. Verily, sieges have their good points…"

"Shut up and come see this!" shouts Marie Laurent. Having removed herself somewhat from the others, because of some movement she thought she heard in the yard behind the house next to their own, she has now come running back and is extremely agitated. Corolère follows her, then he, too, returns, his face pale as a winding sheet.

In the garden, someone has set up what appears to be a scarecrow: a wooden cross with the proportions of a man, topped with a straw hat and clothed in rags; for a face, a stuffed flour sack upon which hath been painted a hideous grimacing expression.

"This is not a good sign," says Blaise.

"Who is it?" asks Ignatius.

Blaise does not reply, but he is very alarmed. He takes a bowl of soup and begins to eat voraciously. Now it is Marie Laurent's turn to speak, and all the players turn in her direction.

6

MARIE explains to the company that if the Straw Man's face is looking in their direction, it is to be taken as a portent that, for them, the end of the world is at hand. However, if the face is turned away from them, then the end of the world is at hand for everyone else. From which it may be seen that it is well to remain on the Straw Man's good side.

"That is the true reason that the good burghers of Quebec leave us alone," says Marie. "They know he is down here, and they are afraid to come near. Have you not heard mothers say to their children, when they are bad, that if they be not quiet, the Straw Man will get them and eat them? And they are right: the Straw Man is capable of anything."

"At one time I was a clerk of the law," Auguste interrupts her, "and in England, a man of straw is one who earns his living by giving false testimony in court. He signals his profession by placing a straw in the buckle of his shoe, so that unscrupulous lawyers who are in need of a witness, or are desperate to corrupt a jury, may know their man. That is all your Straw Man is, a pawn in a bit of shady dealing, nothing more. This fellow here is put out but to keep off crows. There is no need to − "

"Don't come all over the professor with me," Marie replies hotly. "I know what I know. It was the settlers in New England who gave this Straw Man his name. During the time when he fought with the Abenaki, he ran a Dutch sharpshooter through with his sword, and then erected the corpse in his own cornfield, held up by a wooden cross, in the imitation of Christ, with his face turned towards the south. He took this holy figure as his emblem of war. The practice soon spread, and others took it up, and in such wise was born the legend of the Straw Man. So that now, when farmers see a scarecrow planted in one of their fields, they know that the Straw Man is coming to devastate the land and kill all the men on it, and that this is a warning whereby if they have good sense, they flee into the bush for their lives! Now he is here, I tell you, in this town, up to his old tricks, and scarifying everyone, in faith. Blaise," she concludes, "you tell them about the Straw Man."

Corolère is apparently too busy finishing his soup to give immediate reply. He is happy at last, having a full belly and, a semblable rarity, an audience that seems desirous, if not eager, of hearing what he has to say. He pauses to consider that this is an opportunity to demonstrate to the players his skills as a story-teller, which greatly surpass his facilities as a hangman.

"He was one of my first clients," he begins slowly. "A matter of a duel fought in Montreal between a certain lieutenant and a young cadet, the two having exchanged angry words when they were both drunk. The lieutenant was the Straw Man. During the duel, he slipped and grazed the boy with his rapier, pricking him in his private parts, but so lightly that he was quite unconscious of hurting him. But the wound festered, and the boy died three days later, grateful, I have no doubt of it, to take leave of his agony.

"I did not know what they expected of me, since the cadet was already dead and the lieutenant had disappeared, but the law is the law. The case went to trial, and both were found guilty of duelling, which the king hath condemned. The hearing was, perforce, not a lengthy one, since neither of the accused were there to defend themselves. Lawyer Auguste may know, though I do not, how it is that a dead man can be tried, but I know that he can be, for I attended his trial. For duelling, the cadet was discharged, and his family was fined. As for the Straw Man, though he was no more in evidence than the dead man, yet was he stripped of his rank, dishonourably discharged from his regiment, and fined as well. Further to that, he was sentenced to an hundred strokes of the cat, after which I was to hang him high and dry, like a common criminal. In absentia, of course.

"It was the first time, I do confess it, that I took any pleasure in carrying out the duties of my office. If all public executioners would but do as I, there would be much less suffering in this world. There was no difficulty about it. I placed the dead man in a pine coffin and confined him at the bottom of a small root cellar, so that his smell would not offend, and I then fabricated a mannequin of him, the which was intended to represent him. I made it with my own hands, and as I am quite adept in that way, it was a good likeness. I was rather pleased with it. Since it was market day, and hence a good day for setting an example, I carried the mannequin to the gallows in rue Saint-Paul, beat upon my tambour, read out the sentence and laid on the mannequin with an hundred best strokes of the cat, after which I cut off its right hand."

For once, Blaise did neither faint nor swoon. Unhappily, though, his pantomime was performed entirely without an audience, since a victim that does not suffer is of interest to no one.

"I then bound the real body to a board and dragged it behind my horse through the streets of Montreal, with its face pressed down toward the ground, a punishment known as disfiguration, or defacing of the corpse, which is usually reserved for suicides, but of late is also applied to duellers. As fortune would have it, it had snowed the night before, and I did not completely obliterate the face. I was supposed to then throw the corpse onto the dung heap, but having been made the recipient of a generous sum by the family, I conveyed the body to them instead, they being desirous of giving their son a proper, if discreet, burial.

"I did not, however, hasten my corpse to that end which awaits us all. Before delivering it to the family, I conveyed it to the king's physician, who dissected it while I watched, thereby showing me a great many things useful to me in my trade. Such as the location of the liver and the stomach and the heart; what brains are made of, and bile, and other things of like nature. The doctor also gave me a large tip. And finally, but this I would ask you not to repeat to anyone, I sold two of the corpse's fingers to a gambler, the none other than Monsieur Hébert, who wanted to make a good-luck charm of them. There is money to be made from the fingers of a hanged man. His worship, too, paid me a handsome price.

"It was much easier in the case of the Straw Man, and also more agreeable. First I collected the fine, which presented little difficulty since the absconded man left all his belongings behind. I sold a good portion of them, paid the fine with the proceeds, and kept the rest for myself. I then made a second mannequin, which surpassed the first because I had some of the condemned man's clothing, such as his uniform and sword. I carried the mannequin to rue Saint-Paul and read out the judgement against him with all the solemnity I could muster, then I tore off his lieutenant's stripes, whipped him to within an inch of his life and cashiered him from the army, worthless dummy that he was. My superiors later commended me for the skilful way in which I handled this difficult assignment, but I must admit I enjoyed the ceremony, having had experience in such matters. Do you but recall that I was once a drummer, and you will not wonder that I took no small pleasure in ripping the stripes off the sleeve of an officer.

"I could not hang the mannequin, having too much mangled it in the whipping, but I had a better idea. The law says that the condemned man being in absentia, then I am obliged to perpetrate his punishment on an effigy. Do you not agree that mine is a very peculiar profession? I procured a wooden board and some colours and painted a likeness of the lieutenant hanging by his neck. Since I had plenty of time, I also drew thereon a crowd of spectators, the street, even myself, although I am something hidden from view. Such effigies are intended to warn the condemned man of the fate that awaits him should the law ever take hold of his collar again. And one would have to agree that the strategem works, since there has not been a duel in Montreal since that time, nor hath the lieutenant returned to that place. By gad, it is the most agreeable way of meting out justice that I have heard! And when I tell you that I am able to draw beautiful theatrical designs, you may believe me. I have the proof of it. What then, how say ye to it?"

Feign would Corolère continue his tale, but that he hath run out of matter with which to extend it, which is a pity since, of a sudden, a crowd of fresh listeners hath gathered about the wagons. The good Ursuline is here, and several French dragoons, but most of the newcomers consist of Canadian militiamen, who seem to have at least momentarily cast off their habitual expressions of the deepest melancholy. They have heard about the appearance of the Straw Man and know what he is capable of, and it is good news to them that he is in our vicinity. The players ask them many questions, and everyone is speaking at the same time, but I am able to provide my patient readers with the following summation of the proceedings.

The Straw Man calls himself Saint-Ours, but he is of no relation to the Saint-Ours family, having merely taken the name, partly from mischief and partly to honour the memory of Jean-Baptiste de Saint-Ours Deschaillons, a seigneur and recipient of the Cross of the Order of Saint-Louis. Deschaillons was the king's lieutenant in Quebec and took in the Straw Man and his brother when they were but children. Neither is the Straw Man related to François-Xavier de Saint-Ours, captain of the colonial regular troops, who is here in Quebec with Montcalm's army.

He is not even from New France, our Saint-Ours, but was born at Fort de Chartres, in the Illinois territory, where his father was an unlicensed fur trader, of whom there are a great many in that country. His mother was a Protestant from New Sweden who was abducted by the Malecites when she was a child and sold and resold three or four times before the Straw Man's father purchased her for a flintlock and a bottle of firewater, which he considered a good bargain since she was so fair. She was a strong woman with skin the colour of fresh bread, and she never seemed to raise her voice. The couple had two sons.

At length, the father left to join La Vérendrye's campaign to discover the whereabouts of the Western Ocean and to sail thereon to Japan, and very likely is he in that country now, since this one hath no further report of him. At the time, Jean-Baptiste Deschaillons was commandant of Fort Michillimackinac, and since he had been something of a business partner of the Straw Man's father, he felt himself to be under some obligation to the sons. Accordingly, upon being recalled to Quebec, Saint-Ours brought with him the two boys and placed them in the seminary. They had, at the time, attained to the age of ten and eight years respectively. François-Xavier de Saint-Ours acted as their godfather: the elder boy was given the name Pascal, and the younger, the future Straw Man, was called Benjamin. Their mother, like their father, now disappears from this account and, for aught I know, the face of the earth.

Never had the seminary harboured two such devils as were Pascal and Benjamin. They were as ignorant as clay, having almost no knowledge of the French language, having lived no sort of life but that of the forest, and would have been removed from the seminary a thousand times had not Monsieur Deschaillons undertaken to keep them there until such time as they were old enough to join the free troops of the marine. Deschaillons was very kindly disposed towards them, which is why they were called the little Saint-Ourses, to which they did not seem to object over much. To distinguish the brothers now, the one from the other, the elder is called Saint-Ours des Natchez, and the puisne, Saint-Ours des Illinois.

They were good enough lads, at heart. Though feared because they were as strong as a team of oxen, yet could any accord be had from them by the application of kindness. Benjamin was the more intelligent of the two and remained longer in the seminary; Pascal joined the marine regiment at the age of thirteen and is now a captain in the service of the government of Louisiana, in the Arkansas territory, where he is engaged in much the same occupation as had been his father before him.

Benjamin Saint-Ours des Illinois, in the meanwhile, left the seminary of a sudden to join a group of *coureurs de bois* who were leaving for the West Country. He travelled widely, according to report, and after a while journeyed south to join with his brother in some business of trafficking with Indians, whose languages he had acquired with no small facility. They did much trade with the Dutch in Albany and Boston, which they knew to be against the law, but, like their father, they followed no law but their own. Benjamin stopped for a time in Philadelphia, where he learned to speak English and where he made the acquaintance of Pehr Kalm, the great Swedish naturalist, by whom he was engaged as a guide when the latter journeyed into Canada. After that, he worked for no one but himself.

He was something of a terror in New England long before the commencement of the war. He was a sight to behold, and even the French officers of the regular colonial army gave him a wide berth. They sent him to fight with the Indians in his own part of the country, with the Wild Oats and the Odawas, with whom he set fires to English farms, tortured English prisoners and killed their wives and children. When Fort William Henry fell, he permitted that the prisoners be tortured and eaten by the Wild Oats; he is even rumoured to have tasted of human flesh himself.

Then came this matter of the duel, after which it appears that he fled to Boston, joined Rogers' Rangers and returned north with them to attack the French here. Suddenly, scarecrows began to appear in our fields, their faces turned towards the north, especially in the vicinity of Fort St. Frederick, and the authorities began to wish they had not ordered the hanging of Lieutenant Benjamin Saint-Ours, even in effigy, after all.

He came back to the French side after receiving the promise of a pardon and Cross of the Order of Saint-Louis, and since then he hath ever turned the faces of his straw men to the south, which we count as a good thing. The French officers do not like him, but they would not say so for all the livres in the world. Last year he was in Louisbourg during the siege, but managed to escape before the bastion fell into the hands of the English.

The little Ursuline wants to know if we are likely to see him soon, to which the reply is that all we know is what is happening in the surrounding areas, and that it seems to be heating up for everyone. Jericho asks if this Master Benjamin Saint-Ours des Illinois is handsome, and whether he intends to return to France after the war, to which inquiry Marie Laurent laughs, "How do you think he can return to a country he was not born in and which he has never seen?"

Ignatius inquires if the story of Saint-Ours eating human flesh is true, and is assured that it is. Colonel Bougainville saw him do it, and denounced him for it to Montcalm, who did nothing because he had need of him.

Barnaby says that were Saint-Ours to join the raiding party against the English batteries, which at this moment is being organized by Dumas, then he, Barnaby, would sign up immediately, and having delivered himself of this pronouncement, he casts in Jericho's direction a look meant to be at once melancholic and importunate.

Bernard whispers a word to Auguste, who stamps his feet on the ground three times and asks a question that freezes the entire company in their tracks: "Which way is the scarecrow looking?"

Everyone runs to the garden to have a look. The scarecrow is facing neither north to Quebec nor south towards the English, but has his face turned towards the ocean. Everyone breathes a sigh of relief, and begins to talk of other things.

7

THE world is coming to an end.
Telemachus sensed it before we did. He moaned in his sleep all the night before, could not be quieted in the morning,

and then the first ball struck the roof of Notre-Dame-des-Victoires. Bernard unchained the beast to see where it would go, and it made directly for the cellar of the building behind which the Straw Man had erected his effigy, followed closely by his trainer and the other players, who reasoned that animals must have a better instinct than humans for protecting themselves against cannon shot. The bombardment lasted the entire day, without interruption, and turned the greater proportion of Lower Town into an inferno. When finally it stopped at the approach of five of the clock that evening, the players had aged an hundred years.

They passed the day expecting every hour to be their last and were loath to leave their place of security even when the cannonading had ceased. In point of fact, they did not leave it until three days later, and then only at night, for the very compelling reason that they preferred a death by bombardment to one of starvation and thirst, such as awaited them in the cellar. Telemachus had earlier left the lair, and by the same ratiocination that induced them to follow him into the cellar, they did now follow him out of it. Upon emerging from the puleyn, they were very nearly asphyxiated by the excessive smoke that blanketed the town, but happily a north wind blew up and they were shortly able to see the stars. Lower Town had been reduced to a heap of smouldering rubble. Every second house seemed to be in flames, and all were missing a roof or a wall.

Jericho whimpered at the sight, but there was nothing to be done. There was no food, no one to take pity on us. Auguste was about to suggest that the troupe remove to the Upper Town when Ignatius noticed a sack on the ground beside the scarecrow. Upon opening it, he found it to contain a haunch of dried venison in a quantity of oat flour, whereupon Fleurdelysse and Marie immediately set off to fetch some water and a little oil, and thence to make a loaf of bread. Ignatius knelt on the ground to thank the scarecrow, but embarrassment overcame him at the last moment and he recovered himself: though he doth not believe in God, he finds in that no excuse for prostrating himself before a graven image, as he were a pagan.

Someone said, "Where is Barnaby?" Huddled as they had been for the past three days in darkness, they had not noticed that Barnaby had disappeared at the start of the bombardment. They called for him, but he did not answer. No grave matter, they decided; they would look into the mystery after they had eaten.

Very soon Fleurdelysse and Marie have oatcakes ready, and during the meal Blaise notices a curious sort of cannon ball at the bottom of the garden. "It is the newest invention of the English," he explains. "Two balls joined together by a length of chain, a contrivance that doth thrice the damage of an ordinary ball. Imagine," he says, "if such a device had done for the Captain. I assure you, we would not now be worrying ourselves over the disposal of his body." This serves to remind the players that in their panic over the bombardment, they have completely forgotten about the molasses crate containing the poor Captain's mortal remains. They decide they had better look for it, this time forgetting that they still have not the slightest idea what to do with it.

Blaise and Auguste, taking advantage of the evening's lull, returned to the house in rue du Sault-au-Matelot to retrieve the Captain in his makeshift coffin, and now they come back with an empty crate.

"Where can the body have gone?" everyone asks, and everyone, with the exception of Auguste, turns suspiciously to Corolère.

"Don't look at me," protests he. "Upon my word of honour!"

But the players persist in looking at him, so much more intently than they dare to look at the most likely perpetrator of the corpse's disappearance, which is to say none other than the bear, Telemachus, who, it is suddenly remembered, hath not appeared as hungry of late as might have been expected, had they but thought of it. They do not think of it now. Rather they fix their reproachful regard on the Executioner, while Bernard ruffles Telemachus's neck fur and pointedly thanks the animal for having saved their lives.

Blaise, in the meanwhile, continues to plead his case. "I never ventured from the cellar," he says. "I was with you the whole time." And so forth. The more he protests, the more the others become convinced that it is indeed the bear who has committed this outrage, and therefore the greater the severity with which they accuse Corolère, who finally casts his eyes pleadingly upon Bernard and then turns deathly pale, whereupon Bernard assumes an air of innocence and the others decide it is time to change the subject.

Suddenly, Barnaby is here. It is a splendid entrance, perfectly timed. His face is more pallid than usual, and his Pierrot costume is in tatters; the others can see his pale, bare backside through the holes in it.

"Where have you been?" they all demand to know. "You look dog tired! Are you not a bit starved? We have saved you a little..."

Barnaby, who has never received so much solicitous attention, begins to cry, "I cannot...never more....will I...anything to do with...I swear!"

They give him something to eat, and shortly thereafter he goes to sleep.

Sleep seems a good idea for the rest of the troupe as well. "Let us nestle in the arms of Morpheus," says Auguste. Barnaby will tell his story tomorrow. The English will recommence their bombardments in the morning, and it is well to restore ourselves while we can during this little respite. Even cannoneers must sleep at night, like the rest of the world, and that at least is as it should be. We can sleep knowing that we are still alive, that our bellies are almost full, and that the troupe is reunited and complete once again.

Except for the Captain, of course, but even his absence is beginning to seem normal. And then there is me, the prompter, who makes up the number again, after a fashion.

Between bouts of bombardments, which cause the walls of our cellar to tremble, Barnaby gives an account of his misadventures. He had, so he tells us, volunteered for Dumas's raiding party, which crossed the river to annihilate the English battery positions at Pointe-Lévy. The players listen to him less for the fascination of his account than for the distraction it affords from their dread at the trembling of the walls. Even the bear is paying attention.

Dumas and his men failed at their objective in a most lamentable fashion. With his militiamen and a few Indians, he managed to cross the river during the night, but, upon reaching the far bank, they found the night to be so dark that they could not discern the English emplacements. The men panicked and commenced firing upon one another, while the English soldiers remained quietly in their encampment, unaware even that they were under attack. Just before first light, the party returned to this side of the river in disarray. It was altogether a disgraceful affair.

Barnaby, who had to fire a flintlock for the first time in his life, actually succeeded in killing his man, except that it was no man, but one of the seminarians from the Royal-Syntax Regiment, whom he mistook for an English grenadier and shot at point-blank range. No one noticed his error, such was the general chaos surrounding them, and perhaps by way of atonement, he picked up the boy's lifeless body and carried it, heedless of the danger to which the extra weight subjected him in his retreat, delivered it to the boy's family, telling the mother that her son had died "like Achilles before Troy." Barnaby was then hailed as a hero by his comrades, with no one but himself to know that he was, at best, but a well-intentioned blunderer, and he swore before the troupe that never again would he take up arms with a company of criminally incompetent novices such as he himself was.

The actors settled down to habituate their nerves to the cannonade. The English are nothing if not methodical and are therefore happily predictable: the bombing commences at nine of the clock in the forenoon and terminates at five or thereabouts. One can, therefore, leave one's shelter in the evening for the purposes of provisionment, without fear of being blown to fragments. There remains, of course, the possibility of being roasted alive by the many fires caused by the incendiary bombs, or crushed by a suddenly collapsing house. But guided by Blaise, who knows the town like the back of his hand, the players are so far emboldened as to make their way into the Upper Town, where they plunder abandoned houses until they have found enough food and supplies to last them for a month. (I should drop all pretense here and tell you plainly that I accompany the players on these forays, and that willingly. "Come with us, our little prompter," they say to me, little guessing how much pleasure they afford me by addressing me thus. It is from this time hence that I begin to feel a part of the troupe.) Auguste and Ignatius have retrieved all the goods that were in our wagons, now sadly flattened, and for once we have the means to make ourselves relatively comfortable. Blaise and Barnaby occupy themselves with the water, with such diligence that the barrel is always full, and we can even have a wash from time to time. Life is good.

Best of all, almost every morning, we find that food has been placed for us at the foot, as it were, of the scarecrow. Oat or bran flour daily, venison every third day, and occasionally dried fruit such as figs or raisins. Sometimes there are even little sweetcakes in the sack. Just the other day, there was in it a pound of chocolate, of the kind included in French officers' ration kits. Marie Laurent did not know what it was at first, poor thing, but when she had tasted of it she averred that she was now more determined than ever to get to Europe, if there was food like chocolate to be had there. Once there was a small satchet of a sort of herb, which Fleurdelysse identified as tea, an infusion of which she said made a good beverage in cold weather, and was even better drunk with the chocolate.

And so we may be said to have made a life for ourselves in our cellar. Barnaby's too-white skin, where it peeps through his costume, hath ceased to amaze us, numbed as we are by custom to the sight of it. We have broken through the cellar wall common to the house next door, which doubles our living quarters, and there we have consigned Bernard and Telemachus, because, not to make too fine a point of it, the bear stinks, and moreover is infested with fleas that are not particular about their hosts. Marie, Fleurdelysse and Jericho sleep on one side, that on which there is the least dripping, and the men sleep on the other. We spend our days in waiting; we breathe out when we hear the bombs falling above us in the town, and we inhale when they fall about our ears here in Lower Town. Some hours pass more quickly than others, and we spend our days longing for nightfall.

After dark, we partake of our meagre meal and talk incessantly; sometimes we even laugh as we sit around our little fire, which Fleurdelysse is diligent to keep alight. The players tell one another stories to pass the time, and the good Ursuline, who still visits us, loves to attend them. But we do not sing, for fear of attracting the attention of marauding soldiers.

The stories the players tell are always those that they already know. Each takes his turn, except me, of course, who hath nothing of my own to say and know only how to listen. Auguste tells of the Easter miracle, injecting much mirth into it, though he is careful not to distort the facts over much, as we know the plot as well as he does. He adds enough of his own touches to make us laugh. Marie Laurent tells such vivid tales of Blaise's botched hangings that we all, not excepting Blaise himself, double up with laughter. By retelling these familiar stories, we are able to believe that we are still alive. It is like unto pinching ourselves; it reassures us.

We talk often in a ribald manner, because we think about ribaldry constantly. The men are in a perpetual state of readiness, and the women are always moistened. Perhaps it is the imminence of death that provokes the love hunger, the urge to create new life being stronger than usual. Even Jericho ventures to speak of it from time to time, but perhaps that is intended mostly to shock the little Ursuline. If so, she does not succeed at it. The Ursuline was a woman long before she was a nun, and she is quick to see that Jericho has never felt within herself the base desires to which she gives such ardent expression.

And yet, life is all but insupportable at times. When it is excessively hot outside, we suffocate in our cell and are eaten alive by mosquitoes. When it rains, there is no escaping the torrents of water by which we are inundated; and when it stops, we are drenched in humidity and stink of mildew. Happily we are not plagued by rats, all the rats having long since been eaten during the siege, but Indians and soldiers prowl without our cellar walls. Just the other day, one of them made an attempt at Telemachus by threatening to discharge a ball into his fur, at which Bernard was greatly alarmed. And then, of course, there are the flies. The bottle-green flies are here in great force, since we have taken to hanging deserters from the exposed rafters of ruined houses. Corpses stink far more egregiously than a bear, which at least hath the excuse of being a bear.

Upon leaving our cellar this morning, Jericho emitted a cry of horror when she perceived the scarecrow: blood was oozing from the stumps of its straw arms and feet. Upon closer inspection by Auguste, who went up to it and removed its hat, it was found to be not a scarecrow at all, but rather the corpse of a man. It was no longer held up by a wooden cross, but rather impaled on a stake. Jericho very nearly fainted at the sight, and the others rushed out, inquiring of one another what this new omen might portend. Barnaby said that most likely this was Lieutenant Stillborne, and that the Straw Man must have infiltrated behind the English lines and killed him, and brought him here either as a trophy for himself or as food for his cannibalistic Indians. At this, Jericho took herself off some distance and began to weep, and we comforted her by saying that Barnaby was only speaking out of jealousy. At last I took a closer look, and saw that it was not Stillborne at all, but another man whose face I had not seen before. Fleurdelysse knew him: it was her former owner, Monsieur Hébert. He must have been killed in combat – no doubt from a ball in the back, Marie Laurent remarked drily; that is, by a French ball. That afternoon, the bear ate of the cadaver with much appetite, and no one tried to stop it.

This morning the scarecrow was back. There was no sack of food at the base of it, but rather the sleeping figure of a man. Marie, being the first to leave the cellar, saw him there and ran back to fetch the rest of us to come and look. Now we are all standing about, silently watching the stranger, as hushed and respectful as though we were in church. Auguste, speaking in a whisper, asks Blaise if this indeed be he, to which Blaise replies that he knows not, never having laid eyes on him.

Whoever he is, we have not seen his like before in this town. His face is painted like that of an Indian, and his uniform is a patchwork quilt of elements from both the French regular troops and the Canadian militia. He wears a set of captain's stripes on each sleeve, and the white tunic of the corps of marines, but his woollen tuque and red sash are those of the militia. For the rest, he is adorned as a Native: loincloth, moccasins, buckskin jacket. He stirs, as though having been summoned by Blaise's reply, and sits up, emitting a wide yawn, then stands and gives good morning to Auguste who, as the leader of the troupe, is urged with much smiling by his comrades to speak to the stranger, yet finds himself unable to do so.

Fortunately, Ignatius can always be counted upon in a moment such as this.

"Straw Man, I presume?" says he, offering his hand. "Delighted to make your acquaintance, sir."

To which the stranger replies, "Straw Man? No, sir, I have not that honour. You do mistake me for this gentleman here," he says, indicating the scarecrow. "My name is Saint-Ours des Illinois. Benjamin."

HAVING introduced himself in so singular a manner, Saint-Ours, alias the Straw Man, took himself off as he had brought himself in: with no more ado, and without speaking another word, he reached for his flintlock and powder-horn and walked off as unselfconsciously as a labourer might pick up his scythe and saunter off to the fields.

Auguste is sorry that he did not properly thank the man for the food that hath been left for us during the preceding three weeks; he is, after all, the director. Jericho would have liked time to correct the first impression she made upon the stranger; with her face smudged with soot and her dress in tatters, she looks more like Cinderella than the fair Colombine. The others, too, are chastened, in their case for having so feared someone who seems, on the face of it, to be no more than a man, take him for all and all. As for Bernard and the Ursuline, their regret is at not having seen the Straw Man at all, since they were in the cellar all the time, attending to a splinter that had become embedded in Telemachus's paw.

There is no bombardment this morning; for once, we can hear ourselves think, and so we take advantage of the quiet to exchange our impressions of Saint-Ours, who now suddenly seems less an enigma than had hitherto been the case. Blaise remarks that he had not imagined the man to look as he had, and that the effigy he had made of him must not, after all, have been such a very close likeness, which was, of course, an observation about which we were not obliged to have an opinion, our not having been favoured with a view of his handiwork. In any case, the man made a strong impression on Jericho, who hath finally ceased her perorations on the chivalric virtues of Lieutenant Stillborne. Marie and Fleurdelysse, having foreseen this rapid change of heart, exchange knowing, if clandestine, glances with one another. Barnaby, for his part, is keenly aware of Jericho's interest in the newcomer, and so he quickly invents something derogatory to say about him.

"This young upstart – Benjamin, did he say his name was – was not, I think, with the Dumas expedition, in which I myself very nearly lost my skin. I did not see him there, do you know? Which is not to say that he is a coward; I would not infer such a thing. But it does make one wonder, does it not?"

The rest of us find this bit of chicanery so appalling that we can think of nothing to say to it, and so we say nothing.

Auguste suggests that we hold a small reception for Saint-Ours to repay him for his generosity, to which Ignatius, wanting to contribute something and not knowing what else to say, says, "We could ask him to join our troupe! Could he not be the Captain, when the war is over?"

Jericho shrugs her shoulders at this, as though to say that she has never in her life heard a more ridiculous suggestion. The rest of the players laugh, which makes Ignatius pig-headed. "Why not?" he says, looking around at the troupe. "He is tall enough, and strong, and he may even have some talent. He is bound, at any rate, to have more than his predecessor." At this, the bear utters a belch loud enough to awaken the dead, and everyone becomes quiet, partly out of respect for the Captain, partly out of embarrassment. Then the bombardment resumes, and we all stop thinking about anything. We find it is easier that way.

That evening, when we crawl out of our fastness to reoccupy our particular hell on earth, the scarecrow is once again gone from the garden, and Saint-Ours hath returned. We are heartily glad to see him. Ignatius asks politely how he busied himself during his absence, and Auguste tells him to shut up, even though he, Auguste, is secretly glad that Ignatius hath so far presumed with Saint-Ours. The latter responds, but as though to a question not asked.

"This is a good place for you to seek shelter," he says. "The worst of the bombardments are over here, there being nothing left to fire at in Lower Town, since before long there will not be a house left standing. The English are aiming their cannons into the Upper Town, where there are still many people, and where they will do the most damage. I myself am not moving from this spot. I have my own cellar not far from here, but I prefer to sleep outside under the stars, when it is not raining. I am hungry."

We scurry about to find him something to eat. When Fleurdelysse brings him water to wash his face, he favours her with a word. His every gesture we inspect for our reassurance. He is, after all, truly like other men, in that he eats when he is hungry, and even goes to the trouble of washing beforehand. What is more, his manners are very agreeable, and his speech is almost as accomplished as our own. The stories about him are obviously fabrications, the legend of the Straw Man being particularly unjust.

We long to question him more closely, but do not dare. However, he has but to drop a word, and we pounce on it like cats upon a mouse, expanding it into a pronouncement, and hoping it will lead to more. For an example:

"It is going to rain tomorrow," he says between mouthfuls.

"Is it your opinion, then, that the rain will dampen the English powder?"

"Will the bombardments cease on that account?"

"Do you think the Redcoats will become discouraged by the bad weather, and depart?"

To our discouragement, he continues eating without making reply to our inquisition. Happily, though, he always finishes by saying something, albeit we have had to tailor our curiosity to his oblique manner of monologue, which is often charged with unlooked-for meaning.

"We are one against his two," he will say. "It will require a miracle for us to beat him. And they have grape and canister shot, and cannon bullets, in almost infinite supply. They have been hammering away at us for three weeks now, and could easily continue unabated until Christmas. It is as though they have come prepared to create a desert. If Montcalm is lured into the battle of which he dreams, the sort that is engaged in in Austria and Flanders, as I am told, then the French army will be crushed. Our only hope is to hold out until Martinmas, let us say until November, after which the English will be forced to weigh anchor and cast off to avoid being trapped by the winter ice in the St. Lawrence. And, having once left, they will not soon return, since an expedition of this magnitude must needs cost a fortune. When they do return, they will have to start all over again. As will we. But all that I can tell you with any certainty is that it will rain tomorrow. That I can guarantee."

In such wise did we learn, every day a little more, about the progress of the war. About Saint-Ours, however, we discovered little, until Ignatius embarrassed us once again by asking Saint-Ours what he did during the day, since he did not seem to belong to any particular regiment. Saint-Ours did not appear to resent the question; in fact, he seemed almost glad to have been asked it.

"I fight my own war," he said. "The French officers affect not to understand my preference for harassing the enemy from Amherst to Niagara or St. Frederick, and for my part I do not like to wear their uniform, even though I find theirs more becoming than the British Redcoats. I feel more at ease among the Canadian militiamen, who fight only to protect their farms and their women. There are days when this war seems not to be about them at all, and certainly they will tell you that to be ruled by this king or that makes no odds with them, they not having had the honour of meeting either. Never forget that the Canadians fight like devils because they have no choice, but you can not count on them for long. This is not to be wondered at. A few days ago, a French officer attempted to inspire an enthusiasm for battle in his militiamen by promising them that he would see to it that their widows received a pension of forty livres per annum. The next day, half the company deserted. I am happier campaigning with the Wild Oats and the Outaouais, whom I have brought down from the Hinterlands. At least they know how to fight, and when they see that the fighting is none of their business, they go home. They make war only to gain some advantage for themselves. They are mercenaries, like me."

One evening, when Saint-Ours was off somewhere else, the question came up: why was he fighting on the side of the French? We could think of nothing that would invoke his loyalty to our side, and as a mercenary he would surely have far more to gain by having sided with the eventual victors. The task of posing this question to Saint-Ours fell, naturally, to Ignatius, and the reply made Jericho's head to spin.

"The English are here to stay. They never can return to their homeland, even if they wanted to. This is especially true of the Scots Highlanders, who have no homeland to return to. And that is why they are going to win this war. They have no choice in the matter. The French think of nothing but getting back to France. To talk to a French officer for ten minutes is to know that he is here for no other purpose than to advance his career; that his body may be in Canada, but his mind is perpetually turned towards Versailles. Montcalm wants a pitched battle because he wants to die, which is as quick a way as any of returning to France. Bougainville is another story. I know him; he is more dangerous. He wants to return alive and weighted down with medals. Even the habitants, at least those with money, have but one ambition: they want their children to use the war to advance their status in the country. La Vérendrye was born here, but he has been an officer in the French army and fought at Malplaquet. Bienville, the Governor of Louisiana before Vaudreuil, was born in Montreal but lives on his pension in a very nice hotel in Paris, a city upon which he had not laid eyes until his retirement. Merchants, farmers, tradesmen, seigneurs, soldiers, they are all alike: all they want is a new start. They are but killing time here, and the dead are the only permanent citizens of this country. I am not so different. If we win the war, I will prosper, and be sent to France or somewhere else. If we lose, like every other officer I will be called to France. I will go to Versailles to receive my Cross of Saint-Louis, and to see if it is true, as they say it is, that the courtesans there piss in the corners of the chateau, and the king wipes his arse when he receives ambassadors. Like them, I am only passing time here. I know it better than you, because I am not from here."

At times, we cannot fathom him at all. Only the other day, we asked him why he dealt in war, given that he is so fond of life.

"I desire only to know if life is real," he replied.

In any case, Jericho now speaks of no one but Saint-Ours. Like most of us, she hath sat late into the night, alone with him, but unlike us she never tires of hearing him talk. The smallest detail enchants her.

"He never knew his father," she says. "Or his mother. In that we are alike; I have no family left, either. I told him about my father, a king's notary, and the house we lived in in Montreal, and what we ate. He is so interested in everything. He asks me many questions, but not once has he asked me what I was doing in Jericho. He says he is interested only in my career as an actress. He is a true gentleman, this Monsieur de Saint-Ours. Moreover a gentleman of means, who plans to return to France as soon as possible. He will take me with him, if I ask him to."

Even Barnaby has found something good to say about Saint-Ours, that is, that he knows French but poorly. By becoming his speech master, Barnaby hath placed himself in a position of ascendancy over his rival, a vantage point from which he hath been unable to survey until now. For once, Barnaby hath cause to style himself a scholar.

"But this is not to be believed," he pontificates, "that there are words that a king's interpreter, a master of all the languages of the Interior – Sioux, Fox, Illinois, Sauk, Ojibwa – for which he receives four hundred livres per year, plus a further six hundred livres in his capacity as a captain of the navy, that there are words, I do repeat myself for effect, of which he is ignorant. Are we to credit it, that a man who is on the receiving end of a thousand a year, not counting the fortune he made before the war selling furs, illegally I might add, in Detroit and Hudson Bay, is woefully deficient in certain basic aspects of the French tongue?

To what end, you might well ask, is the world coming? I took it upon myself to explain to him what holly is; he had never seen it. Neither had he the slightest idea of angelica; I had to tell him that it is a plant that grows in France, whose stems are preserved and eaten. I am astounded that he was not cognizant of it. 'How can I be expected to know what angelica is,' he demanded of me, 'since I have never tasted of it?' Well, as I told him, the word is in all the dictionaries, is it not? But I am helping him, lexicographically speaking, that is to say, I am instructing him in words. He appreciates me, I do believe. I had, of course, to explain to him what the word appreciate means: it is to augment in value or esteem. I have reason to doubt that any of you knew that until this moment. Yesterday I taught him the words catapult, clown and China clay. Tomorrow we will do domine, dungeon and dickey seat. I think it is best to proceed alphabetically. All the new pedagogies say it is the most effective method. Our Saint-Ours is avid of learning, for which I can forgive him much."

To this, Ignatius makes no reply, but he hath rendered Saint-Ours a better service. While rummaging about in an attic in rue Sainte-Ursuline, he found a store of books belonging to a French officer killed during a bombardment, and he sold the books for a good price to Monsieur de Saint-Ours, as Ignatius now calls him, who is so avid of learning, as Barnaby hath observed, that he cannot stop at any price when it comes to books. Ignatius and he spent an entire evening going through them, volume by volume, page by page, so charged were they with the potentiality of pleasure. There were, among others, *L' Histoire de Tom Jones*, by someone named La Place, and Monsieur Diderot's *Encyclopedia*. Ignatius recounts of this marvel to Auguste.

"What most amazed me," he says, "is that when I told him I had read of those books, by which I meant only to warn him that I was aware of their great value, he offered me twice what I had asked for them! Saith he that a book once read must be worth more than one that hath not, for the reason that its value hath been appreciated by someone else. I, who have never read a book in my life, would have thought the reverse, that a book that hath not been read must needs be valued more than one that hath never been opened, seeing that it is still new. If you take my meaning. What think you of that, Auguste?"

What Auguste thinks is that he has no idea what Ignatius is talking about, but he is careful to keep that to himself. He knows better than anyone that Saint-Ours is our hen who lays the golden eggs, and that we must endeavour to keep him attached to us at any price. He hath so far seemed well enough disposed towards our troupe, not least because we are as outcast as he is, but there is much to be gained from cultivating his friendship. With this in mind, Auguste discreetly asks Marie Laurent if she hath considered replacing her absentee sergeant, who might already be dead, with a captain with so brilliant a future ahead of him. To Blaise, he hints that it may not be amiss to make his apologies to Saint-Ours for having painted his effigy dancing the airy jig in Montreal. "It would be a mark of kindness, would it not? After all, it cannot be every day that a hangman hath the opportunity to request pardon of his victim."

To which Blaise replies, "On the contrary; I do it all the time."

"Be that as it may," says Auguste drily, "it might be mistaken for a friendly gesture."

The only one among us who is silent is Bernard. Telemachus hath disappeared, and he is inconsolable.

9

THE world is taking its time in coming to an end. We have become accustomed to the walls of our cellar shaking with every bombardment; to fires breaking out from one end of town to the other; to the far-off cries of soldiers whose limbs are amputated by the surgeons; to blood running in the streets from children cut down by grapeshot while rummaging for food in the trash heaps; to the brilliant blue-green flash of flies on dangling corpses. What we cannot inure ourselves to is the hunger. We cannot stop thinking about our stomachs.

Saint-Ours does not come by so often now, and our little supply of food, so providentially left for us at the foot of our scarecrow, has likewise sadly diminished. Until recently, Saint-Ours was one of those charged with following the movements of the English ships, one of Bougainville's ideas, but a few days ago, he told us he was finished with that, that he would waste his time with it no longer. The English navy hoists anchor every morning, allowing their ships to drift downstream with the tide, which makes the fleet advance and retreat like one who cannot bring himself to enter a strange house, and yet knows he must. The French spend the whole day running up and down the shore, keeping pace with the ships, to prevent the English from landing on our side, as they are daily expected to do, so that when General Wolfe finally does decide to invade, our soldiers will be too exhausted to repulse him. And all the while Montcalm passes the day in argumentation with his war council, or in tilting at windmills on his horse, to habituate himself for battle.

All of which irritates Saint-Ours to the point of distraction. He hath decided to rejoin his Indian guerrillas, saying he will lie in wait for Rogers' Rangers, whom he is impatient to engage in battle because they, too, take no prisoners. The Rangers, made up to appear as Indians, descend on outlying farms, terrifying the population and diverting blame to the Indians; Saint-Ours's force does likewise, diverting blame to the Americans. The two forces rival one another in cruelty, both in combat and in torture, anonymity abolishing all inhibitions.

To remove our minds from our hunger, we talk. Obviously, we talk of Saint-Ours, thus avoiding having to speak about ourselves. His every phrase is examined, held up to the light like a precious jewel. Jericho is his most tireless interpreter.

"The other day," says she, "I told him the sad story of the early death of my parents, and when I asked him if he remembered much of his own mother and father, do you know what reply he made? He said, 'My mother is a village, and my father is the forest.' Is that not sweet? Do you not think that the most marvellous sentiment? What do you think, Barnaby?"

Barnaby is happy to respond, Marie Laurent being engaged in sewing the seat of his trousers, where they had been so revealingly rent by the war, and so putting him in a pleasanter frame of mind than has lately been the case. He avows as how he, too, has grown fond of Saint-Ours, "having forgiven him for juxtaposing himself between myself and thyself, to wit, you, which is to say, Jericho." He hath devised, moreover, a theory concerning Saint-Ours's rhetorical skills, which fails utterly to astonish us, since Barnaby inevitably devises a theory about everything. We having nothing better to do, however, attend to his deliverance of it.

"It is my considered opinion that Saint-Ours's penchant for the laconic phrase, the mot juste, if you will, derives, ironically, from his very ignorance of the language, of which I have already made mention. The richness of his expression hath its direct cause in the paucity of his vocabulary, and it is this that lends to his conceits their undeniable pith and charm. Just yesterday he made the most poetical sentence. He said, 'It hungers here.' I imagine that when he interprets all those Native tongues of the Hinterland, he is of that genre of interpreter who substitutes but three words for the hour-long haranguing of a Chippewa chieftain, so that one suspects him of having left out the burthen of the disquisition for the purpose of advancing his own designs. It is a grievance commonly levelled at interpreters, that they are more partial to their own interests than to those of France, of which, of course, they have no direct knowledge. We reproach them for this as a fault, but secretly we approve of it."

During his long conversations with Saint-Ours, Barnaby hath learned that the latter did not begin to speak French until late in life, and that the only books he ever held in his hands before entering the Quebec seminary were the rough catechisms printed on birch bark by the Jesuit Chauchetière for the edification of

Indian children, in which are illustrated the history of the saints, the sacraments and the seven deadly sins. Once arrived here in Quebec, he was taught to speak and read like the rest of us, and acquired a rudimentary knowledge of geography, mathematics and, above all, Latin. He has, says Barnaby, little Latin, but he cherishes it as the sharpest arrow in his linguistic quiver.

"Whilst travelling in Canada as a guide for Pehr Kalm," continues Barnaby, "our noble young savage had much to learn from the eminent Swedish scientist, but since Kalm spoke neither English nor French, they could communicate only in Latin. It was, to be sure, a language far superior to the dog Latin of the seminaries. In Quebec, he had much admired the priests who seemed able to deliver themselves as effortlessly in Latin as they did in French, and he could not know that no one in this country has more than a few words of that language, especially not the peasants who have been mouthing the *Te Deum* all their lives without the slightest idea of what it means. Kalm pointed out to Saint-Ours that in Canada, clerics speak Latin only during Mass, and that the Bishop of Quebec himself refused to meet with the philosopher for the simple reason that our worthy prelate was only too aware of his inability to make himself understood in Latin. This realization must needs have caused a great consternation in Saint-Ours, and he took to despising anyone who pretended to a learning he did not, in fact, possess. Saint-Ours, however, knows the Latin names for a great many of our native plants. It was he, for example, who told me that the tamarack is called in Latin *Larix laricina*, and that a beverage made from its needles boiled with the liver of a beaver, when imbibed, is an effective tonic against the cough. That is something to know, is it not? I myself was unaware of it..."

There arises in the cellar a ground-swell of admiration for Saint-Ours, who is most assuredly not merely a courageous and useful fellow, but also a scholar, perhaps even a great physician, did he but know it. Ignatius excites our opinion with the information that he hath observed Saint-Ours rubbing his body with a live toad to rid himself of lice and fleas, but Marie and Fleurdelysse astonish us anew by claiming that that is no mark of great learning, since everyone is aware of that remedy. The enthusiasm ebbs soon after that, and we wish the women had kept their own counsel, for we now no longer talk of Saint-Ours, which leaves us with nothing to think about but our hunger.

Auguste has forbidden us to talk about food, but since food is all we think about, our being unable to talk about it places us at liberty to think about it all the more. It is, under the circumstances, an extremely difficult topic to obliterate from our minds, the more especially when, through the chinks in our cellar walls, there drifts the enticing odour of burning wood from the town. Such smells cannot help but bring to our recollection the image of those alchemical fires by which, in another life, are converted base ingredients to golden nectars and succulent sauces: how a pig, which we do so misprize to see wallowing in the filth of a barnyard, is transformed to roasted pork, stuffed and dripping on the spit; or the pumpkin, the lowly pumpkin, which sits out the greater part of its life in the mud at the bottom of a kitchen garden, yet doth redeem itself of its humble origins when nestled in a bank of coals, or sliced and grilled in the bakehouse, sprinkled with cinnamon or sugar.

Each hour of the day hath its own hunger. In the mornings, we want berries: strawberries, blueberries, raspberries, hawthornberries, serviceberries – it matters not so that they be washed down with thick cream and sugar. In the evenings, it is fresh bread and cheese. Likewise every hour hath its taste. At the hour of sunrise, we dream of the coarse rye bread we eat with onions and garlic; the next hour, the mouth fills with the memory of beef broth. Noon is green peas with butter. Mid-afternoon, fresh-picked corn, lightly boiled and served with more butter. At the dinner hour, we vacillate between fresh rainbow trout, filleted, rolled in flour and fried in a skillet with bacon fat, and the grilled chops sizzling on the cookstoves of the habitants, who welcome strolling players into their country kitchens. If we are fortunate, as we too often are, the night will bring the stench of rotting corpses to our nostrils and wipe all thought of food from our minds, and we may wake the next day with our stomachs distended from the bountiful feasts that fill our dreams. We swallow a mouthful of water, and wait for the hunger to take us again.

Our esurient state doth make us gentle. It quickens within us a deep sympathy for the bones we tossed so disdainfully from our table, without sucking out their marrow, as all good bones deserve. We weep for the tiny morsels of roast beef that fell from our forks, unobserved, and the duck's poor wing, which we so negligently burnt in the fire, and which we would now tenderly cosset in a soft blanket of fresh white bread, if we had some. We make for ourselves firm resolutions. Never again will we complain of Ignatius's somewhat perfunctory cooking; we will even thank him for it. Everything he makes will be delicious, we will devour it all, we will lick our plates. From now on, we will praise the food we once despised: broad beans for Auguste, sheep's kidneys for Barnaby. We even long for foods which we have never tasted of: thus Fleurdelysse pines for pears; Marie Laurent craves coffee.

That we do not die of starvation is due to the good Ursuline, who hath resorted to stealing the rations from the pouches of soldiers who die in the hospital. And to Bernard, who spends most of his day looking for his bear in the ruins of the town and brings back what he picks up there, when there is anything to pick up. Two days ago, Saint-Ours returned with a sack of dried corn; we boiled it up and made a salmagundi of it by the addition of the heel of a pumpkin, some flour and a small measure of pork fat. It was so good, the corn so tender and sweet, that we forgot for a while that Saint-Ours is the Straw Man.

The salmagundi so raised our spirits that we were emboldened to ignore Auguste's edict against talking about food, and we talked about food throughout the entire meal, as people do who take full bellies for granted. We exchanged recipes, we compared tastes. Blaise confessed that, so fond was he of corn on the cob, that he ate them without butter or salt; Marie admitted to a weakness for wheat bread smothered in cream and sprinkled with maple sugar, and the others applauded her discernment. We were feeling extremely well disposed, at least until Barnaby ventured the opinion that the best omelette in the world was made with fine herbs, to the which Ignatius counterproposed that an omelette was not an omelette that did not have onions in it. Barnaby begged to differ, and petulantly asked his esteemed colleague how he, Ignatius, could pretend to know the first thing about omelettes, never having set foot in France, where in his, that is Barnaby's, humble opinion, the omelette was the very prince of foods. There followed a spate of harsh words and an invitation, which was accepted, to step out of doors to settle the dispute in the manner of gentlemen, and the next day both Barnaby and Ignatius sported gloriously blackened eyes.

The only one among us who did not join in the food talk was Jericho. She continues to refuse even to think about food, the blame for which she lays at the door of our chief troublemaker, Ignatius, who, no sooner had Saint-Ours returned with the sack of corn than he blurted out one of his confounded questions, in his impatience to know whether it was true, as had been rumoured, that Saint-Ours hath tasted of human flesh.

"I only want to know," said Ignatius, "what it tastes like."

"As did I," replied Saint-Ours. "I saw nothing wrong in it. It is not so different from eating bear, and bear is the animal whose name I have taken, since indeed it was my brother and I who adopted Saint-Ours Deschaillons, and not the other way around. The bear is the most powerful animal in the forest, and is its king. So respected is he that the Algonquin do not presume to speak his name, calling him instead Short-tail, or Black-meat, and when they kill him for food, or to make clothing from his pelt, they first ask his forgiveness, and after, they place his head atop a high tree and burn tobacco to it. I have learned from Pehr Kalm that it is not otherwise in the northern parts of Europe, where, too, in former times, his name was not pronounced, and he was known as Beowulf, the wolf of bees. I have many times eaten of bear meat, and have covered myself with his fat and slept in his skin. We love what we eat, and we eat what we love. That is most true of our heroes and princes, for it is written in the scriptures..."

"But to eat a man!" interposed Ignatius.

"The taste is peculiar, that is all. When I die, my fellow animals will devour my flesh – flies, fish, ravens – and my soul will dwell in the constellation Ursus, under which I was born, and will one day return to earth in a new body. That is what the Indians believe. Each to his own."

The players shivered, especially Jericho. "But – "

"Like Ignatius," continued Saint-Ours, "I was curious. Among the Indians of Hudson Bay, where I lived for a time, it is held that he who eats the flesh of a human being is condemned to eternal sadness. The Mississaugas believe that he becomes a Windigo, an evil spirit. I wanted to know if they were right. And, as you can see, nothing happened. I have since come to question the beliefs of the Indians; I follow only those that appeal to my fancy. I am no longer convinced, for example, that when I die, my soul will go to live in Ursus; only on certain days, when I am in good spirits, can I credit such a belief. I have grave doubts; I waver from this belief to that. It all seems to me to be so many words. Once, with my friends the Wild Oats, I took part in one of Belestre's raids; we massacred an entire German colony – men, women, children. We took only four prisoners. One was a young girl who was ill; they split her skull open to see why she would not cry. The boy they adopted, without asking his opinion of the matter. They tortured a young soldier to death because he was so thin. And a fat man, a baker I think he must have been – we cut him open like a meat pastry and drank his blood, which the Indians call his broth, and ate the rest of him in one night. Again, nothing happened to me, I felt no different the next day. I have also consumed the flesh of a Negro, and found it tastes no different from that of a white man. I would do it again if I had to, but no longer out of curiosity. And I would rather eat a bear than a man."

The others made no reply to this. Only Fleurdelysse and Marie were not dismayed by his words, being themselves too well acquainted with misery to pass judgement on another brought into its desperate domain. They listened quietly to Saint-Ours, and smiled when they saw Jericho vomit up her corn.

And now Bernard has returned, his face as long as ever. Telemachus remains unfound. Saint-Ours rises from his bench and puts his arm around Bernard's shoulders, offering him some food from his own bowl. He likes Bernard and is moved by his unhappiness. "Your Telemachus," he tells him, "is without doubt holed up somewhere and is as safe as we are. He will come back to you, Bernard."

Bernard permits himself a small smile.

10

MONSIEUR de Saint-Ours, it so transpired, was accurate in his prediction, as our little prompter would say, were the latter still among us. He is, however, no longer able to perform his old function, and so it hath fallen to me, Auguste, to take up his tale. I am, after all, the director.

Montcalm engaged the enemy, as he had long dreamed of doing, according to the accepted rules of warfare, and succeeded in losing the battle and the lives of six hundred French soldiers and militiamen in a matter of a few minutes. Montcalm himself was killed and rather hastily interred in a mortar hole at the exact centre of the Ursuline chapel. Saint-Ours, with his Canadian militiamen and with Dumas and a number of Indians, made raids into the English army's flanks and killed a great many of them, including General Wolfe, who was conveyed to his flagship mortally wounded, whereupon he died. Quebec surrendered this morning at the insistence of the merchants, after five days of negotiations.

Monsieur de Ramezay did well to raise the white flag. He had six thousand mouths to feed, a third of them wounded soldiers. Our Ursuline and the good Bernard brought Saint-Ours back on a litter and would have placed him in the Captain's molasses crate had they not discovered our prompter already in possession of it, having crawled in to die along with the others. Fleurdelysse brought Saint-Ours back to our camp, though he was already more than half dead.

No one believed that it would end like this. We were exceedingly gay on the eve of the battle. Saint-Ours strode into our camp with several of his comrades: a lieutenant of dragoons; four militiamen, including a captain; and a Wild Oats chieftain called the Cat. They had somehow managed to liberate the hind quarter of a horse, three days hung, an huge sack of turnips, a demijohn of Spanish wine, five pounds of chocolate and a bottle of Cognac. We made a feast of it such as we will not forget, lo the Final Trumpet sounds.

Jericho required coaxing to join the festivities, her ardour for her beloved Benjamin having cooled noticeably since his avowal of having feasted on his fellow man. She remained some distance apart when he arrived, and did not, as hath been her tireless custom, pester him with a swarm of questions. Bernard, too, seemed not to have the heart for a feast. Without Telemachus, he was a changed man. The Ursuline finally convinced them to join the rest of us, however.

Although we were on the very threshold of starvation and would not be thought likely to pick and choose at what was, for many of us, our last supper, we hardly touched the horse. The habitants have been encouraged to eat their horses throughout the war, but they would not hear of such an outrage. To them, a horse is a noble animal and a useful one, here as elsewhere, and our habitant is as attached to his steed as is any chevalier of France. It would take more than a famine to reduce them to the eating of horseflesh. To such an extent that one day, at the beginning of the war, a group of Quebec housewives marched upon the residence of Governor-General Vaudreuil himself, the same who had decreed that henceforward horseflesh must replace beef in the general diet, and did protest that never in this life would they eat of it, and they threw the butchered haunches of their horses on the ground at the governor's feet to make a show of their determination, so that the governor was obliged to say he would have them imprisoned if they did not disperse. Likewise were we loath to partake of it now. But then the Cat, the Wild Oats, said to us, through Saint-Ours his interpreter, "You have but to make a pretense of it."

And it is true. Everything here is pretense. There is a king, somewhere, although we have neither seen nor heard him, and we do not obey him, in faith: we rob him at every turn. The militiamen told us brazenly how, upon being called to duty, they did present themselves at their recruitment posts in a state approximating nudity, so that they must needs be equipped cap-à-pie with new clothes and weapons. Some among them hath in such manner acquired four new suits and flintlocks. They steal from the king without scruple, saying, in their phrase, that they take nothing from him at Easter that they would not take the whole year long. When there was no war, they sold their wheat at grossly inflated prices, saying that, after all, it is the king's money.

The government functionaries purchase their own supplies, which they do buy from themselves at double the price. Nor is it otherwise across the border, for it is well known that Yankee merchants continue to buy our furs, and we from them in return their Brazilian tobacco and Jamaican rum, though we are at war. As the lieutenant of dragoons told us during our final feast, the gold epaulets on his shoulders were woven by Huguenot artisans in New York; he had them smuggled hence, since to have them sent from France would have cost too much and taken too long. Pretense. Our colonial administrators pay us with playing cards, which we all know perfectly well to be worthless. The habitants convert them into silver jewellery as quickly as possible, in anticipation of leaner days. Everyone here is for their own advancement, and look but to their proper interests. Even Saint-Ours admitted with a laugh that he was still in regular commerce with his merchants in Albany, and had been since the beginning of the war.

In like manner we make a pretense of going to Mass, of professing the sacraments, of respecting our priests, and praying, and desiring to go to heaven when we die. Even when we complain, we do but make a show of our indignation. Let pretense reign, then, we said; let us make a feast in earnest.

After conferring with the Cat, Saint-Ours delared that the horse was not, in fact, horse at all, but moose. Whereupon Ignatius averred that he had eaten of horse before, and that this was not like any horse he had ever tasted, being very much more marbled, in the manner of pork. We replied that if peradventure he did not like the taste of pork, he had but to think of some other viand that was more to his liking. Barnaby rose to say that although he was, perforce, speaking from an unusually advanced state of deprivation, yet was he in possession of an uncommonly discerning palate, and he did attest to the world that upon his honour, this was most certainly a side of very good beef. To the which Jericho, to show herself more refined than Barnaby, clamoured at the top of her voice that never in all her days had she tasted such a fine duck as this. In the end, our poor horse savoured of every manner of creature: goose, mutton, pheasant, wild boar. Even Bernard, who had not laughed for a fortnight, found it amusing. Only the Wild Oats ate it as a piece of horse, because he wanted to know what horse tasted like.

The wine and the food having loosed our tongues, we exchanged pleasantries, sang songs, told stories. It had been a long time since we felt so unwary. Jericho sang a bawdy ballad which, under less unrestrained circumstances, she would have professed not to have understood. I installed Marie in a wooden crate and sawed her in half. Ignatius produced a succession of gold sovereigns from the Wild Oats' nose, and then made them to disappear again into his own pocket, and Barnaby regaled the gathering with tumbling tricks and obscene contortions. Even Saint-Ours joined in the festivities by imitating for our amusement the cries of numerous wild animals, to which the Cat gave appropriate replies. I do not now recall who suggested the storytelling contest that ensued, but the challenge was to tell the most shocking tale imaginable, with the winner to receive the first drink from the bottle of Cognac.

The Cat almost won with the first story, which was about his having seen his people capture an Huron and eat his heart. The applause was long. The lieutenant of dragoons had been with Montcalm at the siege of Prague, and he told of the death of thirty thousand troops from typhus during the retreat. Neither did Saint-Ours acquit himself badly in his relation of the massacre of the Fox and Natchez nations by the French, who killed hundreds of warriors, not to mention their women and children, as the expression goes, but his voice broke in the telling of it, and so he failed to stir our imaginations. The little prompter said nothing when it came his turn; by my faith, I cannot even recall the sound of his voice.

Barnaby won the prize, to no one's astonishment, with his account of the punishment of Damien, who was drawn and quartered before the French court for having stabbed at the king with a penknife. For a playwright, Barnaby is a truly gifted actor.

The women did not long pay heed to our oratorical jousting. They sat somewhat down-stage, talking amongst themselves, whereupon I insinuated myself close enough to them to eavesdrop without being detected at doing so, and heard Marie Laurent exclaim, "Go to it, and then you may tell us what *he* tastes like."

At which Fleurdelysse explained to poor Jericho that Saint-Ours was right in saying that to love is to eat.

"Do you not say to a child that he so beautiful you gone eat him up? It is not different between a man and a woman. To love a man is to want to devour him. And if a man desire you, doan he nibble at your lips at the start, and lick your neck? And doan he then descend to suck your breasts, and bite at your thighs? And after that, doan he taste of your nether lips with his tongue, and then stuff you like a turkey, and do you not do the same for him, and take him into you, to consume him withal?"

Marie, the meanwhile, was biting her own tongue, so impatient was she to add her own delicacies to Fleurdelysse's menu.

"Never forget, Jericho, that a woman tastes of the sea and a man of the earth. Put your hand between your legs and smell: it is the salt scent of sea creatures, you will have remembrance of it. And when you have eaten your fill of a man, you will say his seed hath the taste of mushrooms, and the odour of the forest floor. A man or a woman with no smell have ceased to exist. The sea and the earth, Jericho, forget it not."

I perceived that poor Jericho was on the point of swooning, but whether from repugnance or desire, I knew not. She turned white, whilst her two counsellors laughed like loons. They were revenging themselves on Jericho, it seemed to me, who hath ever considered them to be less than nothings, an executioness and a slave.

From across the camp, Barnaby's voice sounded triumphant.

"This took place three years ago," he was saying, "in France. I read of it in the gazette. First, they distended Damien's guts with water. His shoulders were then broken by means of the strappado, and the executioner crushed his heels with his boots. The villain's hand was thrust into a brazier alive with coals, and his fingernails were drawn out with pincers. Molten lead was poured into each of his wounds. After that, four horses were tied to his limbs, and he was torn asunder. This took one hour. His arms and legs became disarticulated, and yet he did not come apart, so that the executioner was obliged to cut at the muscles with a poignard. Both legs and one arm were thus removed before the man expired. His body was tossed onto a woodpile ten paces from the gibbet. And all that, mind you, as punishment for inflicting a scratch on the royal person. Behold, ladies and gentlemen, the grandeur that is France!"

Never had Barnaby received such applause as he did on that night.

The entertainment continued well into the morning hours, whereupon we all went to bed, our heads heavy with wine and our stomachs full of horse. But I did not close my eyes, for I wanted to see if Jericho would profit from the advice of her two counsellors. Unseemly curiosity, I do confess it, but it was stronger than I.

I did not see much. Jericho crept up to Saint-Ours in the darkness, awakened him, then thrust her hand under her skirt and held it out for him to smell, saying, "I am the sea." But it was the Ursuline who was sleeping in Saint-Ours's place, and she merely replied to Jericho, "Yes, I know, my little one, so am I. Go to sleep, now." Saint-Ours, meanwhile, was with Marie in another corner; they were coupling noisily against the wall, like condemned prisoners. Across the way, the little prompter slept the whole of the night with Fleurdelysse.

At the morning tocsin, Saint-Ours and the Cat rose and immediately began preparing to leave. Jericho ran to Marie and Fleurdelysse and cried in their arms, so that the two women knew that for once she was grieving for someone other than herself, and they pitied her, that she had not tasted of the man whom she would now never know.

We tried to detain him. "Do not go," we begged him. "Stay here with us. We are your friends, Benjamin!" The Ursuline asked him to at least say a prayer before going into battle. To please her, because he had, I think, grown fond of her, he bent to his knees and said grace, which was the only prayer that he could remember.

He then rose to his feet and departed our company, saying, "I am going to do something real in a world that is but pretense. Fare thee well."

It was with much heaviness of heart that we watched them go. Marie the executioness above the rest.

That day was very hard. We had not expected that the English would land so close, or that the battle would be so quickly over. The French officers blame the loss on the Canadian militiamen. The Canadians were in the front ranks, to protect the French soldiers with their bodies. They were given the order to fire and advance, at which it was the turn of the English to fire and advance, and so the battle would continue until there were none left standing, as is set down in the best books. But the militiamen, no fools they, had their own ideas about proper warfare. After the first salvo, they threw themselves to the ground to reload, whereupon the French soldiers behind them, bearing the brunt of the English salvo, became disorganized and the rout ensued. That is how it was explained to me.

Bernard and the good Ursuline had such difficulty retrieving Saint-Ours and placing him in the Captain's molasses crate that we wept with them. Even Jericho. Bernard was so distraught at Saint-Ours's death that we did not have the heart to tell him that it was Saint-Ours and the Cat who had shot his bear, and pretended it was horsemeat.

I do not rightly know what will become of us now. No doubt we will be sent back to France. There is a ship that makes the crossing once a year, called the *Auguste*, and I would sail with her if I could but find the money. I believe that I would bring good fortune to a vessel that bears the same name as my own.

We thought we were witnessing the end of the world, but the world hath not ended. It is, however, much depreciated. And we are still hungry.

BOOK TWO
THE DUMMY

1

WOULD someone have the kindness to tell me what I am doing here?

And while they are at it, they might also tell me who I am, who the people are who seem to be in charge of me here, and, if it is not too much trouble, where here is.

I seem to have been conscious for some time, although I still sleep for long periods. By following the course of the sun as it crosses the blue expanse of window above my bed, I can determine when it is morning, afternoon and night. The nights are growing cooler, and during the day the light has a rusty tinge, as at the end of August.

Now it is night, and I have time to marshal my impressions. My room smells of the sea, but the odour no doubt issues from the porpoise-oil lamp that burns on the wall beside the door. I might be in the bowels of a ship. I say that, although I have never in my life been aboard a ship, so far as I know. Did someone once tell me what a ship smells like? Or did I read it somewhere? Do I know, it suddenly occurs to me, that I can read?

Yes! I do know that! It comes to me of a piece: a memory of myself as a child, turning the pages of a catechism printed on birch bark, and a priest correcting my pronunciation. A Jesuit. Father Sixte! Yes, that was his name. I can breathe more easily now; for a moment, I feared myself unlettered. Such relief is fleeting, since I do find these long, sleepless nights difficult. However, the small certainties I can detach from this curtain of

fog that surrounds me requires such prodigious efforts of concentration that I can perform them only when I am alone. For
which reason my insomniac nights have become so precious to
me.

The couple that have charge of me are good people, like
father and mother to me. He is a giant of a man; she is a beautiful Negress. They speak to each other in such familiar terms I
must conceive of them as husband and wife. Every morning,
they get me up and feed me, usually with a kind of creamed oat-
meal mixed with maple sugar, which they spoon into me with
the tenderest felicity. At noon they bring me vegetable broth and
bread; they dip bread into the broth and place it in my mouth,
then wait patiently for me to chew and swallow. At night it is the
vegetable broth again, but this time with a soupçon of meat
added, a hint of mutton or beef. Not a varied menu, but a whole-
some one. I feel my strength returning.

They must not know the extent to which I have regained my
senses. When I first opened my eyes I was afraid to close them
again, and I feared that my guardian angels would sound the
alarm. But no, they seemed unconcerned that my eyes would
open from time to time. To be safe, however, I endeavour to
have them closed whenever they enter my room.

It is a very spare room: a chest of drawers in which are kept
my bedclothes and nightshirts, a chair, my bed, a wash stand.
There is, too, a night closet, to which they carry me when my
needs occasion it. This morning, when I had eaten, the giant
picked me up and brought me to it. Either he is as strong as a
bear, or I have become so thin that lifting me is a trifling matter,
for my transposition seemed not to have caused him the slightest effort.

When I had finished, the giant washed me in the presence of
the Negress, who did not so much as avert her eyes. He is very
gentle of touch, this colossus, and has caused me not the slightest discomfort. When I was first restored to consciousness, I
found these attentions somewhat humiliating, but now that I am

accustomed to them, they infuse me with a feeling of happiness, of bestowed benevolence, nay, even of love. I look forward to our daily ritual with keen anticipation. That being said, I prefer when it is she who performs that particular office.

Most mornings and afternoons they walk me about the room a short while, and each day in my bed they undress me, bathe and rub my body, and exercise my arms and legs as I lie on my back. Happily, the giant is always in attendance during these exertions, otherwise, were I alone with the Negress, I fear that my manhood would assert itself. Even as it is, I must distract myself with silent prayer to prevent any outward show of virility.

I make no mistake, however: I am a prisoner in this room. They always bolt the door behind them, from within when they are within, and from without when they leave. They always come into my room together, never alone, why otherwise than to prevent any attempt on my part to escape? From below, I sometimes hear a man speaking with a foreign accent, and his voice has reminded me that there is a war, and that I have played some part in it.

Prisoner though I be, I am no ordinary prisoner. We seem to be in a great house, a manor house, perhaps; on the first day that I was able to rise from my bed unaided, I could see from the window that my room was on the top floor, directly under the eaves. There was much stone and half-timbering, a stout wooden enclosure roundabout, and a coach standing in a great courtyard below. So weak was I that I was obliged to return to my bed and await the following day to further my intelligence.

Now that I think upon it, I ought to have known that this is a manor house, because there was ice in the pitcher of water that was brought to me the other day. If there is ice in August, then there must perforce be a cellar, and there are no cellars beneath the habitants' houses. A hole is dug under the manor and covered over with planks; at the recommencement of winter the hole is filled with snow and then pumped full of water from the well; this water freezes during the winter, and remains in solid state throughout the year. I take my hat off to my gaolers; they have chosen my prison well.

I do not know what they intend to do with me, but I am familiar with the options: exchange for another prisoner, ransom, execution. In war, anything can happen.

Now that I have set my deductive faculties in motion, certain aspects of my situation are becoming apparent. My wounds tell me that I must be a soldier; in the dresser, there is an officer's tunic and a moth-eaten periwig. The tunic must be mine; two nights ago, I tried it on and it fit me like a glove. It is shot through with holes in several places and smells strongly of powder, though it seems to have been a long time out of service. Would that I could conjure my rank from it. Colonel? Captain? I think I should prefer to be a captain, since I would not then be obliged to wear the periwig.

I have determined to make my escape at the earliest possible opportunity. I have a vague recollection of fire, a clash of swords, tears cried for nothing; when I close my eyes, I see houses burning in the night, women weeping. The memory of female voices inflames me: I feel my manhood stirring, stiffening. My humours returning.

Each day brings new discoveries. This morning, I noticed that the rays from the sun falling on my coverlet were blue, red and purple. It has taken me the rest of the day to explain this curious phenomenon, but at last I think I have it. Bird droppings on the window pane. Now is the end of summer, and the birds are gorging themselves on blueberries, raspberries, hawthorn-berries; their droppings, coloured by these fruits, function as prisms on the glass. This deduction reminds me that autumn is approaching. The armies will be removing to their winter quarters, and travelling in that threadbare uniform will soon be unwise. I must leave before the cold weather locks me in.

Today, in fact. If need be, I will even wear the confounded periwig.

◆

My memory is returning piecemeal. Not as completely as I would wish it, but returning all the same. I can recall the events of the past few days exactly, but details of my life before coming to this pass remain foggy and disconnected.

I dressed myself in the officer's tunic that was in the chest of drawers. I also found therein some buckskin leggings and a pair of moccasins. I put them on, not knowing what the weather outside was like, and having no intention of coming back to change my clothes.

I could not set out unarmed. An ancient halfpike hung on the wall, and although it is a weapon more suited to an infantry sergeant than to the captain I hoped I was, I was glad enough of it. I left the periwig in the drawer; if it turned out that I was a colonel, I would have to set a new fashion for bare-headedness in colonels.

The giant and the Negress, who had both treated me well, I decided I would merely knock on the head. The door to my room opened quietly. As stealthily as a wolf, I crept to the top of the staircase that led down to the kitchen immediately below. From my vantage point, I could see that the door leading into the great courtyard was standing wide open. All I had to do was descend the stairs and throw myself through it: if the giant should try to stop me, he would be a dead giant, or at the very least a stunned one.

I could hear the Negress in the kitchen, singing as she worked. I could even see her as I descended the stairs. She was kneading bread dough. Her blouse hung loose, and from my position slightly above her I could see her breasts. I was very nearly overcome with desire for her; a fine mist of flour had mingled with perspiration at her breast and formed there a white crust that I longed to lick away. She seemed more beautiful to me than ever, less mechanical, absorbed as she was in her labour and the sweet song she was singing. She was a woman, no longer the nurse I knew. I wanted to speak to her, to say a gentle word of farewell, but something held me back. Then, taking a deep breath, I uttered an Indian battle cry, a high-pitched howl meant to curdle the blood of an enemy, and in three bounds I was out the door. Behind me, the Negress herself gave such a penetrating shriek that for a moment it was I who was very nearly petrified with terror.

My dash to freedom, the unaccustomed movement, the rush of activity, was all so new to me that I was already close to fainting from fatigue by the time I reached the courtyard. I tried to run, but was obliged to stop two or three times, nearly dropping to my knees to catch my breath, ere I gained the enclosure. Once there, I could scarcely manage to pull myself to the top of the wooden fence that separated the manor grounds from the open fields beyond. Had anyone been watching, they would have assumed they were seeing a tired, old man making a break for freedom.

Someone was watching. At the top of the fence, I turned and saw the giant emerging from the stables, a heavy hammer clutched in his huge hand. I caught the sound of his voice as he called to me and advanced in my direction. I decided to stand and fight, and raised the halfpike menacingly. Luckily, the giant changed his mind and turned in the direction of the kitchen door, where the Negress was still shrieking wildly. I dropped to the ground and made off as best I could.

The field was covered by low, thorny bushes. Running upright through them proved almost impossible, and I found myself more often than not crawling on my hands and knees. This had the salutary effect of rendering me invisible, but no one seemed to be following me from the manor house. I must have scrambled in such wise for a good hour before coming upon the scent of running water, from which I suddenly longed to drink and refresh myself before pressing on. Although it was autumn, yet was the day warm, and I was working hard.

At length my course brought me to a small stand of trees. I stopped to rest, then resumed my scuffling progress through the brush in the manner of the Iroquois, when they would stealthily approach the habitation of settlers in days gone by. Perhaps it was the memory of those days, touched off by my suspicious mode of ambulation, that so transfixed the three men I came across in the field. Farmers, to judge by their pointed, wide-brimmed hats and their canvas clothes. They were clearing their acreage, and were no doubt ill prepared to apprehend an Iroquois brave crawling straight out of one of their horror stories and raising himself to his full height before their very eyes, halfpike in hand. They dropped their implements and stood in slack-jawed amazement, stupefied with terror; nonetheless, I was desperate to learn from them what they called this place. To my astonishment, however, not a word escaped from my lips. Nothing could I utter but a series of hoarse croaks, struggle though I might, at which the three simpletons ran off in such panic as they had seen the very devil incorporate himself before them. Their precipitate departure had, however, two happy consequences. One, they left behind their midday meal – a crock of water flavoured with honey, a small loaf of coarse bread and half a leg of ham – which I devoured ravenously, being very nearly faint with hunger. And two, it was from them that I learned my name, for they had run off crying, "Monsieur de Saint-Ours!" Saint-Ours. I liked the sound of it. It gave me the sensation of having become reacquainted with an old friend.

Feeling refreshed, I made my way towards a body of water I could see glimmering to my left. When I reached it, I deduced by its size and current that it was a river and quite a large one; there was a small village on the far side, which confirmed my impression. I bent to drink from it and found the water sweet. Had it tasted of salt, I would have known that I was below the Ile d'Orléans, that is, downriver from Quebec. I was in fact upstream, but where, or how far, I knew not. But I at least had had the pleasure of finding my river again.

I worked my way along the riverbank, in what I took to be the direction of Quebec, for two long hours, being careful to keep myself hidden in the tall reeds that grew close to shore for fear of being discovered by the search party that must of a surety be combing the countryside for their escaped prisoner. At nightfall, completely exhausted, I found a dry spot somewhat above the water line and fashioned for myself a makeshift shelter out of bulrushes. As I was about to crawl into it, however, I noticed that the ground beneath me had previously been disturbed. With the aid of my halfpike, I dug in the soft sand and gravel and discovered a cache, exactly like those left here and there by Indians and *coureurs de bois* before the war. The cache contained everything I needed to make good my escape: a measure of dried meat, a tinder box, a piece of punk with which to make a fire, a fully charged powder horn, an awl, a knife, lengths of moose-hide thong, and a drinking gourd. Enough to keep me going for at least four days.

I tasted of the meat: it was bear. I experienced the first moment of pure happiness since my escape. I had drunk from my river, I had learned my name. I knew who I was. And now, in this ecstacy of freedom, I had rediscovered my self.

Calm again, at peace with myself, able once more to find happiness in the small pleasures of life, and having ascertained my true identity, I no longer fought against sleep. I did not even take the time to complete the roof of my shelter, but simply rolled myself in the odoriferous moose hide with which the cache had been wrapped. I was naturally nervous that, once asleep, I might not reawaken for a long time, as must have happened to me once already, but exhaustion soon overcame my anxieties.

2

I AWOKE early the next morning to the sound of geese honking overhead. I felt rested and strong, the sensation of well-being that had so elevated my spirits the night before having not departed from me.

Having slept in a normal fashion, I believed that the lethargy that had pervaded my movements until then had gone forever: no longer would I drowse away my mornings, waking from time to time indifferent to the hour of day or the state of the weather. My first clear thoughts were these: my mother is a star; my father is a bear; I am alive. Standing beside my river, I joyfully merged my own water with his.

After eating the remainder of the bear meat, I resumed my course of the day before. My plan was to find a canoe, with which I would put a greater distance between myself and my erstwhile captors. By now, the alarm must certainly have been sounded.

When the sun was at its highest, that is at mid-day, I came upon an apparition that to me seemed much better than a canoe: a horse, well saddled and shod, grazing among the reeds. I lay on my stomach among the rushes, perfectly hid, and waited for its master to appear, for I had determined upon the instant that that horse was to be mine.

Its rider soon showed himself. He was an English officer, a major; his red tunic was faded and worn. He came walking through the reeds with a concentrated expression, as though he were looking for something. Or someone. Presently he called his horse to him, reached into the saddlebag, and withdrew a small cooking pot, which he filled with water from the river. Then he made a fire and set the water on to boil.

Having spied on him for what I deemed a sufficient length of time, I fell upon him as he was eating. A sharp blow to the head with my halfpike and he lay senseless at my feet. The exertions of the previous day, combined with the nourishing viands, had restored in me the better part of my strength and agility. Before my illness, I would doubtless have issued the officer a formal challenge, but my failed health had instilled in me an unwonted caution, a reliance upon subterfuge. The weak think more deeply than the strong, as I was beginning to learn.

Having invited myself into the officer's mess, I commenced to partake of his dinner. I then bound and gagged him, as he seemed on the point of regaining consciousness. To further inhibit his escape, I entwined his torso in a fishing net that I found in his saddlebag.

He awoke in a fury of resentment. He commenced to groan loudly, then slowly progressed from painful lamentations to a curious sort of stifled barking, his eyes wide in supplication, almost as though he would have discourse with me. I brandished my pike-staff at him, and his impertinences soon ceased.

It was a fine day. I had acquired the wherewithal to facilitate my escape and, what was more, had now taken a prisoner whom I might, at some future date, be in a position to exchange for a considerable ransom. To that end, I resolved to conduct him to the nearest village, where I would be able to ascertain my precise whereabouts.

Tethering my prisoner to his own horse, I climbed into the saddle, and together we set off, me happily astride the animal, he following miserably in tow behind. My soldier's instinct had returned in full; I must at least have been a captain, and even contemplated the periwig of a colonel if such I turned out to be. My recent malady seemed to have rendered me more susceptible to humane consideration, however: my prisoner often stumbled and fell, whereupon I stopped to allow him to regain his feet rather than continue unconcerned, as doubtless I would have done in the past.

After an hour's travel, we came upon a crossroads marked by a large crucifix, such as are often seen in the countryside of New France. The sight of this wooden Christ pinioned upon a rough-hewn cross stirred my heart, for it resurrected in me an image of myself as a child, gazing up into His doleful face. Just then, a group of farmers appeared on the road, armed with pitchforks and flintlocks of the kind once used for trade with the Indians. They appeared to be militiamen on their way to fight an urgent battle, and I raised my hand to them in salute.

In a swarm, they hurried towards us. Their arrival was not marked, as I had anticipated it would be, by expressions of gratitude to me, who had taken an enemy prisoner on only my second day of liberation, but rather with an inexplicable show of sympathy for the English officer! They even prevailed upon me to release him from his bonds. I tried to stop them with a word of command, but, as had been the case the day before, though I could formulate the proper phrases in my head, I was damned if I could bring my tongue to utter them. The militiamen pressed about the prisoner and looked up at me with a pitying expression on their faces. One of them asked me to descend from my mount.

"Monsieur de Saint-Ours," he said, "if you please, sir, do not persist in this sad enterprise. This is Major Stillborne, master of the neighbouring seigneury. Please allow us to release him. He is a friend to us all, a brave gentleman who wishes no harm in the world, and who I am certain you will come to hold in high esteem yourself when you have regained your proper intelligence, begging your pardon. He was coming to inquire after your health, as is his custom. Sir, if you would kindly allow us..."

I was utterly dumbfounded, utterly. A cabriolet pulled up, drawn by a fine matched pair, and the militiamen lifted the major into it with many tender solicitations. The major, for his part, once his bonds and gag were removed, seemed incapable of anything more than to hold his head in his hands and complain about his discomforture. To my amazement, I was able to understand everything he said: I had not known that I could comprehend English.

When the major had been safely despatched to his own manor, the habitant who had spoken to me took me by the arm and told me he was going to take me home as well, adding that it was not far, and introducing himself as Master Séraphin. "Notary of Sapinière," he added, "and the voice, if I may so put it, of your authority here. I have been occupied in your affairs since you were brought here in so, er, uncommunicative a condition, following the Siege of Quebec. You are our seigneur; it is to you we owe our allegiance and our faith, and it is for that reason we have cared for you as we would a child, although you are in fact more like our father. To put it plainly, Monsieur de Saint-Ours, we are your servants, and we love you."

The road was by now quite encumbered with people who had come out to stare at me. They gaped at me as though I had returned from the dead. The men doffed their caps, the women curtsied, the children ran up to touch me. As for my prisoner, I quickly decided to heed the advice of the notary. These people seemed so docile, and at the same time so persuasive, that it was impossible to resist them. Certain I was that they intended to do me not the slightest harm.

As we progressed along the road, Séraphin laid before me many details of the seigneury, using long words that I did not understand. Seventy tenant farmers, twenty-four of whom were widows. A thousand acres ploughed and planted, four hundred more lying fallow. Two hundred head of cattle. Three hundred of horses. Five score of sheep. Eighty farmers' houses, of which ten were vacant. I was given the agreeable information that, in the past year, my tenant farmers had milled hundreds of sacks of wheat and three hundred of rye, and harvested one thousand bushels of turnips, apples, pears and wild cherries. My lands were the best managed in the region; the income from them was enormous. Or would be. Naturally, the habitants had not been paying all their rents; since I had been asleep for such a long time, they considered that I would have few expenses. But the arrears would soon be made up. I had the notary's word for it! I had many distinguished neighbours, among them the Sieur du Bec and Major Tristram Stillborne, the unfortunate gentleman whom I had just...

I had stopped listening to him. Had the war ended, then? Was this territory through which we were passing French or English? Where were my men? These questions and more raced so violently through my brain that I began to feel nauseous, and wanted nothing so much as to lie down and go back to sleep.

We arrived at the very manor house from which I had so

recently made my escape. The Negress and the giant were standing in the doorway, the latter appearing somewhat less gigantic than he had hitherto seemed to me. It was as though, in my weak state, I had lent him a stature commensurate with the degree to which his strength had been greater than my own. There were also waiting a well-dressed woman and a man wearing a blue waistcoat and holding a curious sort of writing table in his hand. They sat me down at a table that had been carried out and placed in a small stand of well-tended poplars; they all stood around smiling broadly and talking, evidently overjoyed at my presence among them. All I could make out was Monsieur de Saint-Ours this and Monsieur de Saint-Ours that.

I, too, tried to speak. I had a thousand questions to which I fervently desired the answers. But nothing came out of my mouth. I was consumed in silent rage! At length, the man in the blue waistcoat advanced towards me holding out his writing table. "I am Toussaint, your secretary, sir," he said. "If you are having difficulty formulating words, perhaps you would do us the honour of writing them down."

I racked my brain for several moments, but all that would come to mind was the Latin word, *Pax?*

The notary and the secretary read what I had written, exchanged brief glances, and then the secretary responded, "Yes, sir, peace has indeed been established between England and France. Everywhere there is peace now, not only here but in Prussia, in Spain, in Russia....It has been two years, sir, in Europe. Here in Canada, five years. Yes, sir. Five. Canada now belongs to the King of England, and we are all loyal British subjects. Yes, it is odd, sir, when you think of it. You go to sleep French and, hello! you wake up English. I quite see that, sir. It wasn't quite that sudden for the rest of us, I'm happy to say. We hardly noticed a thing. We weren't consulted about it, you know. But such things must perforce occur more frequently when you sleep for a very long time, as you have done, sir.

"As for us, it has not made much of a difference one way or

the other. The goings-on all took place far away, and everything was settled months before we even heard about it. We were a bit taken aback, as you can imagine, sir, when we found out we were English, but it was not as much of a jolt as you might think. We still speak our own language, as you see, although that's not the kind of thing you can expect to change overnight, is it, sir? Chartres held out until just last year, nearly six years after Quebec. It's amazing, isn't it? The world just seems to take its good old time about these things. We were not under martial law for more than a year, or was it two?

"The English have been very kind, when you consider all the things they might have done to us. There was no pillaging. They left us our churches, our farms, and our wives. They even punished any of their own soldiers who behaved disrespectfully towards us. The only person they hanged, so far as I know, was an old crone named Corriveau – a witch she was – who poisoned her husband. We would have hanged her ourselves in the old days, eh, sir? After the hanging, they left her to rot in an iron cage. Since then, there hasn't hardly been anything to write home about, as you might say."

Throughout this long discourse I sat like a stunned ox. When the secretary had finished, the well-dressed woman approached.

"I am Clémence," she said, "your housekeeper. You have been asleep for seven years, Monsieur de Saint-Ours. During the Battle of Quebec, a ball fired from a French cannon very nearly took your head off, sir. Fortunately, it had already gone through three men before finding its way to you, and its force was greatly diminished. Some friends of yours found you and placed you in the care of an Ursuline, and she brought you back to life."

"At the Augustinian hospital," interrupted the notary, Séraphin, "where the victorious English were treated alongside the vanquished French by the nursing sisters. Your companions were Major Stillborne, although he was only a lieutenant then, and General Sir Guy Carleton, who is now the governor of the

Province of Quebec. You were fortunate to have been placed in such well-connected company in that house of death."

A man whom I had not remarked earlier now came up to my chair.

"Dr. Ambroise, your physician," he said. "I, too, was at the Siege of Quebec, serving in a medical capacity. You were my patient throughout the terrible winter that followed the surrender. You had a great many wounds on every part of your body. Some of them were old and had re-opened. But you recovered, I am happy to report. You were a healthy man, sir. Physically, at any rate. It was your mind that worried us; you suffered a tremendous cerebral perturbation, a sort of mental concussion, and we could not say whether you would remain comatose for the remainder of your life, or if you ever woke up that you would retain your cognitive faculties. And now, here you are, God be praised, sound as a shilling! Excepting, of course, for your power of speech. As to that, it is much too early to say. Perhaps…"

It had become difficult to hold my head up. All this, coming upon me so quickly, was proving too much for me to bear. Exhaustion overcame me in waves. I wanted nothing more than to lie down on the grass, but I dared not move. Suddenly there were children running around the side of the house, two boys and a girl, the latter very dark-skinned. They were extraordinarily beautiful. Dazed as I was, yet could I not refrain from smiling at them, albeit in the manner of one who has nothing to say.

"The children," began the notary, but then he hesitated and, turning to the Negress, took up again in his erstwhile spritely tone. "This is Valentine, your maid and cook. She was born a slave and came with the seigneury as part of its chattel. You gave her her freedom, in your boundless generosity, when you acquired these lands…"

This time I managed to stand up and point my finger at my chest, as to say, "Me? Seigneur? When did that come about?"

"As to that," said the notary, "there was no great difficulty. You were well known as a trader, and before the war had amassed a great fortune. Before returning to Quebec to rejoin your regiment, you instigated arrangements to purchase this seigneury, which had formerly belonged to the Saint-Ours family, who are now reestablished on the Richelieu River. Their land here had reverted to the king.

"I remember it as though it were yesterday. I had just opened my practice in this region, having removed hither from Montreal, where business had fallen off. You came to see me, to seek my counsel regarding these transactions. Acting on your behalf, I bought up all the land hereabouts, paid the back taxes owing to the king and consolidated it into a seigneury. It took three years. There were a few obstacles at first, some small recalcitrances, but in the end, business is always business. While you were sleeping, I made you Benjamin de Saint-Ours, Seigneur de la Sapinière. Oh, no, please, no need to thank me..."

3

I GRABBED the writing table from the secretary and wrote another word: *Amici.*

"The others?" he asked. "Oh, I see. Yes. Well, they did not wait for you. After the surrender of Montreal, the year after the battle of Quebec, all the French officers returned to France. All of them: Bourlamaque, Bougainville, Lévis, Vaudreuil. The lot.

"The Canadian seigneurs, most especially those who had children and were anxious about their futures, also packed up and emigrated to France, where nothing awaited them but their dead ancestors. The rich merchants likewise. Most of the priests, as well, at least those who could afford it. The only ones who stayed behind were the poor and those who were too sick or too seriously wounded to make the journey. Like yourself, sir. The less fortunate ones, as you might say – the patriots.

"There was a time, early on, when you were thought to be

sufficiently recovered from your wounds to rejoin your regiment. It was under the command of General Amherst, who was then the Governor of Montreal. The negotiations for your seigneury here were still incomplete, and Mr. Stillborne, who had by then been made a captain, and who was desirous of marking his promotion with a seigneury of his own, put in an offer for these lands. It was thought by those in authority that your presence here, saving your grace, sir, would be inimical to a lasting peace.

"Passage was accordingly booked for you aboard the *Auguste*, a French vessel that was returning to her home port. You were being looked after by the director of the largest theatrical group in the country. He had offered to take you; in fact, he and his troupe refused to leave you behind. But at the last minute your place was taken by a seigneur whose fortune, if I may be so bold, sir, exceeded your own, and who had made several judicious disbursements in certain quarters. In any case, when the ship sailed, you remained in Quebec, still bed-ridden. And a marvellous thing it was, too, because the *Auguste* went down off the coast of Acadia. There were almost no survivors, sir. One there was who made his way back to Quebec, however, having suffered a thousand privations, not least of which was his dragging himself through the forest primeval in the dead of winter. He was the Seigneur Luc Lacorne de Saint-Luc, the same who had stolen your place on board the *Auguste*, and upon his safe arrival in Quebec, he took his oath of allegiance to the King of England and determined to remain in this country, saying he would never in this life set foot in France. After that, few ships returned to France full of well-heeled refugees. It was no doubt Saint-Luc's example that persuaded the authorities to leave you in peace. And so it is, sir, as we tell ourselves, that the Fates have preserved you among us, your tenant farmers, sir."

I had again ceased to listen. Having just learned that I was a wealthy and respected seigneur, that life had not changed under King George, and a great deal of other things, I knew not what response I could make. I could follow what was being said to me only with the greatest difficulty. I wanted nothing more than to go back to sleep.

The former giant caught me as I slipped from my chair. The notary Séraphin introduced him to me. "He is Zacharias, your manservant and jack of all trades. He does everything that needs to be done around here. He has a heart of oak! Clémence and Valentine also look after your needs. Dr. Ambroise and I live in the village, not far away. I pray you, do not hesitate to call upon our services if you have need of them. Your secretary, Toussaint, resides in the manor house with you and manages your affairs. He is very attached to you."

Supported by Zacharias and Valentine, I made my way into the house. Seated at the kitchen table were the three children, the black girl and the two boys that I had seen earlier. No longer having the strength to write, I merely pointed in their direction and looked inquiringly at the secretary.

"Ah, the children, yes," he said, clearing his throat. "Ahem. Yes. Well, you know, although you have been in a…for want of a better term…an unconscious condition, certain of your faculties remained, shall we say…er…"

He was interrupted by Valentine. "Do not listen to him, master, he speaking gibberish. What he mean to say is that your body was far from dormant even though in your mind you were sleeping. You did not seem to object to the comforts of female companionship during the long, cold nights. In short, sir, the children are yours. The girl, Marjolaine, is mine, that is, ours. The taller boy, who hath your eyes and hair, that is Jeremy. You knew his mother in Quebec; she was on the *Auguste* when it went down. The other boy is Nicholas. We do not know who his mother is. A girl from the village, we suspicion, who took advantage of your weakened state when we were not in the house. She must have heard of your returning strength. Any rate, she left the little one alongside of the well in the courtyard, with a note naming you the father. He been raised with the other two, and he most resembles you in the matter of temperament, sir."

This time it was the notary who broke in. "You are under no legal obligation to recognize them, sir, none at all. These children belong, as you might say, to everyone here." At this, I caught Valentine casting him a dirty look. "But they are very well-behaved, quite civilized, well-brought-up children. Especially the youngest..."

No, it was decidedly too much to absorb. To learn in an hour that one has been asleep for seven years, that in that time a war has ended and a peace signed without our knowledge, that I am not only a seigneur but the father of a family, and to have no memory of any of it! I simply could not take it all in.

Despite all the kindness that had been shown me that afternoon, I could do nothing but take off my clothes, even as I stood in the kitchen before the entire household, and mount the stairs to my room, where I promptly went back to sleep.

◆

I slept for fourteen months. I awoke on St. Martin's Day; the very day, as I learned upon rising, upon which the local habitants traditionally come to pay their respects and to pledge their allegiance to their seigneur.

No sooner had I opened my eyes, it seemed, than there they were, hats in hands, a dozen or so of them, each paying me the most extravagant compliments and presenting me with gifts. One gave me three fat capons; another a brace of partidges; others brought me two hares, a dozen eels, four sturgeons, a quarter of dried moose meat and a sack of nuts. I acknowledged their bounty and dismissed them with a wave of my arm; I still had no words with which to thank them. My housekeeper, Clémence, ushered them into another room, where they were each given something to eat or drink before being allowed to leave. Valentine brought me one of the drinks, something she called tea, the taste of which I much enjoyed.

By this time I was well awake, and I did not sleep another

wink for the next four years! It is difficult to explain, difficult
even to formulate an idea of what it is like. I sleep one year out
of five; I endure seemingly interminable periods of insomnia,
which allow me to make up for the time I lose in sleeping. I feel
as though I am living three lives at once, rather as though I had
sold my soul to Satan. If I were given my choice in the matter, I
would assuredly prefer to be awake during the day and to sleep
soundly at night, like everyone else. But I have never been like
everyone else, never like others from this place.

The notary, Séraphin, comes to see me. Indeed, if I did not
put him bodily out of doors at times, I am persuaded he would
stay for months on end. He says he is fond of the cooking here;
I strongly suspect he is rather fonder of the cook.

He has explained to me my rights and obligations regarding
my tenant farmers, as well as their tradition of respect and allegiance to their seigneur. I learned that I was a captain of militia,
and in the case of "troubles" – an invasion, peradventure, or an
insurrection, I was obliged to assemble a company of my fellow
parishioners and to place it and myself at the disposition of the
governor, who could send us wherever it pleased him to deploy
us.

Troubles? What troubles, I wondered, could possibly befall
us now that the kings in Europe were no longer at war? I could
think of none. Captain of militia? Why not general, nay, since
they were passing out titles, why not emperor? Perhaps, when I
next awaken, I will find myself a pope or a sultan. They can
make of me what they will, it seems. A circumstance that does
not please me.

What troubles we have are entirely domestic ones.

First there is the secretary, Toussaint, who is ever at odds with
the notary, Séraphin. The other day it was over the question of
whether or not I take precedence over the priest when I enter the
church. They quoted articles of jurisprudence and codes of conduct at me until they were blue in the face. I asked them – still
by writing on the tablet, of course – where the church was. They

told me that there is one in the village, but that it has been closed for several years, since the diocese is too impoverished to despatch a priest to us. I then settled their dispute by pointing out that since there is no priest, then I obviously take precedence in the church. Excepting that, since I never go to church, precedence goes to the first to arrive, on the basis of first come, first served. The logic of this observation failed to diminish the ardour of their argumentation.

The discussion served to call to my mind the last time I had been in a church. It was a German church, somewhere in Pennsylvania, and it was during the war. I had entered it for the purpose of setting fire to it. When the flames had extinguished themselves, the walls were still standing, and I remembered saying to myself how well made they must have been. I still recall the *Te Deum* and one or two other prayers, perhaps because I can remember so little else. Try as I might to forget them, the words remain inscribed in my brain. My memory seems to have a mind of its own. Despite appearances and the disputations of my learned advisors, I am not the one who takes precedence here.

A few days ago, I heard the children playing with a dog outside my window. The sound moved me to inquire of Valentine, through my secretary, since Valentine cannot read, whether or not I had fathered other children since Nicholas. She told me no, that neither she nor the other women of the household presumed to come to me during my recent dormancy, since the children did not seem to please me. No one made the attempt, I asked? Yes, she admitted, Clémence had ventured it several times, as during my previous dormant state, but I was always unresponsive to her then, and have remained so.

In other words, I thought to myself, I had been as a virgin for a year and two months; little wonder, then, that I awakened with my member as hard as a rod of iron, and that it had rarely been in a state of relaxation since. Oddly, though, I did not seem able to fix my desires upon any particular person, certainly not upon any of the women in my household. None the less, I have, since that day, summoned Valentine to my bed, having first formally forbidden her to allow herself to become with child without asking my permission. She is very kind to me. And the children, too, are agreeable.

My strength having returned in its entirety, I feel quite able to leave the manor house and make the rounds of my seigneury. I am curious to see it. My tenant farmers are very hospitable, and it is difficult for me to habituate myself to the thought that they are so out of duty rather than through any natural generosity of spirit or real affection; they treat me well because I am in a position of authority over them. They took me fishing through a hole in the ice covering the frozen river, and we brought up several eels, which we cooked and ate with much relish. The habitants like them smoked or grilled; I prefer them raw. I am not insensitive to the fact that they were somewhat shocked to see me eat raw fish; I judge that to be a good thing. If they hold it a mark of savagery in me to eat food that has not been altered by the hand of man, then they may believe me less the seigneur than they had hoped.

In the spring I helped them make maple sugar. I watched them sow their fields and remove the bounty from them in the fall. We hunted moose together. I did everything that a habitant does, and still I was bored. They pointed out to me which women in the village were widowed, which were hoydens, which were grasping. They taught me well, and I profited much from their benevolence. Deep down, they were very good for me. Among themselves they call me the Dummy. They apparently think I am deaf as well as dumb.

The notary, the secretary and the doctor all bring me books to read, and I read them. It is no doubt on that account that I write more easily now. I never wrote so much in my life! Or so it seems to me. Still, despite all this physical and mental activity, I am bored. Bored beyond endurance.

By chance I read an article in the Quebec *Gazette*, which the notary forgot in my office one day. It consisted of an obituary notice for a certain Seigneur Lauzon, Cross of Saint-Louis, who died peacefully in his bed, surrounded by his numerous descendants and, by the grace of God, lovingly remembered by his tenant farmers and his children. The article intrigued me. The following day I called for my secretary and asked him what was meant by the Cross of Saint-Louis; the words excited some portion of my mind, but I could not succeed in remembering what it was.

He told me that the Cross of Saint-Louis is a distinction that can be bestowed only by the King of France, upon those who have distinguished themselves in combat. Montcalm, Bougainville and Vaudreuil have been given it, he said. As have the Saint-Ours of Richelieu.

"And have I received this cross also?" I demanded to know. "I have been a captain once, I am told, and am now a captain again."

"No, seigneur," said the secretary, "you have not. What is more," he added, "you may never receive it, since you are no longer a subject of the King of France, neither do you live on French soil. If the king in his wisdom determined to award you the Cross of Saint-Louis, you would have to return to France. And what is even more, the English governor has forbidden Canadians who have not already returned to France to accept the Cross of Saint-Louis. Even if you chose to return to France now, you would have to have someone present your cause to the king, and you have no powerful connections at Versailles. True, Monsieur Bougainville is still among the living, but he rarely appears at court; if he agreed to represent you, then you might harbour some small hope in that direction. Otherwise..."

I sent him away. An idea had come into my head. And a very good one it was!

4

I HAVE discovered a cure for my boredom: I will have the Cross of Saint-Louis. To accomplish this, I realize, will require the performance on my part of some signal service to the King of France. I do not apprehend that to be very difficult, since Bougainville hath done it and he is an idiot. Even now, I foresee the day when I will be presented to the king at Versailles, and His Majesty himself will encircle my waist with the Girdle of Fire.

The signal service I have in mind is the return of Canada to the Bourbon throne. In short, I will reconquer the country, for the which I need only some paper and ink. Small things, to be sure, but who knows how many glorious enterprises have had their beginnings in such humble materials? I will begin first thing in the morning. No – I will begin immediately.

Here is my plan. It is of primary importance to arrive at a precise appreciation of the state of the Canadian militia. I must know exactly how many trade flintlocks are in circulation, how many men in fighting trim, and so on. I do not think there can be under five thousand who have intimate experience of military service and of the bush. I will need to make a list of them, and then to mobilize them, appoint their officers and give each their marching orders for the day we fix upon for the achievement of our objective, which is nothing less than the reconquest of Canada.

There are in the country, at present, three thousand of English soldiers – no more, if my secretary is to be believed, and I consider him to be well informed, seeing that he reads a newspaper at least once every month. If we act swiftly and with guile, we can disarm them with very little effort. The English colonists are also few: we need only to convince them that no harm will come to them if they do not resist, and that they will moreover be allowed to retain their goods and chattels, so long as they swear allegiance to France. I will guarantee their freedom to cultivate their land and to use their own language in the courts. That is what our current masters have done to tranquillize the habitants, and it seems to have worked!

I hereby declare myself General of Militia. We will take Quebec, Trois-Rivières, Montreal, Louisbourg, Frontenac, Toronto and Detroit. That will be our occupation during the autumn, for I have no intention of initiating hostilities during the summer, when the habitants are too busy getting their crops in to take an interest in anything else. I know my men too well for that. And if we make good use of the fall, the English will be unable to send reinforcements until spring – May at the earliest – by which time the country will be ours.

As soon as the Reconquest is accomplished, I will send dispatches to Versailles, London and New York. I will inform the English colonies to the south of us that they have nothing to gain by collaborating with England, that they will not be attacked by us so long as they remain neutral. I will also send envoys to all the Indian nations, to bring them to my side. The Saulteux chieftains will send me a war party to ensure my personal safety, and I will receive foreign plenipotentiaries entouraged only by an Indian colour guard. That will impress them.

At that time, I will declare myself marshall, and name generals, colonels and captains. They will become inebriate with honours and distinctions. They will love me. They will follow me to the gates of hell. It will be fine.

◆

I am most happy. All day long I have been writing. And all the night as well.

I stop only to take walks in the seigneury. The habitants wave but rarely speak to me, which I count a good thing since I do not wish to be distracted from thoughts of my project. I have no way of replying, in any case; to them, I remain the Dummy. How surprised they will be when they learn that this Dummy is about to lead them into combat, that some few of them will die on the field of honour. I contemplate them going about their daily occu-

pations and my heart goes out to them, but I tell myself that
what I do, I do for their good. They will have to make of that
what they will.

Meanwhile, the household is very smoothly run. My health
and business affairs are in capable hands. Clémence, my housekeeper, looks after all my needs, brings meals to my study and
fetches me more paper when I run out. Valentine also attends to
her duties and is raising the children in exemplary fashion. The
children remain cordial towards me. I could not ask for more.
Toussaint, my secretary, manages the seigneury with a masterful
hand. Every night the four of us – Séraphin the notary, Dr.
Ambroise, Toussaint and I – play at cards together. Sometimes I
find myself envying their simple lives. When I think of the storm
that will soon come crashing down upon their heads, I must
remind myself that great deeds are not accomplished by faint
hearts. I feel closest to my manservant, Zacharias, who, like me
but for different reasons, is a man who keeps his own counsel:
we understand each other's silence perfectly. I spend long hours
in his quarters, watching him work or perform his simple
domestic tasks, and I forgive him everything, even his atrocious
manners at table. The other day I saw him place his empty plate
on the floor for the dog to lick. "That's how I wash my dishes,"
he said to me. The feeling of revulsion I apprehended in myself
I took to be a sign that I am well on the way to acquiring the
refined tastes of a seigneur.

Last month I wrote to the Governor of Louisiana, suggesting
a joint campaign on the Ohio River, from where we could be a
real threat to Virginia and the Carolinas, thus assuring the neu-
trality of the American colonies. I also wrote to the King of
France, in the greatest possible secrecy, obviously, asking him to
send a naval squadron, which I myself will command to the
retaking of Hudson Bay and Newfoundland, after which it will
be positioned for a possible blockade on New York and Boston,
should the northern colonies prove recalcitrant. Apparently, I
was once a captain of marines, and must therefore have learned

how to navigate a ship. The campaign will get me out of the house, in any case, and will no doubt do me a world of good.

For the most part, however, my enterprise progresses on its own. I intend that quite literally. There are times when heaps of papers appear on my desk filled with words which I have not the faintest recollection of having written. Thus, one morning upon my return from my habitual walk, I found there the completed texts of the Act of Surrender of the English Army in Canada, a Notice of General Mobilization of the Habitants, and a meticulously worked plan for the rationing of food in Montreal. With not so much as a blot upon it, and none of my usual idiosyncrasies of syntax or spelling. I suppose that I am working so feverishly on so many aspects of the project, which require such intense study and consideration, that there is little to wonder at if some of them slip from my recollection. Still, it is disconcerting, especially in the matter of certain replies I have received to messages I do not recall having sent. I would swear that I have sent no dispatches; yet has word of my intentions apparently spread, for people are already rallying to my cause. This is good; this is very good.

One response, however, has very nearly broken my heart. It is from my brother, Pascal, with whom I have not been in touch, so I am told, since the days when we were traders together. We have had little to say to one another, it seems, since leaving the seminary in Quebec, but while there we were as inseparable as two fingers of one hand. The last time I saw him he was removing the scalp from a woman he had just killed, and I asked him how he was doing. He intimated that things could be better.

Pascal de Sainte-Foy, as he is called now (having also been raised to the peerage), wrote that the Louisiana Territory has belonged to Spain since the Treaty of Fontainebleau of September 13, 1762. (This my secretary neglected to tell me. It is unlike him to disappoint me in such matters; I depend on him to know everything that I do not.) Pascal says he himself did not receive word of the transfer until three years after the treaty had been signed. Since his knowledge of the territory represents a valuable trump card for the new king, and since he is particularly familiar with the area bordering the vice-regency of Mexico, where he has long had clandestine commerce, he was urged to pledge his allegiance to the King of Spain in return for the rights to great honours. At present, he is a colonel, entitled to a new uniform every four years, decorated with the Order of Santa Isabella de Castillo, and has been made the Alcade of Santa Fe. Hence his new name. He answers only to the Governor of Cuba, a man upon whom he has never laid eyes, and no doubt never will.

He says he is looking forward to being reunited with his wife, who will come from Grenada. She is a sort of Creole princess, it seems, without a sou of her own but distantly related to the Viceroy of Peru. He begs me to understand that he cannot participate in my Reconquest, not the least because he has not been authorized to do so by his new sovereign. He has, however, apprised the court of Spain of my intentions and, if all goes well, and if the mails continue reliable, I should hear from him again in two years. A great pity, but there it is.

I have also heard from several private American citizens, one of whom, a certain Dr. Franklin of Philadelphia, claims to know me. They all say there is nothing to fear from them in the matter of England; they are as disgusted with London as am I. Imagine it, they write, "We do not even have access to furs from Canada; our own storehouse, as it were, and it is being treated as though it were a separate country!" I do not recall having written to Dr. Franklin, but I am very heartened by the tenor of his response.

My joy in it has been diluted, however, by a new set-back.

Yesterday a letter arrived from the minister of the Royal Navy, from Versailles, forbidding me absolutely to act in any further capacity without first consulting with him. He adds that I must also give up my aspirations for the Cross of Saint-Louis, even should I succeed in returning Canada to the throne of

France. Pursuant to a change in the rules regulating the order, the cross is no longer given to persons of modest birth, i.e., to persons such as myself. It is no long sufficient to have distinguished oneself upon the field of battle, writes the minister; one must also be of noble birth. "You being the son of a simple trader, an unlicensed one at that, and about whom nothing whatsoever is known, and the fact of your not even knowing who your mother was, disqualifies you absolutely." I am a seigneur, but I am not an aristocrat.

Do I then waste my energies?

The minister's letter gave me pause, to be sure. Where, I ask myself, is the sense in conquering a country and presenting it to a king who manifestly does not want it, or know what to do with it? Furthermore, I must kiss the Cross of Saint-Louis goodbye, and my presentation at Versailles. I will write to the king once more and tell him that I will not accept the Cross of Saint-Louis even were it offered me; I reject it absolutely. I have better things with which to occupy my time.

My plans for the Reconquest are in place. Why not proceed with them at the earliest possible opportunity? Nothing could be easier than to rid the country of the English, and after that, who knows? No king has ever set foot on this soil; I might fill the role as well as anyone.

The idea fires me with enthusiasm! Not a second to lose! I must have ink, more paper, hurry, Clémence! I will bring my secretary into my confidence: he writes better than I do. He will be useful to me.

◆

I was right. Toussaint has proven more valuable to my purpose than I had anticipated; he is, if anything, more enthusiastic even than I. After speaking with him, I have unhesitatingly promised him the secretaryship to the royal household, minister of foreign affairs and chancellor of the exchequer. (I have no idea what an exchequer is, but the title sounds well, and in any event, it was his idea.)

His compliance is very important, particularly by reason of his learning, which is vast in many of the areas in which my own is perforce deficient. He is preparing me for my role by providing me with a great number of books, an entire chest of them belonging to a French officer who had been killed in Quebec. He assures me that the chest contains everything I need to know, and the knowledge I glean from it will prove extremely enlightening, I am certain. Toussaint was secretary to the Governor of Trois-Rivières during the time of the French king. He therefore knows much about court procedure, the little networkings of power, royal etiquette and what have you. I could not have chosen better.

With my permission, he has taken the notary Séraphin and Dr. Ambroise into our confidence. I believe he shows much discernment in this. Since joining our conspiracy, both have left off playing cards and getting drunk on the local rosé each night, and have launched themselves into efforts that will ensure the continuance of the kingdom. The notary is drawing up a civil code, and the doctor is compiling a list of ordinances pertaining to public health. I have named Séraphin the attorney-general, and Dr. Ambroise physician to the king and surveyor-general.

Everyone is very busy and supremely happy, not excluding the women, Valentine and Clémence, who go about their daily tasks smiling and singing, no longer having to worry about us getting in their way. A studious atmosphere permeates the household; it has even affected the children, who are learning how to read from Toussaint, who has added public education to his already bulging portfolio. Zacharias is the only one who will hear nothing of my project, but, as I have said, I pardon him everything.

A present has arrived for me: a huge pendulum clock, a gift from my friend in Philadelphia, Dr. Franklin. Although I rack my brains, I have no memory of my having had correspondence with him, but the clock is of the latest Swiss design, a pure mechanical marvel. The notary and the doctor spend hours sitting before it, watching its pendulum swing back and forth.

Valentine and Clémence contend with one another for the privilege of dusting it at least a dozen times a day. Even I find myself
running my hands over its exquisite cabinetry from time to time.

Such frivolity exasperates Toussaint. We are engaged in a project that will determine the future of this country, he fulminates,
and here we are wasting time on a device that measures only the
time that has already passed. It pleases him to chide us, but I
doubt the sincerity of his indignation. Why, just the other night
I caught him peering into the mechanism with a magnifying
glass, lost in wonder. His condemnation of laxity in the household is no doubt rooted in a similar tendency within himself.
Will he turn out to be one of those whose aspirations to greatness conceal the pettiness of their own souls? It is a question I
sometimes ask myself.

5

TOUSSAINT hath announced that it is time for me to marry.
Our preparations for war are advancing nicely, says he, but
nothing guarantees the security of an empire like a judicious
marriage. A marital alliance with one of the crowned families of
Europe would consolidate the borders of our realm and assure
my lineage. All the history books contain illustrations of these
simple facts.

"Well," I said, "if all the history books say so…"

A quest has accordingly been undertaken to find a wife worthy of my imperial person. (In private, Toussaint always address-
es me as Your Majesty or Your Highness. I think the appellations
suit me.) He hath communicated in this regard with the Tsarina
of Moscovy, the Duke of Piedmont, the Queen of Naples, the
Emperor of Germany and the King of Sweden.

I believe he would have me marry into one of the northern
kingdoms, and I admit that my own taste would favour a
princess from Sweden. The sonority of the name always sets me
to dreaming: Sweden…Toussaint, however, is of the opinion that
my taste, noble and guileless though it be, is yet lacking in depth:

a marriage to the royal family of Russia would double my
influence. It is well reasoned. I also like the sound of the word
Russia. But I told him that if the Princess of Russia has a previous engagement, I will accept the hand of the Princess of
Sweden.

"As you wish, sire."

At times, I do confess, I feel that I have been drawn into this
adventure through my love of words. Words that I have read,
words I have heard. I love the noble parts of speech, especially
those regal and ducal; I am partial to words such as viscount and
marquis. I know not why or wherefore, only that I desire from
this enterprise no other reward than to be able to play at such
imperious word games forever.

One small incident has occurred that intrudes upon the pleasure I take in these majestic pastimes. It took place in the
kitchen. I was hungry, and made my accustomed sign to
Valentine that I wanted something to eat. She told me I could eat
shit.

As she went on to explain, she alone had been doing all the
work in the household for the past three days, Clémence having
been visiting at the Stillbornes and anyway having had less and
less to do with the daily management of the kitchen. And with
the doctor and the notary becoming drunk every night, snoring
in the corners – not that she had ever been able to get much
sympathy from them. As for the secretary, he has become impossible to live with in the last few months, putting on airs and treating her like a scullery maid, besides which the children have all
had the mumps and have been keeping her up all night. In short,
she has had her hands full attending to the whimsical require-
ments of a man who, seigneur or no seigneur, has never a kind
word to say to her and ought, by now, to know how to heat up
a meat pie for himself.

Her outburst gave me pause to consider. I boiled myself an
egg and helped her clean up the kitchen. Then, with a view to
receiving the pardon of my precious subject, I awakened my pro-

curer-general and my royal surveyor with the aid of heavy and
repeated kicks from my boot, and sent them out into the courtyard to split wood with Zacharias. Then I shut myself up in my
room to think about the new turn this business has taken.

The last few days have been extraordinarily busy. In three
weeks I have concluded a concordat with the pope, founded a
school of music, told all the Huguenots and Jews of Europe that
they are welcome to emigrate to my empire, established an act
of obligatory education for all children under the age of ten,
arranged huge loans for the construction of cathedrals and the
feeding of the poor, named six hundred prefects, three hundred
generals and two hundred bishops. Only last evening, I levied
taxes on tobacco and rum and abolished slavery. I am a little
worn.

Committing these summations to paper surprised me. Do I
really want to be emperor? I asked myself. And could one truly
work for the public good simply because one thought it a good
idea at the time, and perhaps found it a jolly sort of thing to do?
Had I been lured into it by the very chimeras I myself had created? Where was I being drawn by this pillar of words that may
or may not have any meaning outside the inkpot that engen-
dered them?

Not to put too fine a point on it, I had had enough. I took off
my periwig, announced my abdication from the throne, and
went fishing.

My secretary was barely able to contain his chagrin when I
told him that he was henceforth to cease calling himself the
grand chamberlain. If he could find no other sovereign to
engage his prodigious visionary talents, I informed him, he was
welcome to remain in my service. He sulked for a time. I, on the
other hand, am doing my best to forget the entire imperial project. Even thinking about it makes me feel that I have become an
object of ridicule.

◆

Toussaint, however, is indefatigable. Another idea occurred to him when he discovered, by reading one of the Montreal gazettes, that the English officers garrisoned there were proposing to stage several of Molière's theatrical pieces for the pleasure of the town's French citizens. The advertisement sent him into a towering rage. "What!" he shouted. "Will the rogues steal our literature from us now? We cannot allow this to happen." The next day he founded a national theatre, and now throws all his energies into the composition of works that will reinspire in Canadians the patriotic fervour that they so palpably lack.

He asked my permission to stage his dramas in my barn, which is the seigneury's largest. He would, he said, reawaken the warriors that slept within our citizenry, perhaps even inspire them to create the great nation in which I myself had apparently lost interest. I gave him my permission, and a good thing, too, because it was thanks to this theatre that the past winter was the shortest in my recollection as seigneur.

Every Monday there was a performance in my barn, the building being easily large enough to hold half the parish. Toussaint put on *The Zealots*, a play in three acts that told the story of Dollard des Ormeaux and his sixteen comrades who valiantly defended themselves and Montreal against an army of six or seven hundred Iroquois warriors. I was one of the sixteen, the one who had no lines and who, at the climax of the play, tossed a barrel of gunpowder at the Iroquois. I fought, I died. I have played a similar role in all of Toussaint's dramatics, all of which require someone to die. One day, for a laugh, I suggested that I be the prompter, but Toussaint did not find the idea amusing at all.

After *The Zealots*, we performed *Madeleine de Verchères*, *The Cassock of Father Brébeuf* (in which I played a demented Huron, which required of me only a repertoire of hideous grins), *Sir William Phipps and the Siege of Quebec*, *Monongahela*, *Carillon* and others whose titles I do not now recall. All for the edification of our fellow Canadians, so that they might regain their taste for war and rise en masse to cast off their English oppressors. I was in a position to observe a very curious thing: the habitants adored the plays in which children were maltreated, or priests burned at the stake, or women raped against huge crucifixes. The plays in which the French were victorious were less popular. The audience yawned all the way through *Monongahela*, for instance, and afterwards I overheard several of them say that the French were so hopelessly outnumbered that they must have pulled a fast one on the English, or else rejoiced in the good fortune that God bestowed on idiots. They seemed to take no satisfaction in the fact that the French won the battle; the only Frenchmen admired by the audience were those who were either tortured to death or who suffered some other form of misery. That was the way of it.

I also noticed that what the audience found most appealing about the plays were the refreshments provided for them after the performance. These were laid out in the manor house, in the same room as my fabulous clock. They, too, were fascinated by the mechanism in Mr. Franklin's pendulum, habituated as they were to roughly estimating the time of day by the position of the sun in the sky. They made wagers among themselves, guessing at the correct hour, and the winners were permitted to sit in awe before the swinging pendulum longer than the rest.

Another reward they liked were the small glasses of spruce beer we offered them. Dr. Ambroise, a veritable cognoscentum of pharmacology, marshalled all his prodigious talents in the manufacture of this beverage. With the aid of the secretary and the notary, he boiled spruce branches to obtain a clear broth, which he then passed through a screen, and to which he added molasses and yeast, leaving the concoction to ferment for forty-eight hours, after which he served it well chilled. Everyone agreed it was the best spruce beer in the country. In order to obtain as much of it as they could, the habitants would sit for hours listening to Toussaint haranguing them on the faded glories of New France, invoking for their benefit the glorious days when the colony was still ruled by King Louis. They applauded enthusiastically. I listened to him with but a single ear, even when he waxed eloquent about the Cross of Saint-Louis, which their seigneur was going to receive at Versailles from the hand of His Majesty himself.

Toussaint, at least for a while, believed that his oratory was having its desired effect, that he was succeeding in rallying the habitants' dormant patriotism. He told them that the American colonists were about to rise against their Britannical masters, that he himself had just received a secret dispatch pertaining to that very matter, and that everyone must look to his weapons and prepare for the day of liberation.

They attended him politely. He spoke well, and it is always enjoyable to listen to speeches given by an educated fellow. The men, especially, would happily listen to him all night, as long as the spruce beer held out. But it soon became apparent even to Toussaint that his cause was gaining very few adherents. When the habitants discussed the insurrection among themselves, debating when would be the best time to rise up in arms, they never quite succeeded in agreeing upon a date. One would say that autumn was out of the question because of the harvest. Another would add that springtime was equally inconvenient because of the maple sugaring. No one in his right mind would contemplate rebelling in winter. And the summer, well, the summer was for working the land if they were going to have enough to see them through the winter. And then summer was always bad for black flies in the bush. They might be able to fit it in around Martinmas, offered one of them. No, no, replied another, they had to be here then to pay their respects to the seigneur.

In the end, these pointless deliberations exasperated the notary, who was beginning to find that his patriotic spruce beer was costing him an arm and a leg. He decided to charge a penny a glass for it, and in one week we lost three-quarters of our audience. And the few who came barely sat through the historical dramas that were supposed to galvanize their nationalistic fervour; they came principally to see the clock.

For my own part, I was tiring of my role as the speechless recipient of repeated sword thrusts and an infinitude of arrows and tomahawks. Toussaint became despondent when he realized that his co-conspirators would far rather talk than act, no matter how impassioned his perorations. My own feeling on the matter is that Toussaint lost the better part of his followers when he told them that it would be he who travelled to Versailles to ask for assistance the day the habitants rose up in arms.

The situation continued to decline. Before long, no one at all came to see the plays. The secretary, the notary and the doctor all wondered why. Toussaint had prepared speeches that now would never be heard; the doctor arrived with several new barrels of spruce beer; the notary, who had acquired a taste for the theatre, had just begun to dream of taking on larger roles. But not a single other soul came to the manor.

I discovered the reason from Valentine. It seems a commercial traveller from New England has made the rounds of the seigneury, a Huguenot who speaks perfect French and is said to be very slick. He sells clocks. All the habitants who have saved a few pennies, and even many who have not, have purchased clocks of their own. Even Valentine has one, which she dusts four times a day, to the neglect of my pendulum parlour clock, which she rarely looks at once a week. The habitants, now that they have their own means of ascertaining the exact time, are no longer interested in Mr. Franklin's pendulous mechanism.

Other factors also came into play. The habitants were angry with me for suspending the Martinmas homages. They liked the tradition, but I detested the obligation and wanted to free them from it. I desired to seem less the tyrant; they rather wanted me to be more the seigneur. I was particularly stung by Valentine's revelation that Major Stillborne, the Seigneur du Bec and my nearest neighbour, was much more popular with his tenant farmers than I was with mine. He, according to my own habitants, was a real seigneur.

For the first time in my life I find myself jealous of someone I do not know. It is, I have since been told, a not uncommon sensation. But it puts me in such a towering bad humour that I have shut down the theatre, told the notary to go sell his spruce beer elsewhere, and given Mr. Franklin's pendulum clock to my secretary, who immediately carted it off and installed it in the little cabin he has had built at the edge of my property, where he retired to compose his useless epics. The doctor has given up trying to cure my speechlessness with his noxious potions, in the efficacy of which he himself no longer believes and which give me nothing but diarrhea.

I have decided it is time to look into this Major Stillborne.

6

THE habitants, I soon discovered, have good reason to smile upon Seigneur de Stillborne, as he is a prince among men, a true gentleman. I had set out with the intention of treating him as an upstart foreigner, this English officer whom I had not seen since the day I took him prisoner with my halfpike. Clémence, my housekeeper, hath several times suggested I invite him round for a spot of something, so that we might make a proper acquaintance of each other, but each time I declined to do so. Now, with some vague notion of getting to know mine enemy, I determined to take the measure of the grand seigneur. I also thought it would help me to forget all the time I had wasted putting myself forward as emperor and watching execrable theatricalities in my barn.

I turned up at his manor house armed with my old flintlock, under the pretext of going on a duck hunt, but with the firm intention of shooting the man point blank if he so much as showed a twinge of hostility towards me. Luckily for him, he welcomed me with open arms and insisted I accompany him on a duck-hunting expedition. He had a well-maintained blind on the river, at just the spot where I had captured him those many years before. He made absolutely no mention of that unfortunate incident; it was as though nothing had passed between us at all. We shot a fair bag of game together, upon which he invited me to partake of high tea at his house.

Not for a long time had I made such a magnificent repast, though I eat tolerably well at my own house. Stillborne confided as how his cook learned her trade from Valentine; they, too, dine in the French style at his house, but there they drink real French wine and Cognac, not the dandelion wine and rose-hip cordial we swill at home. The wine alone was reason enough for me to regard him as a dear friend.

He is very rich, is Stillborne. His father was a man of means in Newfoundland, and Stillborne inherited it all, including the right of salvage for every ship that washes up along the entire eastern coastline of that island, which amounts to a small fortune, all of which he transferred to his seigneury at the termination of his service in the English army. He also owns a tobacco plantation in the Carolinas; picked it up for as little as kiss my hand after the war. Not for him the blond weed we laughingly call tobacco in these parts; he has the real Virginia in his house, the very symbol of distinction, as is anything that comes from abroad.

I have been to his house many times since, and he has as often returned the favour. Having had enough of tepid conversations with my secretary, the doctor and the notary, I designate Stillborne my one friend. He understands my hand signals perfectly, and I, for my part, have no difficulty following his English. We talk about the war, the Siege of Quebec, the storming of Havana, where he was transferred after the campaign in New France. We laugh heartily at our antics in those days, upon which, from our vantage point atop this current molehill of peace, we look back as to our Golden Age. We were heroes, the both of us. Heroes together. And he is so well spoken, he makes me long to have words of my own again.

He hath taught me how to be a seigneur and instilled in me an appreciation of lineage. To a man without a future, nothing shines like the past, especially a past that can be invented whole cloth. And to a man of action condemned to eternal idleness, genealogy is a worthy pastime. Between us, we have constructed a fine family tree for myself. Stillborne puts the matter beautifully. The great advantage of having obscure origins, says my dear friend, and I blush that ever I did treat him callously, lies in the scope it provides for one's imaginative faculties. He hath helped me exercise those faculties, to a small extent. Very well, he hath helped me exercise them a great deal.

We began by resolving to our satisfaction the question of my paternal lineage, which, as is well known, is ever the most troublesome. The idea came into my head, fostered no doubt by my estimable friend, that my father must have been Basque; Stillborne had made the acquaintance of numerous fishermen from that country whilst he was in Newfoundland, and ever found them to be of solid, dependable stock. Once we settled on the certain fact that my people were Basque, I quickly became habituated to the idea, and the choice soon proved to be a propitious one.

The Basques are chiefly remembered as the plundering hordes of the mountain regions of Navarre, the same that massacred Charlemagne's rear guard in a glorious battle: a great moral victory, as all lost causes are ultimately called. The people from that country abandoned the fields and took to the sea, and discovered Newfoundland long before the Spanish and Portuguese. Theirs is a nation of sorcerers, Stillborne relates, in which the devil has never made any headway at all, since in order to infiltrate their minds he would first have to learn their language, and this the devil himself could never do, so he gave up on them. Thus the Basques are the most unbedevilled people in the world, a distinction that pleases me greatly.

Herewith the story of my noble ancestry, as fabricated by myself. One day, experiencing a sudden taste for adventure, my imaginary father decided to see the country. Upon arriving at Bayonne, however, he was stopped by the mounted police, who took him for a Huguenot. Huguenots were being persecuted at the time, and my father was sentenced to be tortured and burned at the stake. He did not want to say that he was of no religion, since atheism was considered a worse crime than Protestantism. He could also have been accused of witchcraft, since it was well known that Basque sorcerers celebrated the Black Sabbath in Newfoundland.

Through an interpreter, since he understood not a word of French, my father was given to understand that he could save his skin by making a public detraction. He agreed, and publicly denounced everything he was asked to denounce. That done, he was declared a Catholic, and after a winter studying his catechism with a group of monks, he was, quite literally, booted out of Bayonne.

While he had been imprisoned, he had been chained alongside a man who confirmed in my father his desire to see the world. His cell mate was an Outagami warrior from the western plains of the New World, who had been captured by the French and sent to Bayonne to be sold as a galley slave. While waiting for a ship, he had been kept shackled in chains, and was displayed at public fairs like a two-headed calf.

He and my father became fast friends when my father drew the head of a bear on their cell wall. My father's clan had venerated the bear since time immemorial. The Indian, despite his weakened condition, also drew a bear's head on the wall, virtually identical to that of my father; the bear was the emblem of his tribe. The men broke into tears, overcome as they were by the fact that the two of them, though from vastly different worlds and infinitely miserable, were nonetheless spiritually united by religion. Though unable to exchange a single intelligible word, they recognized and understood each other perfectly.

From a prison guard, my father learned where his new friend had been captured, and he resolved to go to live in that place. The Indian died a few days after this moving experience, but before expiring, he managed to pass my father a talisman: a fragment of seashell upon which had been painted the head of a bear. My father still carried this portrait with him when I knew him, now that I come to think about it. (I have had to stretch my memory on this score, but Stillborne assures me that that is very often the case.)

About the Indian's native country, my father knew nothing more than that it lay to the west. Accordingly, he took ship at Bayonne with some of his fellow countrymen who were sailing to the Newfoundland whaling grounds. He worked with them as a whaler for a year, then joined another ship that was going to Boston, where he remained long enough to acquire the rudiments of English. Calling himself a voyageur, he accompanied an expedition that was heading west to trade with the Illinois. There he left the expedition and set himself up as a trader. He quickly amassed a great fortune and married an Indian woman, one of their captive slaves who, it is strongly suspected, was the direct descendant of a union between an Indian maiden and one of the lost kings of Ireland. (I cannot be certain of this, of course, and Stillborne advises me not to dwell over much upon it.)

When he handed my brother and my poor self over to Monsieur de Saint-Ours, whose name we have taken for life, I vividly recall my father saying to us, "To you, Pascal, I bequeath New Spain; Benjamin, I give you New France. These are the two realms from which I come. From this day forth, this New World belongs to you."

And thus it is that I have become a grand seigneur, the repository of so much that is great and, one might even say, distinct. Yet, upon reviewing my lineage, I still found it weak in certain areas. Stillborne agreed. "But why need we stop here?" he asked. "We have set out on this road. Let us continue to see where it will lead us." Accordingly, I betook myself to consultation with the notary. If anyone understands the kind of genealogy I was after, it would be a lawyer.

It seems that a certain Joseph of Arimathea got hold of the cup from which Our Saviour Jesus Christ drank at the Last

Supper, and kept it in his family. One of his descendants, forced out of Israel by the Romans, landed in Spain with the cup in his possession. Prince Roland, one of Charlemagne's noblemen, found the cup in the course of pillaging a defeated Spanish castle and took it with him. But Roland was killed by a regiment of Basque mountain fighters during his retreat from Spain, and one of the Basques picked up the cup and brought it back to his homeland as a trophy.

The Holy Cup of Christ was passed from ancestor to ancestor until it ended up in the hands of one who eventually would set sail to Newfoundland, and from there make his way to the American West. The cup now resides with the Seigneur de Saint-Ours: my family is ennobled by virtue of having had the Holy Grail in its possession since the time of Charlemagne.

I was, of course, delighted by this turn of events. I never would have been capable of it myself, not being as inventive as a lawyer. I did, however, fall prey to a small doubt, and so I asked my friend Stillborne if he thought my tenant farmers would believe the story. I shall never forget his answer. "Fantasy is truer than history," he said. "We may forget facts, but we never forget what we have conceived in our imaginations."

He must be right.

He, too, has cobbled together a family history, one every bit as marvellous as mine. Stillborne dreams of establishing an English aristocracy on the banks of the St. Lawrence River. He would be descended from a legitimate son of one of the knights of King Arthur's Round Table; he would be a count, then a duke, then a succession of other titles. The only fly in the ointment is that he wants his family to be in possession of the Holy Grail, since, according to legend, Joseph of Arimathea fled to England upon the death of Christ. I told him that it was my family who had the Grail, since it was I who thought of it first. He replied that such a thing was impossible. The legends were quite clear on this point: Joseph of Arimathea and the Chalice of Christ washed up on the shores of England and nowhere else!

This was the only time that the two of us came close to a disagreement. Being gentlemen, however, we decided to let the contentious matter drop for the moment, and to bring it up again at a later date.

So close have we become, in fact, that we are very nearly inseparable. We play at cards together daily, usually gin rummy. We exchange confidences. He advises me on the running of my estate. "It is your money," he informed me. "Although the notary administers it, along with the doctor." He showed me how I might gain control over a larger part of my capital, and hath instilled in me a confidence in my own unsuspected abilities in financial matters – I who had, before the war, been an adept when it came to pecuniary acumen. I had not known, or at least had forgotten, that aspect of my former self, as with so much else. And it was Stillborne who pointed out to me the singular circumstance that the entire household is living at my expense, is in point of fact sponging off me, including the secretary and the doctor. All this was a novelty to me.

Nor is it all. My contact with Stillborne has taught me how to behave like a seigneur – how, when I receive my tenant farmers, to put on airs before them, to carry on for a term as though they were not there at all, and then to lavish warm marks of my affection upon them. The idea, it appears, is to be insufferably rude to them at the beginning, and to show them my kindness and generosity at the end. I must, in other words, be as clever at pretense as they, and they will love me for it. He himself learned the art from his predecessor, who left on the first ship back to France after the relinquishment of the colony.

Stillborne has persuaded me to welcome my former courtiers back into my house. The notary is very happy about this turn in his fortunes. He says that as a seigneur, I have reason to rely upon his services. He cites, as an example, the many young women of the better families hereabouts, the Saint-Ours family among them, who have married English officers and who have become Protestants. Some of them have even gone to live in

England, where they loll about in silks and velours. "Fortunes must marry if they are to multiply," he says. And adds pointedly that Stillborne has a son, Ebenezer, who has been educated in England; in short, the notary proposes a marriage between this young man and a daughter of mine, if I ever have a white one. He is so infatuated with this idea that he brings it up at every mealtime.

The doctor has also reappeared at my table. At one time all of his patients were of my seigneury, but he has since doubled his case load by making visits to the Stillborne estate, where he had never set foot before my friendship with its master. "Concord is the mother of prosperity," he declares.

As for the secretary, he is still long in the face, although I have noticed he never refuses my invitations. Except when we are at table, he chides me on my friendship with Stillborne, saying it goes against nature. Unlike the notary and the doctor, who have tactfully forgotten our imperial enterprise of the previous year and are content to concentrate on building their fortunes, Toussaint nurtures his thwarted ambitions by the continued use of those governing words which he alone loves and understands. He chews and swallows in silence, sometimes looking up at the rest of us with the surly look of a man who is sure of his command of the language. If he goes on in this way, very soon he will be talking about himself.

The last Martinmas at my house was a huge success. My tenant farmers love me since I have learned to treat them like peasants, and call them in to the parlour to make their obeisance to me, and make them stand there waiting while I pretend to be occupied with something else. I even put on my periwig for the occasion. Then I accept their gifts and treat them magnanimously. In return for which I am obliged to pour out quantities of spruce beer, but even that gives me great pleasure.

Stillborne has offered to buy my seigneury; he is thinking of establishing a marquisate on the river. I told him I would think about it.

All this emotion has been telling on me. I am beginning to feel tired again, and, for the first time in five years, I find myself fighting off the urge to go back to sleep. I have left instructions with Valentine to prevent me from oversleeping. And to not take advantage of my condition to engender more children!

I look forward to being told, by whoever is around the next time I wake up, whether I am still English or have become French again. I am what I am, resigned to whatever account is rendered when I am not able to render it myself. It cannot be helped. Perhaps another time, another life. All the same, I wish myself pleasant dreams.

7

HOW handsome he be lying there, my Benjamin, my little baby. I did not wake him up, like he ask me to, and a good thing I did not. If he knew half of what go on in this seigneury, he would not sleep a wink. So I let him sleep as long as he wants. I watch over him.

When he sleeps, I, Valentine, be the real Seigneuress de Saint-Ours. This may seem strange, I know, because when he awake he hardly know I exist. I just the Negress; no one talk to me less they want something from me: fry them up something, fetch them a cup of this or that, keep the children quiet. Not just him, neither, but everyone in this house, they all alike in this respect. Madame Clémence the worst, but I forgive her. I have my own little revenge.

When the whole household be asleep, and specially when Madame Clémence at the Stillborne house playing the society lady, I treat my baby like a king. First, I help him to the night closet, then I walk him round the room so he get some of his strength back, and then I feed him, and shave, wash and scent him up, and put fresh sheets on the bed, and then I lay him down in it and fill the copper tub beside him, and bathe myself slowly, and touch myself all over to make me wet and ready.

Then I slide into his bed, and touch him, and whisper such words in his ear as I would hear from his own mouth: "I am all for you, my Benjamin." It never long before he find his own way into me, and I take my pleasure two or three times before his turn come, and that the most beautiful moment of all, when my Benjamin whimper like a child who lost his mama, and suck my breast like he dying of thirst. I lay my face on his chest, and betimes I cry, and cannot say who the master and who the mistress; the pleasure make us equal and the darkness make us one. There be times when I would like to do this when he wide awake, but mostly I glad he is not. Then I think myself the only woman in the world to have such happiness, and I know that this joy can never be out in the open, not in real life, and so I keep him this way, to be mine in the night. The day will come when he awake all the time, and we be grown old together, and I will pay him back for all the pleasure he have given me as a servant in his manor house.

Madame Clémence suspicion me of going to Monsieur, but naturally I deny it. I tell her it would never cross my mind to take a vantage of him, and my face does not betray me because I know I telling the truth. When I was a suckling chile, at Fort Chartres back when we were slaves in the lead mines there, my mother was Benjamin's nursemaid, and he and I like brother and sister. I do not remember that time, but Zacharias he told me about it, and it natural now that we should love each other and live our childhoods together again, naked and innocent. But it is not good that others know about this. There are not many who would understand such things.

I can tell, from all the questions she put to me, Madame Clémence, that she would like to know what. But she never ask directly. She afraid of words, that woman. She not as free as I.

Anyone can see she in love with Monsieur her own self. She loved him ever since she read what he wrote. Me, I don't know what he put on all that paper I brought him, scribbling away, filling up all those days when he could not sleep. I don't care, neither, because whatever it has to do with is his daytime self, with that doctor and the lawyer and the secretary. Histories of the conquest, battles and treaties, strongholds taken and taken back, stories that interest no one who have better ways to spend their precious days.

But ever since she read that, she crazy in love with him. It like magic, like the words on the paper have more power over her than words from someone's mouth. To me, when words are written down, it like the spirit gone out of them, not like when they come from solid flesh and blood. But it true that Monsieur cannot speak words, and maybe that why they have so much power on paper. To them who can read, anyway.

And anyway, because I always being suspicioned by her, and I see she spend all her time with him, I finally make her confess she in love with him. But she also say he never respond to her. She say she tried everything, can think of nothing more to try, but his heart the only hard thing about him, and it driving her mad. She cry, I think, because she afraid she not enough woman for him; also she want me to pity on her. She think the more I pity on her, the more I'll tell her how to make him respond. But there be times when I truly pity on her, when I see her face as she leave his room, and I decided I would help her, not to console her so much as to make her stop suspicioning me.

I also think I want to measure myself against her, without her knowing of it. I know why she so unsuccessful with Monsieur. If Madame Clémence afraid of words that are spoken from the mouth, imagine how words not spoken must terrify her. Arm wavings that stand for words. Once I heard they all talking together, Clémence, the lawyer, the doctor and the secretary, one of those long, drunk conversations they like to have in the fall, when the days are cold and sad and they rather talk than work outside, like everyone else. I in the kitchen making bread and minding my own business, like always, playing innocent and listening to them jabber on like I somewheres else. They discussing does God exist. Monsieur Toussaint he says aye, God exist, it say so in these books of his, and he give many proofs. The doctor and the lawyer, they laugh and laugh.

Toussaint get a bit carried off then, and say that he even seen his creator with his own eyes. "God poured out of me," he say, "like a kind of fluid. He flowed from my body!"

The doctor he hardly could talk he laughing so hard. "Well, my dear colleague," he say, "if that's God, then I've seen Him often myself. It's a pity I didn't recognize Him. If only I'd known..." And he and the lawyer laugh like a pair of crows on a dead chicken.

Madame Clémence turn very pale like, paler than she usual, and beseech them to stop. That when I realized she not fully trusting the words we all speak, and why she prefer to read them written down.

She take all my advice, but nothing worked. Benjamin would have none of she, as though he aware of what was going on. Clémence told me that all my secrets weren't worth spit, that they come from a voodoo witch. I didn't say nothing, just kep my head down like a good Nigress who know her place. But inside myself I happy, I the happiest woman. My Benjamin is faithful to me! She can play the big housekeeper all she like, but I the real mistress of this place. I the one! He nobody but mine, my Benjamin, nobody but mine.

Clémence cry for three days, but she did not try him again. It must be hard on her, and I so careful to console her that I for-got to laugh. I found myself sincerely pitying on her, and in the end I stopped hating her. That happen when you victory over someone stronger than you, you forget your hatred, you become a good person to spite yourself.

For Clémence, though, this business with Monsieur was finish. She gone back to her old ways with the others, with the lawyer, the doctor and the secretary, always talking talking such foolishness. She gone back to visiting Monsieur Stillborne, too, but that because she feeling worried. And if Monsieur had a con-science, he'd feeling worried, too.

The other day, I forget when it was, a stranger come to the seigneury, a messenger from King George of England, who say he bring good news. He called all the village to a meeting and told them that the English Parliament have pass the Act of Quebec, which was of great benefit to them. According to this act, he explain, all our old customs are restored to us, for example the privileges of the seigneurs and of the clergy, the right to attend Mass, to speak French in the courts, to pay tithes to the church, and a few other suchlike things. We supposed to be happy about that, because apparently not everyone lucky enough to be allowed to pay tithes.

The habitants were none too happy, which is nothing new. Tithes, they say. How lucky for us! Thank you, kind sir. Pray tell us, though, to who we are to pay these tithes, since there been no priest in Sapinière since Moses' day. As for the privileges of the seigneur, it took ours some three years to learn what they were, and he still hardly pay attention to them; what's more, he sleep all the time. No, sir, they tell the king's messenger, thank you for your kindness, but you wasting your time.

But the king's messenger he went everywhere, into all they houses. People ask him to supper so he could explain this new law to them. He told them that we live in a beautiful country and we should thank our stars it have King George of England for a king. And the people listen, mostly because there been't much else to do around here. The doctor took a liking to the man, and invite him here for supper several times.

I didn't like him myself. I didn't like the shape of his head. And the secretary, Toussaint, he hated that man. It was Toussaint who put the rumour out that the king's messenger, whose Christian name was Jean-Baptiste, was a former Jesuit who pass over to the English side after the Battle of Quebec. A turncoat. After that he made fun of the French soldiers in the Augustine hospital, by walking between their cots with a pot of chicken fat and saying he goan give the Last Rites to the Catholics. He put some kinder poison in the pot, and when he rub it on they heads he blaspheme them. "There," he say, "go join your Maker, you credulous idiots, and tell Him I shit on His wafers and piss in His wine!" He even scandalize the major in charge of the hospital, and got hisself thrown out on his ear. Ever since that time, he call hisself the king's messenger. That what Toussaint say, anyhow.

It seem no one believe Toussaint, because his story so wild. No one believes stories that go too far. No one but Clémence, that is; she took Toussaint's story to her heart. She believe anyone who speak bad about religion.

It about this same time that another stranger come to the seigneury, a woman who gone around saying the opposite of the king's messenger. Her name is Charlotte, a widow woman and seamstress by trade, who say she live a long time in New England. To hear her talk, the New Englanders up and rebelling against they English masters any day now, chase them right outen the country. She talk about the republic, and liberty and equality for all men. The doctor, who is a educated man, call her the Queen of Hungry, on account of all she talks about is revolution. The name stuck to her, and now all the habitants call her the Queen of Hungry. I think she like that.

She make the rounds of the habitants' houses herself, pretending to do her work but taking a vantage to preach her own gospel. The American colonies goan rebel and then invade us, else we prepare ourself, she say. We must make a pledge of allegiance to the American Congress, and to Monsieur Franklin, who is Monsieur de Saint-Ours's friend, and that the only way we be saved. Naturally there is no love lost between the Queen of Hungry and the king's messenger; neither one has a good word to say about the other.

People in these parts don't know what to think about all these new ideas. Sometimes they on the side of King George, who personally never did them any harm; they also have nothing against Monsieur Franklin and his rebels. But all of them – Monsieur Franklin, the rebels, King George – they all speak English, and the people here suspicion them. One day they for, the next day they against. It hard to say. I think the only side they really on is they own hillside, where they crops are.

The Queen of Hungry eat with us often, at Toussaint's invitation. I don't fancy her, myself, especially since she ask to be alone with Monsieur one time. She say, "Leave me alone with him for a while, and I see if he really asleep." I was against it. She frighten me. All she say around here is seigneurs are parasites who make themself fat off the backs of the poor. She may be right about other seigneurs, but not my Benjamin. He don't harm no one. All he do is sleep.

Clémence was for it, though. She like to see the Queen of Hungry busy herself with my Benjamin. I think she want to revenge herself on him. I swear, she acting very mean to him. Just the other day, she left him in the outhouse, which we put up outside while his night closet is repaired. Thank the Lord Zacharias had to go hisself that day, and he found Monsieur in there, frozen half to death. My poor sweet man.

She say she forgot, but I sure she did it on purpose.

Ever since that day, I on the side of King George.

8

I WAS awakened by a nightmare. I'm told I have been in a foul mood ever since.

I dreamed I was in the Abenaki village at Odanak, a place no great distance from the seigneury, but to which I have never been. I was purchasing some sort of medicaments from an old woman there, for the doctor to use in those potions of his that never do me any good. She would not allow me into her cabin, and so we conducted our transactions outside her door. The November sky was one vast cloud, darkened by the cold and fringed with orange by a febrile sun. At a certain point I decided that my backside was quite sufficiently frozen, and so I entered her cabin without knocking. What I saw there still causes me to waver between ecstasy and horror.

The old woman was leaning over a basket, giving suck to a litter of hounds with human faces. One had the weasel face of the doctor; another that of a black man who resembled Valentine, my cook; a third looked like Zacharias, my hired man. There was even one that looked like me. A wolfhound, obviously the old woman's paramour, lay curled up in a corner, eyeing me suspiciously but without apparent malice. The woman herself swore at me and I backed out, shaken to my very bones. I tried to lean against a tree but slipped and fell into a patch of icy mud. I could not stand up again, and was afraid the small Indian dogs would eat me. I lay trembling like a newborn baby, and a vile smell surrounded me.

When I woke up I was in the kitchen of my own house, feeling very much out of sorts. I was seated in a stuffed chair with a blanket over my shoulders and a bowl of clear soup in my hands. If only I could have a few moments of peace, I thought, I might be able to make some sense of my dream, but tranquil reflection is not possible in this house. Valentine and Clémence were hurling insults at each other, the former accusing the latter of leaving me to die in the outhouse on a day in November that was so cold it felt like snow. Clémence started to cry, and then threw herself into the arms of a third woman who was unknown to me, and who had been warming herself by the stove. For a moment I mistook her for the wolfhound of my dream, but I was quickly disabused of that notion.

I heard Valentine talking about a certain Queen of Hungary, which reminded me of something. I wanted to tell them to shut up, but I could still not speak. Then I remembered who I was: Benjamin de Saint-Ours, the man the seigneury children laugh at and call the Dummy behind my back. At this point, three men came into the room; I could not recall any of their names, but I knew that they were acquaintances of mine.

"Ah, so Monsieur is awake," said one. "As usual, just in time for the Martinmas gift-giving, as I see. Did you receive a bundle this year? Tomorrow I will show you the seigneury account books — if you're still awake, that is. Valentine will be disappointed..."

I could not follow half of what they were saying, but I recognized the barbed sarcasm in their voices. My new bout of insomnia was not beginning well.

Another man entered. I was certain I had never seen him before. He introduced himself as Jean-Baptiste Something-or-Other, a messenger from the king, he said. Salutations, low bows, et cetera, et cetera. Then they all began to argue, and before two minutes had passed they were yelping at one another like a litter of hounds. To make them go away, I seized a knife from a table beside me and began to clean my fingernails, scowling at them as fiercely as I could manage. They soon left the room, all except Valentine, who went back to stirring her pots. She is a kind woman, is Valentine. Pretty, too. There ensued a mercifully quiet hour, and the kitchen filled with delicious smells, yet was I still disturbed by the memory of my nightmare. Taking a quill and some paper, I recorded the dream so as not to forget a single detail from it. Then Zacharias came in for his dinner, bringing with him the three children who I knew belonged to the house but whose names continue to elude me.

That evening, I caught Valentine lighting the stove with some papers on which there was some handwriting. I thought for a moment they were the papers on which I had written down my dream, but when I gestured to her to hand them over, I saw that they contained a letter addressed to the Empress of Russia. Valentine said she had burned many such letters of mine. I had not wanted her to burn them, she said, but she could not read and did not understand why they were so important, so she burned them. I must have written one to the Queen of Hungary, which would explain why the name had sounded so familiar to me when I first awakened. At any rate, Valentine was quite correct when she said that the letters gave off a very pleasant odour when they caught fire.

She is a wise woman.

•

This morning, the night closet in my room still being under repair, I went again to the outhouse. An Indian came in and sat on the seat next to mine. He said hello, and we then launched into a prolonged conversation.

Using gestures, I asked him what he was doing here, and above all what language he spoke and where it came from. It was not a local dialect, and the sound of his voice took me back in time, an extraordinarily long way back. The more he talked, the more I felt I was returning to my childhood. He said he knew me, but that he hadn't expected to find me here. No more had I, I gestured. He replied that he was passing through the region, and very naturally had decided to stop in to relieve himself at my manor house, as he would stop at the house of any old friend before whom he had no reason to be shy. Again I gestured: Who are you? How is it that you know me?

He paused for a long time before answering.

"I am called Le Chat," he said, "and I was your friend in the old days. It grieves me that you do not remember who I am, because it was I who saved your life when the Scottish artillerymen fired on us with their muskets and threw themselves upon us with their claymores. They would have cut your throat from ear to ear if I had let them. A French ball knocked you off your feet, and you were lying there, unconscious, and I picked you up and carried you on my back through our lines, and gave you to the man whose bear we had eaten the night before, which was so good. I left that place the next day with my Wild Oats, and we were very sorry to have come so far to see the French destroy themselves in such a lamentable fashion. There were fifteen of us when we arrived, and only four when we left.

"The voyage home was very hard. We had nothing to eat, and our canoes took on water without stopping. When I came down with a fever, my friends left me with an Abenaki family in Odanak. I still live there. The year after Quebec, when the English were besieging Montreal, our village was attacked by

Rogers' Rangers, the same band that had caused such devastation up and down the St. Lawrence when they were fighting for General Wolfe. They did what they wanted with us, because they had a score to settle and there was no penalty for killing Indians. A British soldier caught abusing a French family would have been executed on the spot, but with Indians, every atrocity was permitted. It is true, I know, that the Abenaki caused the British much trouble in New England. They were good fighters, like us. But still…"

I managed to ask him how he had saved himself.

"The two women who had adopted me when I was sick, they took me down to the river and we hid in the reeds. We stayed there three days, and when we came back to the village it was no longer there. The Rangers had killed everyone and burned and scalped everything that moved. Men who allow themselves to fall into such ways do not seem to believe that enemy women should be made the same as other women, and so after using them in the usual way they rearrange them, so that they no longer look like women. If a woman was pregnant, they opened her and fed her child to their dogs, who soon ate up everything. It is thought to be a method that impresses the enemy; you will recall that we used it many times ourselves in the old days, and perhaps it was we who taught it to the Rangers, although I do not think the Rangers required any lessons from us. That was the first time I had seen it applied to my own people, and since then I do not believe it a very good method. It is impressive, all right, but it makes for very bad dreams afterwards."

We must have gone on talking for hours. The man's tale and his manner of telling it fascinated me. Several times we were disturbed by urgent knocking at the outhouse door, and shouts from outside accusing us of taking too long, so we went into the house, where I sat him down at my table that he could refresh himself, which caused Clémence to fly into a fury. We would not have an Indian in the house when you were asleep, she scolded, and what was the world coming to, and so on. My old friend and I ate heartily, as though it were nothing to us, and then we went into my room and talked for three days and three nights.

I learned that he is no longer called Le Chat; he trades with the English now and is known as the Cat, or Decatte. I asked him if this change bothered him, and he replied with much wisdom that it was more bothersome to the French, who no longer control the civic state, which is always, as everyone knows, the apanage of the victor. (He did not express himself in precisely those words: I am, of course, paraphrasing.)

"I know within myself who I am," he added. "In my mother tongue I carried a name that I knew for barely an instant and which I have already forgotten. I am no more bothered by that than I was at being adopted by the Abenaki, who have since made me their chief. I am happy here; I am alive, and it is unwise to ask for more than that."

I found his words well reasoned. We separated the best friends in this world, as we had been in the world before, and I promised him that I would come to Odanak to visit him and to relive with him all those good old times of which I have absolutely no memory at all.

◆

I was not long keeping my promise, still haunted as I was by the images in my dream.

They say that one can always make oneself understood with gestures, but I challenge anyone to explain a dream without having recourse to words. I spent a great deal of time at the village trying to make myself understood. In the end, the Cat took me to the home of an old woman who could read dreams. She was not the old woman of my nightmare, as it turned out, but she was wise in many things.

She explained to me that the young whelps with the human faces were simply men. There is in each of us an animal that sleeps, and when it awakens it is either to save our lives or to take away the life of another. "If this dream is haunting you," she said, "it is because you are afraid of the animal inside you. No

more do you love the man who is inside you. You must recon-
cile yourself with the one, and with the other one, too, if you are
to find peace again."

Peace! I was not in search of peace, and I had not thought I
was at war with myself, nor with anyone else, for that matter.
What I wanted from her was to rid myself of this feeling of
dread that overcame me whenever I recalled my dream.
Sometimes, to fight it off, I allowed the images to affix themselves in my brain, and I stared them straight in the face. That
generally made me smile, because I would be looking at a little
puppy that had my own face, calling it endearing names and
throwing kisses at it. Then disgust would overtake me again as
the whelp came up to kiss me in return; I was plunged once
more into a state of lethargy and would remain so for hours on
end, heedless of the knocking on the outhouse door.

The Cat was very good for me. He let me recount to him my
cursed dream again and again and, like the old woman, told me
that I was at war against the animal within me. For days I
ambled about the village like a soul wandering in purgatory,
finding release from the dream only by plunging myself into the
ice-cold waters of the river. I no longer found contentment in the
war stories the Cat loved to tell; I could not bear to hear him say
that I had massacred women and innocent children. Any refer-
ence to those days upset me greatly. I kept asking myself
whether it had been the man or the animal within me that was
acting then, and losing my way in such wild conjecturings sad-
dened rather than comforted me.

All this while, the people at the seigneury were growing dis-
pleased with me, since they did not know what to make of an
absentee seigneur who spent all his time among the Indians at
Odanak. To make matters worse, there was open hostility
between the Queen of Hungary and the king's messenger, and I
was being called upon to intervene. The people themselves were
divided, there was much general confusion, no one knew what
to make of anything. There was little enough I could do that

would please anyone, let alone everyone. Some there were who said there might soon be open warfare at home, and grumbled that I seemed to be completely indifferent to it.

I decided that I had to leave the seigneury, leave it for good. I even wanted to leave, being a traveller by nature, a man of the open road. I have nothing but contempt for village life. The Cat will come with me, of course. We will make our preparations in secret. He is as discreet a man as I am.

9

DURING my enforced idleness, I read that no voyage is successful without it is accompanied by a complete narration of it. I do not, however, wish to encumber myself by bringing with me an escritoire and other accoutrements of the literary trade. I wish to travel light. I have therefore resolved to write my account before taking the actual voyage. I realize that I may have to make certain adjustments to it upon my return. If worse comes to worst, I would not be the first to resort to fabrications and approximations in the telling of a traveller's tale. Pre-writing the narrative might even be seen as a necessary precaution, since, on account of my continuing lethargy, I will almost certainly forget a great deal of what will happen to me on my voyage, and I do not want to run the risk of having nothing to write about when I am safely ensconced once again in my manor. There is nothing wrong with preparing oneself beforehand.

I have at hand several excellent models to work from, among them the narrative of Bougainville, entitled *The Voyage Around the World of the Frigate* Boudeuse *and the Flute* l'Étoile, which I have from my good friend Toussaint.

(I can never remember the difference between a frigate and a flute. I must needs consult a dictionary upon my return. For now, I cannot allow myself to be distracted by words. That being said, I find it difficult to imagine the periwigged milquetoast I knew as Bougainville undertaking anything as strenuous as the circumnavigation of the globe, not even in a flute. I knew him well in Quebec, and I cannot believe this to be the same man. He must have very influential relations in France to have been entrusted with such a mission. He was a well-intentioned young man, and not ill educated, but it ever seemed to me that he lacked judgement. During his time here, he conceived the most hare-brained schemes imaginable concerning the conduct of the war. He once proposed, for example, to incite the slaves in the Carolinas to rise up in revolt against their plantation owners, as if slaves could be persuaded to fight against one master only to replace him with another. He also wanted to convince the Scottish troops in the British Expeditionary Forces to fight against England, as though he did not know that the most loyal soldiers of a conquering army are always those most recently defeated by that army, a truism I have myself verified almost every day here on the seigneury. Poor, naive Bougainville! And we will never know why he failed to come to Montcalm's defence at Quebec. To think he has received the Cross of Saint-Louis and was further rewarded with these voyages of discovery. One can scarcely regret being ruled by a king capable of harkening to such unwise counsel.…All the same, there is something to admire in Bougainville after all: he writes well, it is a pleasure to read him, so much so that I wonder if it were not his skill as a writer that hath provoked such confidence from his king. Well, well, let us leave it for now.)

I shed but a single tear upon leaving this place: the Cat will not be coming with me. When I asked him why not, he said that I had not consulted him, and, in any case, he would have told me that he has already found his true place; it is I, not he, who must go in search of a home. I have always believed that the only true citizens of this country are its dead; I forgot about the Indians. I shook his hand warmly, and he bade me safe journey.

I quickly replaced him in my plans with Toussaint, my trusted secretary. I foresee a bright future for this man, whose ambition is discreet and founded upon a veritable talent for flattery in his pen. Such men have but one fault, and that is to suppose themselves superior to their masters, in whose mouths they put words. They have the courage of their convictions, but seldom the courage to act. Be that as it may, he it will be who records my exploits and carries my escritoire, because I am in no doubt now that I shall be in need of one.

At first he and I disagreed on the nature of our voyage. He had his heart set on a voyage of scientific exploration, which he thought would bring him glory in the telling of it, the only kind of glory, he maintains, that counts in this life. The voyage, in other words, is for him much less important than the account he would give of it. I am more interested in discovering countries, planting flags, bestowing names, things of that sort, for I believe that lasting glory is to be attained more through geography than through literature. But he raised so many objections to this and that aspect of the expedition that I finally gave in to him. The only important thing for me, after all, is to wipe the dust of this accursed country off my boots...

•

Thus did we quit the Seigneury de la Sapinière in the greatest possible secrecy, undesirous as we were of causing the merest hurt to anyone there. We journeyed by foot six days, after which interval we arrived at the town of Quebec. Upon seeing the famous ramparts, my valorous secretary inquired of me whether we were not travelling in the wrong direction, seeing that Quebec lay to the east of us, whereas we ought to have been travelling due west. Our intention, he reminded me, was to discover the Northwest Passage, and therethrough the silks, gold and spices of China. I confessed to him that I had completely forgotten that such had indeed been our goal. Walking had put me in such excellent humour, I told him, that everything else had flown from my mind utterly, for the which I begged his forgiveness, the which he did graciously grant me. To replace ourselves in better accord, thereupon, we sat two days on a public bench in the town square, exchanging views of our projected voyage. In the end, it was my own view that prevailed, since it is I who am financing this trip, the whole adventure having been conceived primarily for my diversion. There will always be time for considerations of science and glory at some later date.

It was a gloriously sunny day, the fifteenth of August, when we left Quebec. Our immediate destination was Newfoundland, and shortly after arriving there we set sail for the Azores with a view to ultimately reaching the coast of Portugal. The wind was from the east and filled the sails fair to bursting. Our sailing companions were rough and unpleasant men, not excepting the ship's captain and officers, who were fiends for corporal punishment and resorted to the cat-o'-nine-tails for the slightest infraction.

It must needs be said that the ship on which we found ourselves was not one of our choosing; rather the reverse, in fact. The threat of another war with America had obliged England to remuster its naval forces by resorting to a method of recruitment known as pressing. Royal Navy press gangs roamed the dockyards along the Thames and in the colonies, compelling sailors into His Majesty's service and forcing them aboard their man-o'-war ships. Thus it was that my master and I found ourselves one evening under escort and much against our will from a tavern in Quebec, and obliged to accept the king's shilling aboard a Royal Navy vessel anchored in the harbour. My master was content enough, since he had long dreamed of sailing to distant shores. For my part, however, I found that my enforced duties aboard the ship prevented me from making scientific observations. My master gave me to understand that I had only to keep my eyes open and write down what I saw later by consulting my memory. I conceded as how he was in the right of it, especially since it was plain that I was to be given so little choice in the matter.

Our ship was a frigate that had endured more than its share of heavy seas and strong winds. Half its crew was composed of involuntary mariners like ourselves, most of whom, however, did not share my master's enthusiasm for seeing the world. The work was not overly arduous, the only difficulty being that although my master could readily comprehend the orders given to him in English, he could make no vocal reply to his superiors. It thus fell to me to reply on his behalf, and I do not speak English. We were usually able to disentangle ourselves by making common cause, but there were occasions upon which we would find ourselves embroiled in woeful misunderstandings.

I will cite a case in point. Having arrived off Louisbourg, on the eastern coast of Ile Royale, a place my master knew well from his having participated in the siege of the fortress some fifteen years earlier, our captain decided to drop anchor in order to take on fresh water and wood. We were situate at 30 degrees east longitude, 44 degrees north latitude, the wind blowing steadily from the west, a light rain falling, and choppy seas portending an oncoming storm. (I take this latter from an account of an earlier voyage, which I had had the foresight to pack in my portmanteau.) My master, who had not yet got his sea legs (no more had I) and who had, for several days past, required my most diligent attention, desired to walk about on land in order to restore himself to countenance. The quartermaster, however, forbade us leave to go ashore, that privilege being reserved for regular volunteers, and not for hands who had been acquired by force. Upon hearing this, my master lost his temper, knocked the quartermaster to the deck with a single blow, and was immediately clapped in irons and sentenced to an hundred of the best, the cat to be let out of the bag on the day following.

I was in no small fear for his life. Although my master is a strong enough man, so severe a punishment could easily prove fatal. I therefore determined to aid him in an escapade, an enterprise that proved to present no great difficulty since every regular sailor on board was celebrating some obscure English holiday to the accompaniment of extra rations of grog. The shackle lock yielded quickly to my knife blade, and before long we were over the side and safely ashore. By sunrise, we had put a satisfactory distance between ourselves and that floating prison.

My master having had enough of sailing for the time being, nothing in the world would induce him to repeat the experience, not excluding even another press gang, which hitherto had seemed to offer him such an inexpensive way of getting about. We were therefore obliged to postpone our plans for a European tour: farewell, Versailles, where my master had entertained such hopes of receiving the Cross of Saint-Louis from the king himself; Madrid, Vienna, Rome, adieu. We will visit you anon. For the nonce, we settled instead upon a walking tour of America. From Chile, we thought we would hop over to visit Japan and India, and upon our return to the New World we might discover the Northwest Passage, as my master had promised me we would do.

Our peregrination having taken us some distance from Louisbourg, we encountered a crew of New England fishermen engaged in drying cod flakes on curious wooden stages which they had ingeniously constructed for the purpose on shore. As they were bound to return to their home port in any case, they agreed to take us on board as passengers for a reasonable rate, and our deliverance to Boston was thus considerably more agreeable to us than had been our conveyance to Ile Royale.

We commenced this portion of our journey on a cold, wet day in October. Reading over my shoulder as I made this entry in my journal, my master asked me why I had described the day as cold and wet when ordinary sensory perception made it obvious to him that we were sailing under sunny skies with a warm southeasterly wind. When I replied that "cold and wet" was the forecast given for this day in my almanack, he regarded me in a state of some perplexity. I explained to him what an almanack was, and he asked to see the copy to which I referred. It was a very expensive one that I had had sent over from France the year before.

He read through it for several minutes, and I watched as a look of amazement and delight spread over his storm-ravaged features.

"Is it possible," he demanded to know by gestures, "to predict the weather an entire year in advance? But this is marvellous!"

His discovery afforded me an abundance of satisfaction, since I know no greater joy than that of kindling a tiny flame of knowledge in a mind that hath hitherto dwelt in a state of the darkest ignorance and obscurity.

"Just so," I told him. "That is precisely the case! See here, where it says in the preliminary pages that the forthcoming winter would be extremely harsh, and many children would die from exposure to the cold. Well, even though this almanack was made in Normandy, is it not true that last winter at the seigneury was an extremely hard one: there was an unusual amount of snow, and no fewer than four newborn infants froze to death in their cradles. Just as the almanack predicted! It also says that the spring would be mild and good for planting, followed by a warm summer with a bountiful harvest in the autumn. And call me a flounder if that was not exactly the case at Sapinière!"

There is no doubt about it, an almanack is a very valuable item. I am never without one, especially when I travel, when there are so many things one needs to know. For example, if it so happens that I must needs miss a day of entry in my journal, I have but to inquire into my almanack to see what the weather was like in France on that particular day, and transcribe an accurate account of it into my own diary. Nor is that all! For an almanack contains a great deal of other useful information, such as recipes for the preparation of grilled meats, jams and marmaladoes, herbal remedies and the like. All there, ready to be copied down in my journal!

We proceeded upon our pleasant journey, my master perusing the almanack daily as a means of fending off the boredom of a lengthy sea voyage, I making copious and meticulous entries in my logbook. At length we disembarked at Boston, a town admired by my master in his youth, although he was much put out at there being no mention of it in the almanack. We quickly engaged a fisherman's barque to take us to New York, which we found greatly enlivened by the agitations of the Republicans, but which nevertheless presented us with an extremely interesting countenance. We continued to Norfolk and voyaged thence as far as the Floridas, whence we made a rapid passage to New Orleans, the one destination dreamed of by every serious traveller.

At dockside we were met by several estimable persons who, having anticipated our arrival, were vying with one another for the privilege of receiving us. In the end, we accepted the invitation of the alcade himself, which was most graciously made, and at his residence we had the very great pleasure of making the acquaintance of the celebrated Countess Manon Lescaut, who invited us to dine with her the next evening. Her plantation is the richest in the country, having in its service three hundred contented Negroes who do nothing but sing and dance all the live-long day. Her table is resplendent with Saxony porcelain and the best of French wines. My master seemed quite dazzled at being surrounded by so much luxuriance, not having been, shall we say, to the manor born, and so I have taken it upon myself to act as his cicerone into this exalted social stratum.

I believe Monsieur might also be something jealous of the ease with which I am able to comport myself with the Countess Lescaut and her guests. When he overheard Madame make certain unmistakable overtures to me regarding the sleeping arrangements for the coming evening, he flew into a towering rage which I found to be not a trifle embarrassing...

◆

I discovered Toussaint writing in my room when I was not there. It was not the first time, and I let him know in no uncertain terms that I would not tolerate it again! He does mistake himself for his better, does this secretary, and I will not have him in the manor; let him return to his own house and never leave it more. So saying, I threw his journal in the fire and propelled its author from my premises with the bottom of my boot. Alas, he tripped on the doorstep and broke his arm in falling, and now I am uneasy in my mind at having wounded my non-travelling companion. I find my fondness for him returning. I must be tired. I am going to go to bed. Perhaps I will dream again of the old woman and her litter of human pups, only this time I will dwell with them a little longer. I do hope so, in any case.

10

MY boy Benjamin, he'll be all alone in the house when he wakes up, which is why this is the last place I plan to be when he does, what with his temper and all the bad news that's waitin for him, he'll be on a rampage for the next five years. There's no livin with him when he don't get everything his own way. I am the only one left here now, his old Zacharias, and even I won't be here much longer myself.

The first thing he'll do when he opens his eyes is ask for Valentine, and that'll be his first surprise. She's gone off alookin for her daughter, Marjolaine, and if I know anything about her we won't be seein her around here again neither.

When the Americans came to set us free, as they put it, they were a might put out when we told em they didn't have nothing we wanted. Some on em were downright mad at us, and the ones that were billeted here took Marjolaine with em when they left. I'll not go into what they did to her afore that, but there were four of em, right there on the kitchen table. There warn't no one in the house at the time cept Clémence, but the Americans didn't want nothin to do with her. They just wanted the child.

Clémence did what she could. She yelled at em, sayin that the girl was the child of a freed slave and the master of the house, the Seigneur de la Sapinière, but apparently they just said that that made it all the sweeter on account it helped make up for all the trouble they went to to free up such an ungrateful country as this is, and all the rest of it. She even told em we were on their side, thinkin it might make em ease up a bit if they knew the child's mother was a Republican through and through. But they just laughed that one off. A freed black is still a nigger, they said, meanin the child, and a good nigger is still worth two hundred dollars in the Carolinas, no matter what they did to her afore she got there.

I warn't around when all this was happenin, but I heard about it. When I did, I did what Benjamin hisself would've done under the circumstances. I went and got his friend Decatte, the new chief of the Abenakis down in Odanak, and him and me followed the trail left by the Americans. But they had too much of a head start and we only caught up with two on em. We had fun with them, though. We gave em the old Indian treatment from the high country, cut their heads off and took their scalps, and then brought the heads back to Valentine to let her know we at least accomplished somethin. Didn't do her much good. Even got us into trouble with Clémence, who wanted to know what we planned to do with a couple of useless American heads. She had a point, we had to admit, so we buried them in the garden. Maybe they'll come up cabbage heads next year, if anyone's here to dig em up.

When Marjolaine got took, Valentine warn't here neither or she would've shot the whole lot on em. But she was off visitin Master Toussaint at the prison in Quebec. Clémence had to give her the news when she got back, and the poor woman took it hard. She cried so loud we thought she'd go an wake up Benjamin. Then she left the next day to find her daughter. I told her, I says, why not wait for the seigneur to wake up and take him with you, you never know, I says, he bein a friend of Mr. Franklin down in Philadelphia, maybe between em they can do somethin, but she wouldn't wait. Well, at least I tried, my boy, at least I tried.

The others have left too, but for different reasons. Master Toussaint, he got hisself arrested by the Loyalists when they looked inside that big clock of his and found a pile of letters addressed to a bunch of American Republicans, including Mr.

Benjamin Franklin. Toussaint protested bloody murder, sayin they warn't his letters, they belonged to Benjamin de Saint-Ours. Maybe so, they says to him, but these here letters are to Benjamin Franklin and they're written in your handwritin, and that's all we need to know for now. You can straighten it out in Quebec. Come with us!

I don't feel all that sorry for Toussaint being sent to prison and all, because he showed his true colours in front of those soldiers and tried to get off by getting my Benjamin in trouble, who never did nothin to harm him. Still, that don't seem reason enough to put a man in prison for, even a rotten pissass scoundrel like Toussaint who shits his drawers if you say boo to him. They said he had dangerous ideas. Well who don't? And anyways, you can't go puttin people in prison because of their ideas. Especially someone like Toussaint, whose ideas are all in his own head and are not exactly shared by anybody else anyway.

Any road, Toussaint is out of prison now. One day the governor, Mr. Carleton, he needed a public declaration translated into French, and someone in his office had the bright idea of givin it to a prisoner who didn't speak any English but could write good French. Somehow they settled on Toussaint. Apparently he let them know that since bein put in prison he had become an avid Loyalist. He polished off a declaration that was twice as long as the English version and didn't have much to do with it in any case, accordin to some, but Mr. Carleton said he'd rather have a useful translator than a gifted one. So they took Toussaint out of prison and made him secretary and official translator for the Province of Quebec! He's got a good job, decent pay, wears suits that come straight from London, and has tea every night with the governor hisself or with some other big wig. Goes out all the time, such as to garrison balls, where he'll no doubt meet some rich daughter and marry her. He landed on his feet, all right, and I have no call to worry on his account.

If my boy Benjamin wakes up and finds out Valentine is gone

and calls for Clémence instead, he'll be in for a second big surprise, because she ain't here neither. When Master Stillborne got out his old captain of militia togs and went out to fight off the Americans, he asked us to keep an eye on his manor house, which we did, on account of him being such a good neighbour. It was mostly Clémence who made sure his rents were paid and the house was kept in decent shape. Then Master Stillborne he was taken prisoner and sent to Philadelphia and is still down there. We don't hear much from him these days. Clémence took it real hard, having a soft spot in her heart for him, I think, since her own seigneur don't ever think of her in that way, not even when he's sleeping.

So she went down to be with him in Philadelphia. She took a room near the prison where he is, and goes to see him regular, takin him in little comforts. The prison there is like the one in Quebec, or so she writes, the prisoners don't get fed or clothed, and have to depend on their friends outside to bring em what they need to keep from starvin or freezin to death. Good thing for Master Stillborne that she's there, or else he'd be in a bad way. The Americans set fire to his manor house to teach him a lesson, and there's not much left of the seigneury. They were harder on him than on us on account of him being one of them. That's the way it usually is. They also made sure they got his plantation in Virginia, the one that used to send up that good smokin tobacco. Anyways, we won't be seein Clémence around here again neither.

We never had the kind of problem that did for Master Stillborne, because everyone here at the seigneury was on both sides of the question, even us. When the Americans took Montreal and sent out all those handbills tellin us they had come to set us free, well, we looked at them and thought they made a lot of sense. And then when the English came and told us that they were here to protect us, we realized that what the Americans said didn't make all that much sense after all, seein as how they put as many of us in prison as the English did, and so we didn't really know what to think, did we? It was like Monsieur Luc de Lacorne Saint-Luc, who fought against the English like he had the devil hisself in his pants during the war, and tried his damnedest to get back to France after the Conquest, but then when he lost everything he had when the *Auguste* went down he decided that the English weren't so bad. Even he was willing to listen to the Americans when they first came up to set us free, but in the end he went back to the English side. That's sort of how it was for all of us. Put it this way: we aren't so inclined any more to be hard on anyone who goes back and forth like a weather vane in a hurricane.

Still, the ones who are best off are them as knew when to stop spinnin and pick a side. Take that lawyer Séraphin, for example. Right from the get-go he was more American than Yankee cheese. You should've heard him readin out the Declaration of the Congress of the Thirteen Colonies to the tenant farmers on the seigneury; he was so enthusiastic about it I thought he must've added a few phrases on his own. Then he switched over to the English side, like everyone else, only before everyone else. And when the English won, they sent him to Montreal as an example. Eventually they made him a judge, and now he too has a big carriage to take him around town in, bigger than Toussaint's carriage, even, because not only was Séraphin smarter than Toussaint, he was smarter sooner.

Dr. Ambroise now, he didn't change horses in mid-stream like his lawyer friend. He was ever on the side of the English, but I think that was just to piss off Séraphin and Toussaint. Those three never did get along. And when the Americans left with poor little Marjolaine, they took the doctor with them because their own doctor had been killed at the Siege of Quebec. The two of them, all alone like that.

But at least we've had word from the doctor. Things seem to have turned out well for him. First off, he bestowed his medical knowledge on a few soldiers who had the good sense to die on him right away, rather than suffer a lingerin, agonizin, putrefyin

death under his long-term care, and so it became pretty clear
early on that the doctor's medical knowledge was a few text
books short of a library. But by then he'd sworn the oath of allegiance to the American republic, with the result that he was
finally able to go to a real medical school.

Which is how he ended up at Harvard College, in Boston.
We got a letter from him. He stayed there three years and then
wrote a paper on puerperal fevers. I don't know what puerperal
fevers are, and I hope I never get one, but they seem to have
done all right for Dr. Ambroise because he's still a doctor today
and has a big practice in Boston. Doctors make a lot of money
down there, so we're led to believe, and it don't look like old
Ambroise is chomping at the bit to get back to Quebec. He even
says we should all go down there and look him up in Boston,
and some of our young people here have done just that. Packed
up and headed south. Our Nicholas, Benjamin's eldest son,
among them. Nick joined the American army and is now who
knows where. The long and the short of it is, Dr. Ambroise
became an American in spite of hisself, and he's a darn sight better off because of it.

It looks like Monsieur is tryin to wake up. I'd better put
another dose of the opium in his milk. Oh yes, we been keepin
him asleep this last little while. It was Clémence's idea. I think
she was jealous of Valentine, if you ask me. Valentine was
always able to have a good time with Benjamin, in his sleep like,
back in the old days when she was still interested in such things.
She was the only one who could. There were a few others,
young women from the village who'd come up to the house for
this or that and slip into his room when everyone was blinking.
That's all they talk about on the seigneury, how Monsieur could
do it with his eyes closed. More than one on em was happy
enough to lose her maidenhead with a man who couldn't talk
about it afterwards. Course that's where them two twins came
from, the boy Josué and the girl Apolline, that were found wailin
beside the well that Easter morning.

Clémence found the whole thing a disgrace, more especially because she warn't having any herself. That's why I said she was jealous, and I bet that's also why she turned to the doctor for help. At first she just asked him for some sleepin draughts for herself, but it warn't long before she figured out that givin them to him might prevent another batch of twin bastards from turnin up at the house. Nothin like a few vials of opium for maintainin public morality. That's the way she put it anyway.

I'm not sayin she was right. I'm not sayin that, but I will say that a bit of opium in the milk came in mighty handy when those Americans were here. If he'd been awake then he'd've gone off fightin against em. Or maybe with em, who knows. Any road, we figured it was best to keep him down. And when the soldiers from both sides came to get him, we had no trouble passin him off as a dead man. Since then, well, we sort of kept up the habit of it. It seems that opium makes a person have dreams that are a sight more fantastical than the ones you have ordinarily. But the doctor's gone now, and we don't have many of his little vials left. Only a few drops, which I'll put in his milk by and by, and when he's sunk into a really deep sleep I'll take my leave, too, along with the rest of em.

I'm all packed and ready to go. I'll head up to the interior, into the Hinterlands. I hear the North West Company is lookin for paddlers and the pay is good. I'm takin Jeremy with me, Benjamin's youngest son. When we stopped him from runnin away with Nick to join up with the Americans, he nearly bawled his eyes out. To make him feel better I promised to take him with me. He's a good lad and sturdy, like his father; he'll be good company for me. Before we head out West, though, we'll make a slight detour to see if we can't do somethin to help his sister, Marjolaine. Just a small side trip I have in mind.

Goodbye, Benjamin. Forgive me. It was my idea to turn you into a seigneur. I put together this place for you after the war, when land around here was going for a song. I told myself I was doin it for you, but now I know I was lyin to myself. You don't help anyone by forcin things on them, or by tellin em stories. But stories are like your opium, my son; they give you beautiful dreams.

I wanted to be a seigneur myself, but it warn't possible for an old outlaw trader like me to rise to such heights in those days. Besides, I didn't have the know-how for it anyway, good manners and all, nobody'd've taken me seriously. But through you I've become the lah-dee-dah landowner I always wanted to be. You were like my mirror, and I used you in order to see my own dreams come true. Toussaint knew that. He always said that all I wanted was to smooth over my own guilty conscience for abandonin you to strangers when you were small. Now I think about it, he may have been right for once in his life.

That's the first snow falling outside. It's November. Me and Jeremy, we have some distance to put between us and this house. We don't intend to leave nothing behind but our footsteps. He's waitin outside, anxious to be goin as all get out. I'll take better care of him, my son. I promise you that.

And now it's time.

BOOK THREE
THE THEOGAMIST

1

MONSIEUR has left. As have so many others. Some of us miss him, others not so much. But whether we miss him or not, we are getting along well enough without him. I am still here, of course, his old friend Pâtissant. One day I hope to be able to take his place in the affections of the tenant farmers.

It started with a messenger from Quebec who came and nailed a proclamation to the door of the church. When the habitants showed up to find out what it was all about, they argued for a good hour or more, until they had exhausted all the possibilities. Some thought it said that another war had started; others decided it was announcing a new tax; still others claimed it was a work order to get them out repairing what they still referred to as the King's Road. Perhaps someone was going to be arrested, someone suggested. Who, then? asked the others. At the end of the day, everyone was still as confused about the whole thing as they had been in the morning, and then of course there were those who said there was nothing to be confused about.

The women quickly tired of all the guesswork. "If the thing is written down," they said, "why not just get Monsieur Pâtissant to come and read it out? That way we will know right away what it says, and there'll be no need to waste everyone's time arguing about what it says."

The men shrugged and admitted the women had a point, and so they sent someone to fetch me. I am, after all, the schoolteacher. I do teach people to read, write and do their numbers, after all. I have my uses. I am very much respected in these parts.

The document in question was a pastoral letter from the Bishop of Quebec enjoining all parishioners not to pay heed to anyone who was going about pretending to be a priest. If these false priests said Mass, they must be reported, and they would be arrested and tried. If they came to our door, we must not let them in. Above all, we must not receive from them any sacrament subject to payment, as that would be a mortal sin. We can not feed, lodge or listen to them. That was all. The habitants went home satisfied. The only pebble that troubled their minds was why the bishop had sent such a letter to this parish, which has not had a priest of any kind for the past thirty years. There were even those among them, the younger ones, who had to ask me what a priest was, and what a bishop was. I told them that a priest was a man of God and a bishop was a big priest, but, judging by the expressions on their faces, they were not much enlightened by my explanation.

The older ones knew, though. There was a priest here at one time, when the seigneury was being run by the original Saint-Ours family, although no one remembers his name. He died and was replaced by another priest, whose name is also long forgotten. For a short while, the curate from Sorel came to say Mass; he was followed by a vicar from Contrecoeur. Each one of these men of the cloth complained that the habitants here were too stingy to support God's work. In the old days, during the reign of the French king, the faith they adhered to had to send a justice officer to collect the tithes due to a priest they had never seen, which caused the habitants to take up their pitchforks and flails and march on Trois-Rivières, where they thrashed the bailiff to within an inch of his life. After that, there was no more talk of tithes around here. Since Canada became an English colony, there has been no priest here at all, and the habitants have been bothered even less with such things.

There is a church here at the fort – the locals still refer to the seigneury as a fort rather than as a village – but no one can recall ever seeing a priest in it. It is an old log building with an earthen floor, containing a rickety pulpit, a small pine altar, a tattered rood-screen and a few wooden benches, including the one that was once reserved for the seigneur, which looks a little less used than the others. The local parishioners think about their church only once a year, when they shut up a pack of starving dogs in it to chase out the rats and feral cats that have taken over the building the rest of the time.

All things considered, it can't be said that religion has fared well at the Seigneury de la Sapinière. There has not been a baptism here in twenty-five years; no one under the age of thirty knows what a sermon or Lent is. They know Christmas and Easter, because those days are marked in the almanack, but no one from the younger generation has been married, and no one of the older generation has received Last Rites or been buried in holy ground. And only the extremely senile can recite a prayer or intone a canticle. In short, the seigneury has been effectively de-Christianized; there is no more religious instruction here than there is in a band of nomadic Micmaqs. In fact, the Abenaki of Saint-François are more religious than we are here. There are no punishments down here for those who do not profess the Holy Catholic Faith. Is there up above? No, we think probably not there, either.

But they wouldn't mind being sent a priest, everyone said. They'd heard that all that religious ritual and ceremony is a thing of some beauty. Having a sabbath day would help to mark the passage of time and also provide an opportunity for the buying and selling of cattle on the church steps, as they used to do in the old days. It would bring them together in body as well as in spirit. They still believe in God, after all. In each home in the seigneury there are crucifixes and statues of the Virgin; everyone knows the religious holidays and many can recite the *Te Deum*. These customs have survived because none others have come along to replace them.

The last time the church was used was when the English soldiers kept their horses in it. Before that the Americans used it as a magazine for their powder and flintlocks. And before that, in the very old times, officers of the Guyenne Regiment would take the women they'd brought with them from outside the parish there to celebrate the Black Mass. No, I think the Bishop of Quebec has been misinformed; there are no priests here, good or bad. Who would want to have anything to do with our old church, which stinks of misery and neglect? Twenty years ago, when the country became Protestant, nearly all the priests returned to France, and none have come back to take their place. No, the good bishop was mistaken, we told ourselves. Such things happen. There was no priest holding sway in the new Saint-Ours seigneury, and if one ever did stray this way he would more likely be high-tailing it out of here as fast as his predecessors had, instead of staying around to preach false gospels. That was what the people of the parish said, at any rate.

But the people of the parish were wrong, as it turned out. A few days later, a rowboat pulled up at the village pier. The man who rowed it hardly took the time to ship his oars before heading up to our poor excuse for a church and closeting himself inside it. A few hours later he came out, went down and collected his belongings from the boat, and then sold the vessel to one of the local eel fishermen, who pronounced it sound and seaworthy. The newcomer said he had no more need of it, because he had come here among us to die.

This attracted a bit of attention, as you can imagine, and they all came to have a look at this curious specimen. He was tall and thin, with a shaved head, and he was dressed in a robe of grey sacking tied with a linen cord. A wooden cross hung around his neck, and his feet were stuck in a pair of wooden clogs. The blacksmith, Boucane, told everyone that evening that the man was wearing the robes of a brother of St. Francis. Perhaps this was the new priest sent by the Bishop of Quebec to chase away the false priest mentioned in the letter. Or maybe he was a new priest from Sorel. Or maybe he was one of the false priests we were supposed to eject from our midst? We would have to wait and see.

But Boucane, not as patient as the others, went up to the newcomer and asked him straight out if he was a good priest or a false one. The man in the grey robe spoke to him softly.

"I am Brother Barthélemy," he said, "a Recollet and a poor sinner like yourself. There is no one living in God's house, and so I have decided to live there myself and to look over the statue of our Holy Mother. If anyone here has need of my ministrations, he has only to come to me and he will be warmly welcomed. He will not even need to knock on the door, for it will open unto him of its own accord."

Satisfied, Boucane told all he had seen and heard to the villagers. Upon entering the church, the first thing the monk had done was chase out the three wild dogs that had taken up residence there and been keeping the neighbourhood awake at night with their howling. One was a female and the two males fought over her like men. The priest had admonished them to go forth and multiply somewhere other than in God's house, and they had instantly and quietly obeyed.

That night one of the male dogs returned to the church with one ear torn half off and blood oozing from his side, having apparently lost one fight too many for his paramour's favours. The Recollet took him in like a prodigal son, bound his wounds, gave him some food and made a straw bed for him beside his own pallet in the small sacristy attached to the main building that had last served as a presbytery. The dog, once ferocious, now behaved like an angel, obeying the good priest's every command. Upon hearing this edifying story, villagers and habitants alike decided he could not possibly be a false priest.

"He is a true brother of Francis," pronounced Boucane, who obviously liked the expression.

The story quickly spread throughout the seigneury. There is a priest among us, a good priest, God has come back to us, we are all going to heaven when we die, and in the meantime, we're all going to church. The story raised a few questions as well, however, and it wasn't long before giddiness turned into guile. A priest means tithes, does it not? How much does he want? Will he make us do long penance for the years we lived as pagans? Will he be vengeful or forgiving? Will he lord it over us from his little confessional? What do we need with a priest around here, anyway? What was wrong with the way things were? And if we have to have a priest, why couldn't the bishop have sent us a proper one, a nice Sulpician, for example, with a black robe and a clean white collar? Someone who looked less like a beggar than this Franciscan, with his grey homespun and his filthy clogs. No, there was decidedly more bitterness than joy in our parish.

The last one to find out about the arrival of the grey monk was the Seigneur de Saint-Ours. Poor man, he had just wakened from a five-year slumber, and he had to use all his powers of concentration to come to grips with what had taken place in the seigneury during his absence. He had two more children, for example, and no idea who their mothers were, as usual. Little wonder that he was morose, subsisting as he was in a perpetual state of startled lethargy. Who would want to bother his head over a mendicant priest about whom we knew so little?

Normally I mind my own business, but in this case, I decided I would see for myself what all the fuss was about. I found Father Barthélemy cleaning up the church. He had already sluiced out most of the dirt with buckets of water and had made a lodging for himself that was humble but respectable. He greeted me with simplicity and gave me a length of log to sit on, explaining that he had been occupied in splitting firewood to prepare himself for the winter. We talked about this and that: the size of the woodshed he would need, what he intended to plant in his kitchen garden, whether he would raise chickens or rabbits to keep him company now and provide for his table in days to come. He was hoping to bring the parish registry books up to date before beginning his ministry in the spring. It seemed he would need the entire winter to put the records into some kind of order.

I could not contribute to this man's poor reputation on the seigneury. It was an honour to have Father Barthélemy among us. He was a man of singular distinction, with an erudition as wide as the ocean. He knew how the real world worked, and it was simple modesty that urged him to venture out into it. He wished only to make himself useful to those who came after him, and he never once backed away from making the smallest sacrifice to bring comfort or aid to people in need. People like us, for example.

He had spent some time in Louisiana, where he performed the function of titular chaplain to the Capucins of New Orleans. He had been born in Brittany, he told me, and studied at the seminary in Rennes. He could have become a Jesuit, but his humility suited him more for the robes of the Recollets. Though a thoroughly educated scholar, he was given the roughest of missions, because he was also as strong as a bull. He could easily have knocked our beefy blacksmith to the ground with a single blow of his fist, and Boucane had killed a bear with his bare hands. Just ask him.

After Louisiana, Father Barthélemy had followed the Acadians sent by Monsieur Bougainville to the Falkland Islands. This unfortunate band lasted little longer than a single season before being transferred by France to Spain, and the poor priest had had to find his own way back to Louisiana. He walked all the way across the American continent, and when he reached Louisiana he had turned north and walked to Canada. He had first been a priest to the Montagnais in Labrador, but he had fallen in love with our country. He wanted to die here, he said, a humble man among humble people, and had come to our village because he had heard that we had no priest. He was awaiting his orders from the bishop.

I visited him regularly, and we talked about spiritual matters while he fashioned new benches for his church. I am afraid I aroused jealousy among the other parishioners; they were jealous of my instruction, and now they are jealous of my friendship with Father Barthélemy. Among others there is the village apothecary, who welcomed the Loyalists when they first came up and had been thrown into prison by the Americans for it, and who since then has talked about nothing but receiving compensation for his treatment. Then there is the bailiff, who initially welcomed the Americans and then turned his coat in time to profit from the English, and who does not like to talk about those days at all. Two false priests who do not like it when there are others around more learned than themselves, though God knows that does not take a great deal of learning.

The apothecary and the bailiff speak badly of our poor monk, who has never done them the slightest harm. They accuse him of having seduced the blacksmith, Boucane, who goes home from his courses completely drunk, his catechism clutched tightly in his enormous hand. When he sobers up, he refuses to say where the Recollet hides his store of spirits. The apothecary and the process-server have therefore determined to rid the village of this turbulent priest.

I could not sit back and watch this good man struggle alone against two such powerful conspirators, but if I helped him, I do confess it, I did so more from idleness than kindness. And the seigneur helped him, too, in a way.

2

MY last period of wakefulness did not go well. First of all, I was awakened by the sound of my own voice: I had been talking in my sleep. I opened my eyes and called for my servant, as if out of habit. Hearing myself speak was a joy I had not felt for years. I began to weep with it and howled as loudly as I could to assure myself that it was indeed me making these strange sounds. Then I started laughing, also as loudly as possible, also out of pure joy at being able to hear myself. I spoke a few experimental words, which came out sounding a bit rusted, but all the same they were my words, and that was enough for me.

"Valentine!" I shouted. "Valentine! Come quickly! I can talk! And I'm hungry, too. Very hungry!"

No one came upstairs. I lost my patience. What was the good of regaining my powers of speech if everyone else had become deaf? I got up and went downstairs; I found it difficult to walk, as though no one had been exercising me during my long sleep. I determined that after issuing my first orders I would have a little talk with all the lazy members of my household, and this time I would be able to do it without having to pass around little pieces of paper. I would be able to speak to everyone at once: the very thought of it made my mouth water.

But there was no one at home. Through a window, however, I caught sight of a woman dressed in the habit of an Ursuline walking along with a measured step. I had no strength to run after her. She seemed kind and gentle, from the back, at least.

I ate what I found in the kitchen and then cleaned myself up, moving slowly, every effort costing me a great deal of energy. Occasionally I would be overcome by a bout of paralyzing nausea. At times I was also overcome by self pity, a sentiment I quickly dismissed because I do not believe that it shows anyone to advantage.

Three days passed, and I felt my strength returning. I began to take short walks. Although I did not stray far from the house, I nonetheless made a few discoveries. I met a man, for example, who was occupying himself in the farm's smithy. I thought I would astonish him by addressing him, but my new-found voice hardly seemed to faze him at all; I essayed to hide my own surprise, telling myself that I had best accustom myself to being considered normal. He seemed a stout enough fellow, much older than I but still keen on his work. I decided not to ask him who had given him permission to work on the seigneury. His name was Boucane, and he explained that he was called that because he fired his forge with driftwood, which though dry retained enough moisture to burn like the fires of hell and smell like the devil.

From there I continued my tour of the seigneury and came upon the small house down near the river. I did not recognize the gentleman who lived in it, but he introduced himself as Pâtissant, the schoolmaster. There was an air of breeding about him, he seemed well brought up and spoke with a French-from-France accent. When he spoke he put me in mind of Bougainville. Suddenly I felt my entire memory quicken: Bougainville, Montcalm, Quebec, Le Chat, Major Stillborne. As nonchalantly as I could manage, I asked Pâtissant the date. He said it was September the fifteenth, in the year 1780. According to my mental calculations, I had slept more than five years.

"And the hour?" I asked, as though that had been what I had wanted to know all along.

"Eleven of the clock," he said, and added with a wink. "In the morning. Monsieur has perhaps lain late abed today?" From which I deduced that Pâtissant was either a fool or a newcomer to these parts. I resolved to ask him at some future date what it was that he taught in that school of his.

The following day I walked around the fort. I saw a large group of people gathered about the remains of the old church, and for a moment thought they were celebrating some kind of festival. I was wrong again. They were making a circle around a man in a grey robe. Hardly anyone even noticed I was there. It was the man himself who saw me and bade the others make room for me so that he could greet me. I desired to speak to him privately, to find out what he was doing that so interested my tenant farmers, and so he brought me into his church, which was more rudely appointed than one of my stables. We spoke together briefly, and his friendliness restored me somewhat to good humour. When I left, I greeted my tenant farmers, but none of them responded at all.

This was a difficult awakening. Everywhere I looked it was as though I were discovering a new continent. Not that I know what a new continent looks like; as far as I know, I have never been on one. But, if one can believe that fraud Bougainville, I can imagine what it must be like. People welcome you warmly to their "new" country, which you wish to make part of your own but which is decidedly not yours to annex. There is a great show of bowing and scraping, much wide smiling, many pleasant exchanges of facile compliments and a rapid ascertainment of the fact that these ingratiating natives want nothing more fervently than your immediate departure from their midst. You know no one, recognize nothing and search in vain for familiar gestures from your own homeland. The natives are not exactly hostile, but neither do you ever feel at home among them. It incites in you a strong distaste for travel and makes you long for nothing more than to return to the country of your birth, until one day you realize with a start that you are destined to remain exiled among these foreigners for the rest of your days.

These thoughts reminded me that I have always wanted to leave this place, but have always been too weak to do so. One day, perhaps…

In the meanwhile, I kept myself as busy as possible. As in the past, I helped my tenant farmers in the fields and split firewood with them. I spent long hours watching my new blacksmith at work; he is also a carpenter. In fact, he knows many trades. But I never learned what it was that had brought him here among us, nor why it was that I so enjoyed his company. The same may be said about the schoolteacher.

The blacksmith was not what one might call chatty, and in this he was the very opposite of the schoolteacher. Pâtissant loved to converse, and it is not too much to say that he was very helpful in my efforts to reestablish a natural way of speaking. My tongue had remained atrophied for such a long time that I had to do painful exercises in order to speak the simplest words and phrases. I asked him if there were not, among the many good

souls who had taken care of me during my recent state of cata-
tonia, a certain Ursuline; he told me that it was possible but he
could not imagine who it might be. Perhaps there was a Sister
from Trois-Rivières or Quebec who came to see me from time to
time. I remained unsatisfied on this point.

For the most part, the women of the village took turns looking after my needs, and I can attest that they did not take unfair
advantage of my unconscious state, except perhaps in the case of
the twins Apolline and Josué. Two beautiful children. I would
very much like to be able to remember something of their mother. At one time I thought I would keep them with me until I
found a wife or a servant, or at least someone to do the cooking
and cleaning.

I kept that thought to myself, however, since I had a strong
feeling that Valentine was somewhere nearby, and I would never
dare to say such a thing in her hearing. She did not like to be
treated as a mere servant. Valentine. I am conscious of missing
her all of a sudden, especially her frank way of speaking. I have
been told of her troubles. I wrote a letter to Dr. Franklin to
inquire whether or not he could do something, but I have not
yet had a response.

But I do have a letter from my brother, Pascal de Sainte-Foy,
dated three years ago. It was here when I woke up. He says he
is married, already with four children, and is the Governor of
Baja California, a position without promise of a future, as he
said. He reproaches me for neglecting to write to him. I would
like to put him in my place, with such long stretches of time during which I cannot even remember my own name. Between now
and the end of the century, I tell myself, I will receive at least two
more letters from him. His postscriptum at the bottom of the
page intrigues me: "My best wishes to the good Ursuline." He
must know something that I do not.

Father Barthélemy, a brave man, comes often to see me. My
visit to his church consolidated his prestige in the parish, and I
suspect that he found in me a kindred spirit that he would never

be so maladroit as to admit openly. Upon leaving his church, I spoke to the parishioners, and since then they have believed that the good Father performed some kind of miracle to restore my voice. I did not want him to disabuse them of that notion; it is his job to give faith to the people. He told me of his adventures, which I found fascinating in the highest degree, and he spoke to me at great length about the court at Versailles, where he had spent some time. What was best was that he was convinced, as I am, that Bougainville, whom he, too, knew well, is an incompetent nincompoop. I enjoyed our visits together; they did me much good, and I meant to find some appropriate way of recompensing him for all that he gave me. But I never did.

As for my tenant farmers, I became used to them gradually, and we have established a rapport that is almost cordial. Before, during the time when I could not speak, they called me the Dummy. Since my recent awakening, when I can speak but only with great difficulty, they have called me the Stutterer. It is a mark of progress, I imagine.

I have also renewed my acquaintance with Tristram Stillborne, my neighbour and the Seigneur du Bec. He has suffered greatly, the poor man. He spent a long time in prison in Philadelphia, and from there he was sent to England, where he spent several more years. He returned to his seigneury a sick and very nearly destitute man. He had a small house built for himself, while waiting to have his great manor house rebuilt, and he gets about with the aid of a small carriage especially designed for invalids. We chat occasionally, but not for very long, because he tires quickly. He has also brought a relative from England, a young woman named Claridge, whom he hopes to establish here. She has an angular face, speaks French with a thick accent and spends all her days reading. Tristram still dreams of his marquisate on the river, something to bequeath to his son Ebenezer, who has remained behind in England.

For myself, I have long since stopped having the dream that used to cause me so much anxiety, that of the Indian crone and the dogs with human faces. Now I dream of women. I want a woman, I tell myself, someone to whom I can be gentle and loving, if I am to flee from these parts once and for all. Let me be frank. The woman I dream of most often is the little Ursuline. I opened myself on this to Father Barthélemy, who acted as my confessor. When he asked me what I knew of this woman, I told him that I had laid eyes on her only that one time.

"So," he replied. "It is a behind you list to hunt. Seek ye and ye shall find. There is no shortage of them around here. In fact, Master Stillborne wants a husband for his cousin Claridge, who is no young filly, I agree, but then neither are you the prancing stallion you once fancied yourself to be, so you can make no difficulty about her age. Neither will she. You can unite your fortunes and help to establish the marquisate to which Stillborne aspires. It will be yours, something to leave to Josué and Apolline."

He knew a great deal, did this good Father, but he understood little. I wanted to find love – true love, not merely a wife.

I was also visited by a gentleman who claimed to be a bailiff and to have looked after my affairs during my last absence. I asked him to give a precise accounting of my books, and they tallied exactly. I asked a few questions about him in the seigneury, and no one had any complaints about him. Still, without knowing why, I was not drawn to the man.

He brought with him his friend, an apothecary, on a day when a winter cough was sawing my chest in half. The latter suggested I try a little vinegar syrup of his own manufacture. It was, he said, a simple recipe. He gathers the flowers of the vinegar tree at the end of autumn, when they are silken as velour. He boils them for a long time in a sugar solution, at the ratio of ten pounds of flowers to two pounds of sugar. To this he adds a bit of gentian and, most important, a measure of rum, one of rum to six of syrup. The cough is arrested instantly and the patient is even inclined to dance.

I purchased two jars of the concoction from him. He told me

that he owned the patent on the recipe, and that he intended to distribute his medicine one day throughout the entire Province of Quebec. "My fortune will be made," he said. "I need only sufficient capital to develop my business." After explaining his plans to me, he prevailed upon me to intervene on his behalf with Major Stillborne to effect an arrangement whereby several London suppliers might furnish him with rum and sugar in quantities sufficient for his purposes. It seemed that now everything depended on the London wholesalers.

The apothecary told me much about Major Stillborne and his marriageable cousin Claridge. I am suspicious of him, but not as much as I am of the bailiff, who never once misses coughing as soon as he steps into my house. He wants me to give him some of the apothecary's syrup, which he could easily ask me but that he prefers to make a pretense of having need of it, a pretense I do not like well.

The apothecary also carries out a service I did not know about. He paints the dead. He makes portraits of everyone who dies within all the parishes governed from Trois-Rivières. Habitants never have time to sit for a portrait when they are alive, he told me. I commissioned a portrait of myself, which he assured me would give me a place in posterity. For me it was simply a means of passing time.

I did not like the result. When he had finished placing me on his canvas, I found my face and proportions accurate enough, but he had given me the eyes of a drowned man. I was not completely put off, but I complained about the likeness and I dickered with him over the fee.

In short, I was even more bored than I had been the previous time.

3

THE truth is, no one likes this new priest. Especially my friend the apothecary, who believes the Grey Robe's presence threatens his business interests. For him it is a matter of commerce; in my case, I am a philosopher as much as I am a bailiff. I have not believed in God since the Bishop of Quebec declared himself to be against the Americans and for King George. The apothecary clutches his pennies; I hold fast to my opinions.

I am not one of the apothecary's cabala, my duties making it impossible, but I have managed to sup with a long spoon, as it were. My friend started by collecting all the fables and rumours about the priest that were circulating about the seigneury. Together, we analyzed the results, assessed their relative weights, then redistributed them in such a way that everyone was soon convinced that we were dealing with an imposter. The habitants never have anything better to do than watch their crops grow, and so they listened to us. When I was certain that the time was ripe, I secretly urged the apothecary to write a letter of denunciation to the bishop.

The Recollet's church has become like the temple out of which Jesus cast the money-lenders. When you enter it you would swear you were in a grist mill except that it smells like a pigsty in which someone is burning a sort of sweet incense that fills you with a sense of dread. Chickens and turkeys roam freely about, laying their eggs under the altar and in the tabernacle. If you remark upon this unholy menagerie, the priest will tell you that his temple is a home to all of God's creatures, great and small.

As a priest, he does nothing. He never says Mass, no one has ever seen him at prayer, he has baptized no one and has never given Last Rites to the dying. (It is true that there have been no births in the seigneury lately, and that people are living longer, but still! He could behave more like a priest and less like a carpenter and gardener whose only effect on the parish is to take Boucane away from his work and corrupt his soul.) And if you happen upon him unexpectedly, you will as often as not find him sleeping on the bench he is making, or else reading from a thick book that appears to have much more to do with earthly than with spiritual matters.

And if that were not enough, he knows how to read and write. The parishioners go to him for their few needs in that department, to draw up their deeds, for example, or their wills and powers of attorney, as though we were still living in the time when the local curate also performed the duties of a notary public. It will not be long before these illiterate peasants stop coming to me, their old friend Grégoire, for these services, for which I have always charged them so little.

I help my friend, the apothecary Gaspard, who is also something of a doctor of medicine, because he lives in constant fear of losing his practice. The priest might at any time tell his parishioners that any remedy prescribed and sold is useless against the dictates of Divine Providence, which always reaps what it has sown in terms of sickness and death. They will no longer go to the apothecary; no one will buy his potions. What is more, he will lose the small stipend he makes by waving his hand over still-born infants and mumbling a few words in Latin.

You can see why it is so urgent that we rid ourselves of this turbulent priest. To obtain a surer grasp on him, my colleague and I went to see him, to ascertain for ourselves what it was he wanted, and was doing. It was the apothecary's idea.

The Recollet was waiting for us.

We found him in his garden, preparing it for spring planting. He told us he intended to plant melons, peas, turnips, cucumbers and lettuce. But we noticed a small open shed at the end of the yard, in which Boucane the blacksmith was standing, holding his hammer. Now, Boucane has been known to us for many years, and it was strange that he did not even look up to acknowledge our presence. Such has been his habit ever since he fell under this Grey Robe's spell.

"Welcome!" said the priest. "You have arrived just in time for lunch. Pray you sit down, my friends." And so saying, he indicated a corner of the church in which a table had already been set for three.

"Had you foreseen our visit?" we asked him.

"In a manner of speaking," he replied. "I have visitors every day, and always set my table for guests. If you will allow me, I would say a short prayer of thanksgiving before we eat."

Father Barthélemy went to the altar, kneeled and recited several words. We could hear him quite clearly, but did not recognize the language in which he prayed. It sounded to us like gibberish. "If he does not know Latin," the apothecary whispered in my ear, "then he is no priest, and we will have our imposter. People in these parts want to hear their Mass in Latin; if they understood what was being said, they would not believe in it. They have to be completely bamboozled before they are certain of being saved. Quickly, say something to him in Latin!"

The priest had gone to his small stove and was busying himself about it. He broke some eggs and whipped up an omelette, slicing onions as though we were not there. I ran over in my mind all the Latin I had taught myself, and said to him, *"Quasi modo infanti gentiles."*

The priest stopped what he was doing and, assuming a grave tone, replied, "One does not speak Latin to clerics."

I did not quite grasp the significance of his reply, but I did catch the expression on his face and it made me laugh, thinking that he was making a joke. The apothecary laughed also, even louder than I. But his scheme had failed, and it was the last time I ever took his advice.

The Recollet served us an omelette of pork fat, garlic and potatoes, with wheat bread. There were raisins for dessert. Taking a bottle of wine from behind the kindling box, he said that he would be a poor monk indeed if he did not offer us a glass of it. It was the wine his order had sent him for Mass. He lives well, this mendicant monk, for all his talk about a vow of poverty.

During the meal, I asked him if it was still the custom to pray only in Latin, or if it was now permitted to use the common languages in parts of the service other than sermons and collects. He replied that Latin was still the language of prayer when praying at the altar, but it was permitted to pray elsewhere in any other language, because God understands all languages.

"Even Basque?" asked the apothecary with a perfidious smile.

"Even Basque," replied the Recollet, unperturbed. The priest was proving to be difficult to catch out.

My colleague asked him what language he prayed in most often.

"Montagnais," said the priest. "It is one of the seven Native languages that I speak. I pray in Iroquois or Abenaki if there are any of my friends who speak those languages present. I am their servant, not their master."

When all was said and done, we had eaten well and drunk exceptionally well. When we left the church, we were completely in our cups, so much so that we very nearly had to crawl home, as Boucane had so often had to do. I only hope that no one saw us.

And we woke up the next day with terrible headaches, which the apothecary attributed to some diabolical poison the Recollet must have poured into our wine in order to steal our souls more easily. We may have had a better idea as to why Boucane was always as drunk as a lord each time he left the priest's lair, but we were no wiser about his authenticity as a priest.

Our mission was not going to be easy. All the habitants had fallen under his spell, from the lowest field worker to the village elders. At first I believed we could rally them to our cause by reminding them of the heavy tithe the Recollet was sure to levy on them. But they simply went to the priest and asked him outright how much he was going to charge them. "Nothing," he replied calmly. "My parishioners are as poor as I am, and I would never insult them by asking them for so much as a penny."

This fell upon the parish like a bombshell. A free priest! Praise God for He is bounteous. Make a joyous noise unto the Lord, for He hath sent into our midst a servant who works for no wages. Suddenly, the church began to fill up with capons and rabbits, smoked eels, baskets of perfect pears and flawless turnips, all to grace the table of a priest who had asked for nothing.

What was worse, it was from this time that the habitants, many of whom still may have nourished some mistrust, began to request certain services from Father Barthélemy. They complained to him of a plague of grasshoppers in the parish. They were worried that there would be no harvest that year, and someone asked him if he could do something about it. The priest replied that he surely could, pointing out that if Monseigneur de Laval could excommunicate the flocks of passenger pigeons that were ravaging the grain fields around Quebec, then he could certainly excommunicate a few grasshoppers. "There are provisions in the Rules of the Diocese of Quebec for prayers that can effect anything. I will use them!"

Several days later, at a ceremony that included the habitants most affected by the plague, the good Father proceeded with the Act of Excommunication. The next day there was a heavy frost. A miracle! No more grasshoppers! Three days after that, he excommunicated all the rats in the parish. Then it was all the fleas. Then a bear that had been seen eating wheat in one of the fields. He could excommunicate any animal he wanted to.

Father Barthélemy remained busy. He began blessing everyone. He blessed the elderly and the children, he blessed the cattle and the seeded fields, he blessed the gardens and the pastures. He blessed the pigs, the horses, the donkeys, even the dogs and the cats. From soup to nuts, he blessed them all.

And when he had done with that, he gave a general absolution to everyone in the parish for all the years they had been without religion because they were without a priest. From then on, everyone was in a state of grace. Everyone, that is, except myself and the apothecary, who would have nothing to do with his pardons.

And even that was not all. He completely won over the seigneur, who would have been better off had he continued to sleep. First, the priest returned his voice to him; that was his first miracle. No one knows how he did it, but even the apothecary had to admit it was pretty strong medicine. From then on, the seigneur could barely stop talking, most often to Father Barthélemy, almost never to us. Too bad, for there was much we could have told him.

I would be very surprised if the Grey Robe hadn't all but converted the seigneur. I often came across them talking avidly of Saint Simon, who lived in the court at Versailles and would have written damning accounts of the pettiness of princes had he been allowed to publish. Monsieur de Saint-Ours swears only by Saint Simon these days, and it is all on account of Father Barthélemy. If he continues in this vein, the seigneur may even start going to Mass. What would happen to our mission then?

My apothecary friend is not a complete idiot. He knows which way the wind lies. He thinks that it might be in our best interests to make our peace with this meddlesome monk. He may be right. The monk is perhaps not as dangerous as we thought; the revenues we have lost on his account we can surely make up some other way. For example, when there is a priest there are more legal marriages, are there not? Legal marriages require legal documents. And the Seigneur du Bec, Major Stillborne, has a poor cousin who needs marrying off. Suppose the priest is able to convince the Seigneur de Saint-Ours, a bachelor, to take her as his wife. The two seigneuries would then be united into one. The road between the two parishes would be very well used. There would be more legal marriages, land transfers, severances; all kinds of business matters would arise. Contracts, deeds, surveyances, the whole gamut! And me the only lawyer around!

The apothecary sees some advantage for himself as well. A merging of the two fortunes would enable Major Stillborne to take Dr. Gaspard on as his personal physician, and Dr. Gaspard is a wizard not only at concocting remedies but also at selling them at a handsome profit. He is a man of science, a true genius.

For example, he explained to me just the other day how bufotherapy saved the life of the founder of the Grey Nuns in Montreal, the Holy Mother d'Youville. Her physician applied toads to a cancer that was eating her leg, and she was completely healed after only three years. She suffered horribly, by all accounts, but she lived to the ripe old age of seventy. Dr. Gaspard says he could cure Major Stillborne, although not completely; no, he wouldn't want to cure the seigneur completely.

There is much good to be done here, but no one seems to be doing it, sad to relate. Happily, we all have our little private projects to keep us busy. What I would like to know, however, is the real reason Boucane goes home so drunk after his nightly lessons with the Recollet.

4

INHERITED the Seigneury du Bec upon the death of Tristram Stillborne. But even now, although I sign all my letters "Claridge, Marquise of Stillborne," in letters as big as this house, the people here still insist on calling me Mademoiselle. They make much of the cold shoulder perpetually turned my way by the Seigneur de Saint-Ours. "Master Benjamin won't have nothin' to do with that old crow," they cackle. They also call me the Dark Continent, because, you see, no man has claimed me. It's not as though I cannot hear them laughing at me behind my back. They call me these things to punish me for what they see as my impertinence, because I came here as Major Stillborne's poor relation and ended up getting everything: his manor house, his lands, his rents. Me, Claridge, the old crow from who knows where, who hasn't even the good looks one strains to see in a rich heiress. Oh, yes, they find much in me to amuse them.

I do have my faults, of course. Two above all: one, I dared to rise to the nobility; and two, I succeeded in doing so. Had I failed, they would be content simply to cast me aside. My misery might even have elicited a sort of sympathy in some few of them. But since I have managed it, I am denied the respect I ventured so much to gain. Dreams come dear, I am aware of that, and life can be a perfect hell for those whose dreams are realized. So I must not complain.

Happily I have become sufficiently philosophical to sustain such minor irritations, such as not being allowed to vaunt my success before this cast of mediocrities. Harder to bear is my inability to correct the wild stories that are circulating about me, or even to snuff out the sneers concerning my supposed virginity. I readily admit in these pages to being completely taken up by my own romantic illusions. I have dreamed, perhaps overmuch, of myself as the beautiful shepherdess whose simplicity seduces the worldly Prince Charming. If I have erred, it has been in confusing my overwhelming desire to rise above my station with sensual contentment. I placed too high a price on my virtue, in the expectation of one day meeting a gentleman who would elevate me to the peerage. I might better have added a tincture of carnality on the few occasions when I actually encountered someone who could make me a marquise. My present age renders me invisible to men, but that is no longer a matter of importance.

Well may they wonder how I acquired, at so youthful an age, such an overweening taste for titles, fortune, esteem. As Colombine, the actress, I would tell anyone within hearing that I was the daughter of the King's Counsel in Montreal. A small deception, the fellow of so many others. I know full well who my father was: he was a barber, he had a large, florid face, his name meant nothing to anyone, and his face is carefully fogged over in my memory, as on a mirror, so that it does rise to disturb me in my dreams. My mother was a hat-maker; of her I have, unfortunately, a very clear picture. She would often take me with her on her rounds to make hats for the great ladies of Montreal. To Madame Bégon's, or to the wife of the governor. I vividly recall the life she would describe to me – how, for example, Monsieur de la Vérendrye slipped on the ice one evening because he had

had too much to drink. I loved such tales of wealthy idleness, ill-tempered indolence, facile grace; I believed from the very start that I was born for such a life.

I was six when my father left. I never quite knew where he went. Later, I convinced myself that he died a heroic death fighting against the Chicachas, but I could never quite convince anyone else of it. I was never much good as a liar. That is to say, I never succeeded in being taken at my word. People seemed to sense the desperation behind my carefully studied self-assurance. The only ones who believed my tales were either those who were so patently credulous that their very belief aroused suspicion in others, or else those whose minds were as desperately inventive as my own, so that our conversations were veritable volleys of lies and fabrications. There is an unwritten code to which all liars faithfully adhere: you must pretend to believe the pretenders: that is the price you pay for being believed yourself, and for having your own false currencies passed around like coin of the realm. And this code can only be broken between two contestants, both of whom are trying to float competing lies, in which case they may denounce each other without let or pity. Strangers always believe you, because strangers always want something new to believe in. I love strangers. Unfortunately, there are very few of them in this place.

Such, then, is the pretty turn I have come to. All my life I have longed to play the role of a marquise, and now that I have not only the role but the real thing, everyone says I am not right for the part. But although such harsh criticism taints my performance slightly, it does not weigh that heavily on my mind. At the end of the day, I am a marquise. Each morning, I look into my mirror, and I tell myself that I have succeeded in creating this role because I never once faltered in my belief that I was meant for it. The others were turned down for the part because they did not know how to dream. There is no hiding a poor performance.

In the final analysis, my ambition was nothing more than a

refusal to accept the cards that were dealt me at my birth. My contemporaries, especially the rough farmers that surround me now, have a remarkable ability to resign themselves to being ordinary. They drift with the tide, roll with the punches. I told myself quite early on that I would not live like that. When my father disappeared and my mother died of some pox or other, I was sent to the hospital in Montreal run by the Sisters of Charity, the Grey Nuns, and I took that as permission to begin my life anew.

This decision caused me much unhappiness. I invented a mother for myself, not because I wanted someone to love me, but because I wanted the privileges extended to young women who had mothers, especially mothers of noble birth. I stomped my dainty foot, angrily denying that I was an orphan. I was punished for these tantrums. Disdaining the drudge work required of all orphans as payment to the nuns for their blessed charity, I insulated myself in aristocratic pretensions. If they ordered me to scrub the floor, I would tell them that the daughter of the Lieutenant-Governor of Montreal does not scrub floors. I would be twice punished: once for refusing to work and once for lying. I would change my parentage and title every week, becoming more and more reckless in my claims. They decided that I was deranged, and so they sent me to Jericho.

Theatre saved me from all that, and by theatre I mean the talent that I displayed for dissimulation and deceit. I stopped saying that I was a princess, willingly accepted my duties at Jericho, and assumed the role of a humble and obedient servant. And at the first opportunity, I slipped out a window and joined Master Auguste's troupe of strolling players. I would have done anything to get out of this hell-hole called New France. Well, perhaps not anything. I had rubbed shoulders with enough fallen women in Jericho to know that a woman's only ticket out of hell is her virtue, and she must sell it as dearly as possible.

There were times when I was ready to raffle off my maidenhead, but then I could find no takers. At first I thought my lack of success was the work of the bear-trainer, Bernard, a commoner but very thick with the Ursuline, who seemed a little too charitable for my liking. Bernard knew how to tie the shoulder-knot, an ancient spell that renders young bridegrooms incapable of performing their marital duty. He cast this spell on me, I told myself, because of the nasty things I said about his precious Ursuline. Or perhaps it was my quiet disdain for the tenets of the Catholic faith that rendered me suspicious in other men's eyes. I'll never know.

Whatever the reason, the men in the troupe ravished me on the stage and reviled me in the flesh. My fabled virtue became my chastity belt, whose lock no one tried to pick. Perhaps, in my heart of hearts, I was afraid I would end up back in Jericho with the imprisoned prostitutes. In Quebec, I believed I was loved by Tristram Stillborne, but he was an English officer and therefore inaccessible. Then I fell for Saint-Ours, the Straw Man, by whom I also hoped to be delivered from my low estate. Unfortunately, the war afforded him no opportunity to fall in love with me in return.

When I played the role of Clémence the Housekeeper, I thought I finally had Benjamin where I wanted him, but I could not penetrate the thick wall of sleep with which he surrounded himself. Oh, how often did I stretch my naked body over his? I could sense that he was willing, but it was ever love's labour lost. I never learned the trick, which other women seemed to have acquired at birth, of turning a tired carriage horse into a serviceable stud. I did not give up hope, but he was always too distracted by all the others who lined up to take advantage of him. That secretary, Toussaint, was forever thrusting greatness upon him for his own ends; I, too, tried to get him out of himself so that he and I might leave the country together. But our good seigneur was not as impressionable as we thought. In the end, I transferred my affections back to Major Stillborne; if I had no hope of returning to France with Saint-Ours, I at least had a chance of getting to England with Stillborne. One way or another, I would get out of this God-forsaken country. But just at the very moment when I thought my attentions to Stillborne were beginning to bear fruit, along came the Americans, who whisked him out of my clutches.

That misfortune set me back, but I was not discouraged. Poverty forced me to attach myself to Stillborne with a determination that anyone would have mistaken for a dedication to duty. But Stillborne was far too intelligent to be taken in by it. I do not think he needed to be clairvoyant, either; once again, my inner desperation was too apparent. Yes, I waited for him outside the prison in Philadelphia, and, yes, I busied myself about him as a maid. I did everything I could to get him back to England, but he would not listen. All he could think of was his marquisate, his little colonial empire here on the banks of the St. Lawrence. He would not return untitled to England; his determination proved as intractable as my own, which is perhaps why we understood each other so well without a word being spoken. But when Stillborne and I finally found ourselves alone, he no longer had the strength to love me as I would have wished. I followed him here because I had no other choice, my privations in Philadelphia having drained me of my resources. My hair had turned grey, I had lost most of my teeth; if no one wanted me when I was a fresh young maiden, I held no hope that anyone would even look my way when I was a faded old maid.

To reward me for my faithfulness, Stillborne tried to marry me off to Saint-Ours, but I never believed it would come to pass; I could see all too well that what Benjamin wanted most in this world was to get away from it, like me. Stillborne did accomplish one marriage, however: his son Ebenezer, who came here to join his own fortunes to his father's, was not long in coming to an arrangement with Apolline, Benjamin's daughter. They loved each other so much that after having only two children together, they decided to marry. Stillborne moved heaven and earth to keep them here, but they would have none of it. The two pigeons took his money and flew the coop as quickly as their little wings would take them. Today Ebenezer is a merchant and a magistrate in Detroit; Apolline is about to have her sixth child. Stillborne died shortly after they left, and I had him buried in our little Anglican cemetery at the back of the seigneury.

Benjamin missed Stillborne terribly, and I took advantage of his misery to become closer to him. I invited him to the manor a hundred times – for tea or a glass of sherry, I would tell him, but he was never in any doubt as to my true intentions. He pretended to be uninterested in me, or perhaps he truly was, but he was always kind to me. He would wear his powdered wig when he came calling, as though he wanted to appear to be of an age with me. I tried everything to get him into my bed: I was cool, I was gay, I threw tantrums, fits of rage or jealousy. Nothing worked.

In the end, I even tried honesty. One night, after dinner, I put all my cards on the table; I told him everything, my whole secret. He didn't seem at all taken aback. The name Jericho meant nothing to him, and he had but a vague memory of his old housekeeper Clémence. You tell a man that you have loved him secretly for twenty years (even if you have not), that you have sacrificed everything to be near him, that his very touch sets off a firework of amorous imaginings, and he replies, with some vague notion of being gallant, "Oh, yes, I remember now. You used to be very fond of my pendulum clock. No one could get it to shine as well as you!" Men have been hanged for less.

After that, I changed my tactics again. He used to like me to read to him aloud from the latest newspapers from Europe, and one evening I was reading about the latest revolutionary atrocities in France. I wanted to dissuade him from returning to Europe, mostly because I wanted to keep him here. I had more or less resigned myself to never becoming his lover, but I did not want to be left alone. I had just told him how a friend of his from the Siege of Quebec, Juchereau de Saint-Denis, after an illustrious career in the French armed forces, taking part in the bloody repression of the revolt on Corsica, had been decapitated by ignorant masses in France. But when I raised my eyes from the journal to judge the effect of my account of the Reign of Terror, I saw that he was asleep. It was as though he was deliberately refusing to take any notice of the horrors in France, a country to which we could now never return. He was even snoring.

When he woke up, I was standing before him. I had unhooked my taffeta robe, beneath which I was completely naked, ready to be taken, as ripe a fruit as any man could wish. He yawned and asked me what time it was. I told him it was a little after fifty years, and that if he loved me as I hoped he would I would save the sheets stained with my blood and use them for his shroud. But my poetry had no more effect upon him than did my nakedness. "Good," he said. "I think I had better go and harness up my horse." I rehooked my robe, but before he left I summoned the courage to ask him why he was so indifferent towards me.

"I love someone else," he replied, having the decency at least to make his voice sound sincere. "An Ursuline who once took care of me. She is the only woman I have ever loved – not desired, you understand, but loved. Through her, I want to marry God. It is a delicious idea, don't you agree? But it makes me incapable of all others. I'm not used to this, I'm sorry..."

I forgave him then, but I have resolved to give him one last try. Perseverance is, after all, part of my nature. I will work on him through his good Ursuline, this stealer of lovers. Not out of rancour or malice, but simply because I, like him, am terrified of dying in this place.

I have a friend, also an Ursuline in Quebec, Mother l'Ange-Gardien. She will help me. She is as bored as I am in this miserable country.

ALL the while I was rotting in Sapinière, I schemed to get Pâtissant to fall in love with the Marquise de Stillborne. It would have created an amusing diversion, had I managed to pull it off. As my friend Father Barthélemy would have said, one's actions are motivated more by self-interest than by reason, and he would have been perfectly right in this case.

First, I let it be known that I was in love with another woman, the little Ursuline nun whom I had seen only once, from a distance, and from behind at that. Sometimes I sang her praises so earnestly that I almost believed I could love her myself. It is, after all, so much easier to love someone you have invented than a woman of flesh and blood, because you can endow her with all the qualities and virtues you admire in yourself and look for in another. I may be accused of toying with love in order to pass the time. Certainly, I was. But it must also be remembered that this was the first time in my life that I had the leisure for such trifles. And it was, moreover, a convenient way of ridding myself of the Marquise de Stillborne.

I decided to ask Pâtissant to help me get the Ursuline out of the convent. He would not refuse me, I told myself. I would tell him that a different kind of love, one actually of my choosing, unlike the mothers of those poor children I find in the house every time I wake up, would be a strong incentive for me to remain in this country. Every time I talked about leaving, such scenes the people here made, calling me a heartless beast. It was driving me mad. They've tried everything to keep me here. When love failed, they dangled titles and fortunes before me; then they resorted to shame and guilt. Fortunately, I kept my resolve.

I unburdened myself of all this to Father Barthélemy, the only man in these parts who understands me and who never contradicts me when I philosophize to him – when I tell him, for example, that man is free only when he has chosen his own servitude. This Ursuline, whom I love, could be the servitude I freely choose, the only kind that would make my life supportable. The good Father heard me out, smilingly, while I told him every thought that passed through my head; I loved him because his silence reassured me of my own intelligence.

I knew what Pâtissant would say. He would take the role of devil's advocate, telling me that this Ursuline was not free to leave the convent, that she was a prisoner of her veil and of her order. (To prepare for our debate, I became as familiar with these arguments as I expected him to be.) I would answer him, as I explained to Father Barthélemy, to whom I told the same story, by saying that I would do everything in my power to set her free. It would not be a crime if she were to renounce her vows, especially if by doing so she was ensuring her own happiness as well as my own. In any case, I would make the attempt, and I would warn him that any obstacle he put in my way, far from stopping me, would only strengthen me in my resolve. The Ursuline's veil revealed as much beauty to me as it hid. I wanted her, I would tell Pâtissant, and if I could not have her I would leave, and that would convince him to help me.

To repay him, I would intervene on his behalf with Claridge of Stillborne, who would be more than happy to have his company in her declining years, which were already all but upon her. How often had she enjoined me to visit her, and when I stayed away too long, what long, plaintive letters she would write. I was neglecting her, I was cruel, I thought only of myself, and so on and so forth. Poor woman, if she knew how bored I was with her constant harping. And the worst of it was that she invoked not the slightest sympathy in me, not the merest twinge of desire, no matter how hard I tried to convince myself that a flirtation with her would at least help to pass the time. Nothing worked. I simply could not contemplate it.

Pâtissant, on the other hand, I thought could. They both loved books, for one thing. If they did not exactly take to each other like moths to a flame, they could at least pass the time in conversation. That would be a lot more than I could do.

So I went to speak to Pâtissant. I found him in his school-house, teaching a class. He was a remarkable teacher; I made a mental note to mention this to Miss Stillborne, as it would raise him in her estimation. I observed him at his work, and I would assure her that it was something to see.

He had opened his school in his own house. It was stifling inside; he did not stint on firewood. He cut and split it himself, as an example to his students of the beneficial effect of physical activity on intellectual agility. Eventually, he confided in me, he planned to have his students split all his wood, since he would never place his own well-being ahead of that of his young charges. Such a self-sacrificing man.

His teaching method was another marvel to behold. He taught everything through translation. Education, he said, was the art of placing the greatest amount of knowledge at the ser-vice of the greatest number of people, and the only way to do that was to translate it. I had not thought of that.

He showed me an example. That day, he was teaching Homer. I had the distinct privilege of witnessing, with my own eyes, Pâtissant making Homer intelligible. Homer is a classical author, and the classics are not supposed to be intelligible. Especially the Greek classics. Every five minutes he would turn towards me and say with his eyes, "You see, it's easy. You have only to speak from the bottom of your heart, using words that you use every day and that everyone understands." As I listened, I gained an understanding of Homer's genius for the first time in my life, as Pâtissant translated it into Northern Creole, which is the only language I know fluently.

"Today, I'm going to tell you a story, if you'll listen. This story took place far away and long ago, a long, long time ago. I didn't write it down, a man named Homer did, and I don't mean Homer Branchaud, the baker, who lives down the road and whose twin brother died last Easter. This was a different Homer, a Greek. I say was because he's dead. Now, a Greek is someone who lives in Greece. Greece isn't a country you can visit by stepping outside your back door. You have to travel a long way to get to it. You have to cross the ocean, and that'll take you up to two months, and then when you get to the other side you have to rent a horse and head south, then make a left turn somewhere around Spain and travel for another three or four months, cross a few borders and rivers, and if you're lucky you'll get to Greece. Modern Greece. Nothing much happens in Greece these days, but in olden times it was a place where a lot of interesting things happened all the time.

"So now we are at the beginning of our story. It starts with a wedding in Olympia, the home of the gods. Yes, I said gods, plural. These gods were not human beings like you and me; they were spirits. Sometimes they were gentle spirits, sometimes they were not so gentle. But whatever kind of spirits they were, it was a good idea to keep out of their way, because when they got mad even the gentle spirits went crazy and did really awful things. Olympia was where they lived when they weren't travelling around doing awful things. It was like their home village.

"Well, there was this wedding taking place in the Olympic village, and there was one goddess who hadn't been invited, and she was some peeved about it, I can tell you. She had a point. Nobody likes to be left off the invitation list, especially when it's someone from your own family who's getting married. How would you like it if your own sister or your cousin was getting married and nobody invited you to the wedding? You wouldn't take it lying down, would you? Well, neither did she. She took it very hard. And it's a good thing she did, because if she had just shrugged it off and said, Oh, well, maybe next time, then Homer wouldn't have had this story to write, and I wouldn't be here telling you about it today.

"So she got mad. And her getting mad was even worse than some of the other gods getting mad, because she was Eris, the goddess of discord. That means she went around causing trouble even at the best of times, just like old Mrs. Beauchemin down the road, who gossips about everyone because she doesn't have anything better to do with her time. So this is what this Eris did: she took a golden apple to where the wedding was, and she wrote on it, 'To the most beautiful woman here.' Then she tossed the apple into the garden where the other gods and goddesses were holding the wedding feast – you know, knocking back the booze and stuffing their faces, just like we do when we have a wedding. When the other goddesses (oh, maybe I forgot to tell you: a goddess is a female god) saw that golden apple, they all cried out at once, 'It's mine! It belongs to me! I'm the most beautiful!' Just like Eris knew they would. There were three goddesses who shouted the loudest and maybe had the most reason to think that the apple was theirs. There was Hera, the wife of the chief god, whose name was Zeus. There was Pallas Athene, the goddess of wisdom, although she couldn't have been all that wise if she thought she was more beautiful than everybody else. And then there was Aphrodite, the goddess of love, who really was something. I mean, she was definitely the fairest in the land, no doubt about it. Everyone wanted to sleep with her, and even at that she wasn't stuck up about it, which is why I said she really was the fairest of them all.

"Anyway, the three of them started a real cat fight, shouting at each other, calling each other names, just like a bunch of school kids at recess (ha ha). After this went on for a while, one of the gods – Zeus, I think it was – who was pretty short-tempered, finally had it up to here, and he said, 'Here's an idea. Why don't you ask the handsomest man on Earth to pick which one of you is the most beautiful goddess? That way we won't have to listen to all this caterwauling, and whoever he picks can take her goddamned golden apple and the rest of you can shut the hell up!' (Ever since then, educated people talk about the apple of discord when they mean the cause of an argument that goes on and on forever.)

"The three goddesses thought this was a pretty good idea, so they all went off to find the handsomest man on Earth. This turned out to be a guy named Paris, who was not bad looking but who didn't have a lot going on upstairs, as you'll soon see. The three goddesses found him sleeping in a field because he was too lazy to work like the rest of humanity because he was so full of himself. The three goddesses said to him, 'Hey! Look at us and tell us which one is more beautiful than the other two.' Well, this Paris took one look at them and said, right off, 'Aphrodite, the goddess of love.'

"Well, Aphrodite thought he made a pretty good choice, but the other two went berserk, as you can imagine. Especially when they found out that Aphrodite had tricked them. You couldn't trust anybody in those days. What she did was, before they had all set out to look for Paris, she had gone down to him first and told him that if he picked her she would give him the most beautiful woman on Earth who wasn't a goddess. This was a woman named Helen. Unfortunately, this Helen was already married, but Aphrodite told Paris not to worry about that, she'd fix everything. (Odd that the most beautiful goddess thought she had to resort to a trick in order to win the prize, eh? Maybe she didn't think she was as pretty as she was. That's the way it is in life, sometimes.) Anyway, Paris agreed, because he was a conceited idiot.

"But the other two goddesses, Hera and Pallas Athene, they found out that Aphrodite had tricked them because Aphrodite, who apparently wasn't all that bright, either, went around telling everyone what she'd done. She wanted the other gods and goddesses to know that not only was she more beautiful than the others, she was also smarter. She picked an odd way of showing it, didn't she? So when the two other goddesses heard what she'd done, they decided to get even with her. And that's how this whole mess I'm going to tell you about got started.

"Tomorrow I'll tell you some more, if you're quiet. I'll tell you about Achilles, the soldier who stayed in his tent instead of going out to fight against Paris and the others. This Achilles – no, not Achilles Métivier, the farmer who lives up the third concession side road, the one with one ear bigger than the other; I'm talking about another Achilles – this Achilles they called the Fleet-of-Foot, because he could run faster than anyone else in the village. He was the son of Pélée and Thétis, who weren't from around here, either..."

I couldn't believe my ears. I had never understood Greek so well! Pâtissant assured me that he taught arithmetic, geography and church history using exactly the same technique, whose principle advantage is that it makes the most complicated subjects comprehensible to the simplest ears. He proved it to me by inviting me to translate the passage from the Bible in which John the Baptist or maybe Jesus chased the merchants and money-lenders out of the temple. I gave it a try.

"Once upon a time there was a man named Jesus. He was a good little fellow, and his mother was very fond of him and raised him up to be smart as well as good. One day, he was going to Mass, and what do you think he saw when he got inside? A whole troupe of merchants had taken over the church, and they were selling things right there: pigeons, cows, sheep. Imagine selling animals in church! I'll tell you what it was like: it was like our church here in the village before Father Barthélemy moved into it. Well, Jesus didn't hang around wondering what to do. He picked up some rope that was lying on the floor and he used it for a whip, and he whipped and kicked all those merchants and shopkeepers right out of the church. Then he turned over the tables of the moneylenders, and he shouted, 'Get out of here! What the hell do you think you're doing? This is my Father's house!' His father was God, you see. Well, when his friends heard what he'd done – they were called his disciples – they said, 'The zeal of your house will devour you,' whatever that means. I think it means something like, 'Watch out, Jesus, there are powerful people who don't like what you're doing, you might not live long enough to regret this.' And they were right. Jesus was a holy man, but when someone thinks he's more powerful than the Church, things start to go wrong…" I don't remember how the rest of it went, but I got out of it somehow.

There was only one thing about Pâtissant that bothered me: he didn't have any students. There were desks in his classroom, but there were no children sitting at them, only mannequins made out of cloth and string. The seigneury children didn't like going to school, he said, so he was practising his teaching method on these dummies, waiting for the day when attending school was made mandatory by the government. When that day came, he said, he'd be ready.

I was so dumbfounded by this that I forgot all about my Ursuline.

6

WE have finally succeeded in ridding the seigneury of that so-called priest, and now that he is gone we can hardly hold our heads up for shame.

It was his success that grated on our souls. Apparently, he was not as grievous a sinner as the bailiff and I had made him out to be, which gave us a reputation for having serpents' tongues. Especially the bailiff. Each time we thought we had him dead to rights, he danced out of our grasp, dazzling the crowd with his antics and making us look like dolts. Even when we were right and he was wrong, we got the blame and he got the glory. Which convinced us that divine justice is not to be found in this world. He was as lucky as a cat. Then the bailiff had an idea.

We finally found out why Boucane went home so drunk after spending the evening at the church. It wasn't because he was getting into the communion wine, as we thought at first. I'm not an apothecary for nothing; I finally figured it out when I got a whiff of the vapours coming out of that shed they'd built beside the church. They were making some kind of illicit alcohol in there!

Then one morning Father Barthélemy came out of his church rolling a small barrel in front of him. Boucane was with him, and for once he didn't appear to be drunk. All the habitants stopped what they were doing and gathered about when the priest called them.

"Come and see, my friends, come here and see one of God's gifts to mankind!"

Boucane took out a mallet and a quoin and, with a single blow, punched a hole in the top of the barrel. Out spurted a stream of golden liquid. The priest placed a tankard under the stream, filled it up and passed it around. Each habitant drank from it in turn, and then asked the priest what it was. Father Barthélemy beamed with pleasure at his little surprise.

"It is beer, my dear friends. Beer brewed by a Recollet using an age-old recipe developed by the Franciscan friars of Alsace. Drink up, drink up!"

We drank up, and then we drank up some more. The beer was cool and smooth, and the froth clung to the sides of our tin tankards. We had forgotten how good beer tasted. Monsieur de Saint-Ours, who had joined us, was delighted.

"How many of these barrels have you made?" he asked.

"More than enough for our needs," replied Father Barthélemy. "But let's empty this one first!"

We drained that one, and then Boucane went and fetched four more, and we spent the rest of the morning drinking the priest's beer. At noon we ate lunch, and that day was the happiest any of us could remember spending in our lives. The beer was so good it washed away any lingering suspicions we may have harboured about the good Father Barthélemy. Even the bailiff and I were won over. And when he explained to us what he intended to do with his beer-making talents, our grudging reconciliation became a veritable hymn of praise.

During the days of the King of France, the Recollets, reclusives within the Franciscan Order who were not endowed with land grants, as were the Sulpicians and Jesuits, and who therefore collected no tithes, managed not only to live well themselves but also to carry out their charitable works entirely from the profits they made selling beer. No one brewed better beer in New France than the Recollets. But when the Franciscans slowly disappeared, the secret of the Recollets was lost. Father Barthélemy had rediscovered it.

"This beer is liquid gold for the seigneury," he told us. He had already sold thirty barrels to neighbouring parishes and to a ship's outfitter in Montreal named Molson. Since he would need a good supply of wheat, barley and hops to make his beer, the habitants could grow these crops and always get a good price from the brewery. The demand would be steady, and the habitants' fortune was assured. There would also be work for tradesmen to make oak barrels, delivery wagons and other items, which would encourage the establishment of a small industry in our district. The bailiff and I both suddenly saw a shower of gold coins falling into our laps.

"Will you need partners?" asked the bailiff.

"I will indeed!" answered the priest. "A good lawyer who can draw up invoices and sales receipts, who knows something of accounting. And you," he said to me. "We will need your knowledge of chemistry in order to improve our brewing and preservation techniques. My skills lie in other directions. As for you, Monsieur de Saint-Ours, all we need is your permission to proceed and you will be a wealthy man for the rest of your days. You can buy as many seigneuries as you please, perhaps even establish the marquisate dreamed of by your late friend Major Stillborne. You can return to France a true grandee, and be certain to receive your coveted Cross of Saint-Louis, which you have so long deserved!"

Everyone applauded the wise Recollet who could see so far into our futures. But what was his interest in all of this? the bailiff wanted to know.

"I am helping to benefit the community," replied the priest. "I am making vice pay for virtue, and in so doing I am founding a second Rome in this country. One day, this liquid bread will buy us a grand cathedral!"

When he left us that afternoon, the villagers were so taken with the good Father that to be blessed by him felt like being blessed by God Himself. No one would have dared to say a single word against him.

The habitants set to work sowing grain; the bailiff, the seigneur and myself, we invested all of our savings in the Recollet's beer. The little lean-to beside the church was replaced by a huge brewery; happiness and riches were at our finger-tips. From that day forth, the Recollet could do anything he pleased. No one complained if he missed Mass, or skipped a sermon, or forgot his prayers, or never spoke Latin. But then he pushed his luck too far.

About this time, an old woman appeared in the village. Dressed in rags, her face wrinkled and weather-beaten, but with eyes that were young and clear, she was pulling a small sled on which was perched a heavy-looking bundle. She trudged through the village without stopping at any house, chewing on what appeared to be the heel of a loaf of stale bread. Villagers followed her progress warily through their windows; a poor old hag who seemed to be dragging misfortune into our lives.

A village dog started following her, then another and another. Soon they were all yapping at her heels, but she plodded along unheeding, as though they were not there. The dogs seemed more suspicious of her than afraid of her stick. Then a group of youngsters, returning from hunting grouse in the woods, showed up at the far end of the village. One of them laughed at the sight of her; another picked up a small stone and threw it at her. When she began cursing them in language stronger even than any of the men in the village had heard, the rest of the youngsters began peppering her with stones and snowballs.

All of this quickly proved too much for her. She could not move, caught as she was between the dogs at her heels and the group of ruffians blocking her advance. She sank to her knees in the snow, covering her head with her hands as though taking shelter from a sudden hail storm. Suddenly the Recollet was on the scene. He dispersed the dogs with a word and chased the ruffians off with a few swift kicks, and then he bent over the hag and, raising her gently to her feet, led her into his church.

We were all ready to believe that we had witnessed another act of divine charity. But then we began to have our doubts when we realized that the old woman was still on the seigneury. When one morning she was seen hanging sheets on the clothes-line outside the presbytery, rumours started to fly, augmented by certain false stories formerly in circulation, mostly initiated by the bailiff. The priest may have need of a housekeeper, but had he acquired a mistress? Idle tongues began to wag in earnest.

We quickly learned which side of the fence Monsieur de Saint-Ours was on. One morning, as he was returning from the last hunting trip of the fall, the seigneur passed a group of villagers laughing and making scurrilous references to the fact that the priest's charity truly seemed to begin at home. Monsieur de Saint-Ours stopped and told them that the next person to make a joke like that would have to answer to him. He said the same thing to the bailiff. He never said one word to me about it, at least not more than two or three.

After that there was not an unkind word spoken about the curate's housekeeper. We soon became accustomed to seeing her about the village, and her presence was even appreciated. When young Janvier was run over by a horse, his parents sent for the priest because they thought he was going to die. Father Barthélemy sent the housekeeper instead. She brought her big bundle with her, which turned out to be filled with all kinds of herbal remedies, ointments and potions. She rubbed the boy's head, which made him stir, and when he regained consciousness she made him drink an infusion of gentian she mixed up on the spot. Janvier slept all that night, and the next morning he was up playing in the snow with his young friends.

It soon got out that the priest's housekeeper performed miracles, too. No doubt about it, that priest had been born under a lucky star. His housekeeper, whom we respectfully began calling the Churchwoman, was soon being prevailed upon to set broken bones, relieve coughs and sneezes, prescribe wild herbs for rheumatism and respiratory ailments. She became a kind of good-luck charm on the seigneury. She even knew how to cure lovesickness without killing the sufferer. Her real name was Virginia.

I didn't like her from the start, and I didn't try to hide the fact. It was as though she went out of her way to ridicule me. Once, when the seigneur was suffering from a raging toothache, she "cured" him by applying a drop of clove oil to the tooth. What a miracle, everyone said. Miracle my foot; every housewife in Europe knows that old trick. Another time I was preparing to take care of Boucane's dislocated shoulder. I wanted to try out a remedy that had been used by the executioner of Danzig to heal the deformed shoulder of the future empress of Russia, Catherine the Great, when she was a young girl: an application of the saliva of a fasting maiden taken every morning at sunrise. Catherine the Great was a close friend of no less a luminary than Voltaire; she must have known what she was about, wouldn't you think? And I had already picked out the young village girl and told her not to eat anything before breakfast, and everything was in place for me to work my miracle. But, oh, no, nothing would serve but that old bonesetter be called in. She had Boucane's arm back in its socket in a matter of minutes, just by stroking it. I strongly suspected her of having stroked more than Boucane's arm, he was in such a smiling, idiotic mood when she came out of his house after treating him. I even said as much at the time, but everyone just laughed at me, saying I was jealous because I couldn't offer him the same treatment. Bah! This Churchwoman was nothing but a charlatan, I told myself.

Things continued to go downhill for me, so much so that I found myself once again taking advice from my former friend, the bailiff. It was I who picked up the pen, but it was his words I wrote down.

One fine morning – not as fine as all that, in retrospect – a new priest arrived in the village. He went directly to the church and spoke for some time with Father Barthélemy. Then he left. Our plan was working faster than we thought it would.

The next day, Father Barthélemy, who had never said Mass in his church because he maintained that religion was above all a state of consciousness, and that the mere fact of sensing God within yourself was more valuable than any practical ritual, announced throughout the seigneury that there was to be a great meeting the next Sunday, at which he would make an important announcement. Everyone went to the meeting. Everyone was there.

"My brothers," Father Barthélemy began, speaking to the masses gathered in the public square because there was no room for them all in the Church, "I have carried out what pastoral duties I could here, and I ask your forgiveness for not having done more. As you are all no doubt aware, however, I never say Mass, and I have been somewhat less than diligent about prayers and sermons. The reason for that is simple: I am not a priest. I am a monk, authorized by the Recollet order to do little more than wear this grey robe.

"I was born out of wedlock, a child of love, as they say, which, for those who commit it, is but a venial sin, but to the powers that be is a serious enough lapse to prevent me from being invested in the full orders of the priesthood. I learned this when I was still a young man in my twenties and eager to devote my entire life to God. I experienced the deepest pain, as you may imagine, when it was pointed out to me that I would never overcome this mortal sin that was my birth. I sought absolution as best I could through prayer, and took up the mendicant life of a wandering friar, which never really consoled me. It has been my destiny to serve my order, my fellow beings and my God without officially being His servant. But here, among you all, my dear brothers, I thought I had completely put my unhappiness behind me.

"But here, also, I find I have been denounced to the Bishop of Quebec. His Eminence has been told that I practise the holy rites of a priest without official authorization to do so. And now a Sulpician has come to me, a fine young man, Father Felix his name was, formerly a priest in France before coming to Canada to escape the revolution ravaging that country. Father Felix came here to tell me that I can no longer stay here. He commended me on my work in restoring the church, but rebuked me for the making and selling of beer. Our brewery seems to have upset the civil more than the religious authorities, the latter being more concerned about my usurpation of the offices of a priest. I must go, therefore I go. I have been told to join my Recollet brothers in Quebec, who will decide if I am to be permitted to remain within the order. I have been happy among you. I have soothed your pains, I have heard your sorrows, and your generosity has given true meaning to the word of God. My place here will be taken by the Sulpician, Father Felix, whom some of you may have seen. Take him into your hearts as a brother. He has already taken you into his own. Goodbye, my friends. God be with you. And with me."

Never have there been tears shed on the seigneury as there were on that day. Never have such tears been shed since. The Seigneur de Saint-Ours himself was barely able to choke them back.

Father Barthélemy left the same day, accompanied by Virginia, still dressed in her rags, and when they had gone we asked ourselves what was to become of our enterprise. It was all the fault of the bailiff, and I believe he has still more disastrous plans up his sleeve. Never will I listen to that blackguard again.

7

I THOUGHT I had taken care of him, settled him down for good, as I had his older brother, Pascal de Sainte-Foy, but I was mistaken. Two wrongs never do make a right. I was told he would, given time, come to see the wisdom in his marrying the Stillborne woman, but, no, he had to take it into his head to marry an Ursuline, a complete fabrication of his imagination. Poor child. I suppose we must forgive him. Anyone who sleeps as much as he does is bound to have ridiculous dreams.

In any case, a letter arrived here at the convent a few days ago, addressed simply, "To the most beautiful...." It was signed Benjamin de Saint-Ours des Illinois, and some malicious person here delivered it to Sister Souillon. That put the cat in among the pigeons. Now it is up to me to straighten everything out, and I have the distinct feeling that it will not be an easy task.

I have been in this convent for a long time, and I have never had cause to complain before. François-Xavier de Saint-Ours placed me here when he no longer wanted me; he had already put my two sons in the seminary at Quebec. We were an encumbrance to him. Still, I mourned him when he was killed on the Plains of Abraham; I believe he had loved me, in his own way. At least he treated me better than my first husband had, who dreamed only of fortunes and titles for his children and a life of unfettered freedom for himself.

Without intending anything of the sort, François-Xavier did me a kindness (unlooked-for favours are often the best). At first the Sisters had little idea what to make of me; I sat in my cell and cried for days on end, grief-stricken at the loss of my three loved ones. When I finally ventured forth, as I was freely permitted to do, I did not know what to do with myself. The truth was, and I believe I can now confess it, that my sorrow stemmed more from the realization that I could abandon my own children without feeling the slightest remorse. I still ask myself why it is that maternity is considered the natural state of all women. It was certainly not the case with me. The children I have loved most have been those I have chosen to love. Those who were born to me, who were not even the products, much less the objects, of love, I cared for out of duty or habit, not from choice.

Gradually I found such comfort in this convent as I had never expected to know. Even when my family in New England found out where I was, as they eventually did thanks to François-Xavier, who thought they would come and remove me from his conscience forever, I refused to have anything to do with them. I insisted on staying here and taking my vows. The convent had become my homeland.

I am not the first woman to have been captured by Indians, and to have subsequently become an Ursuline. Before me there was Esther Wheelwright, who became Sister Esther Charron. And there have been others, too. The convent has much to offer a woman who has seen too much of men, and too many of the horrors men perpetrate upon themselves. During my first years as a novice, I worked alongside the other Sisters, making Indian artifacts which our order sent back to France and sold as authentic handcrafts, one of the convent's chief sources of income. I needed no instruction, being already skilled in such work, having lived so long among the Malecites before being sold to my merchant husband. When the English took over Quebec, I was given the task of teaching their language to the young ladies of good family who attended our school. In short, we adapted to our new situation, as did everyone else who stayed behind. Assuredly, it is to my knowledge of the English language that I owe my recent elevation to the office of Mother Superior. I have taken the name Mother Saint-Exupère.

I have never been the most religious of the Sisters here, but the convent has afforded me peace, a refuge from a world that is in a constant state of war, and in the end I think I have come to believe in God. Such faith did not come to me through prayer, however, but rather gradually, a slowly growing sense that I am safe here, protected from want and privation. Even during the siege, when I saw that my duty was to aid my fellow citizens without a thought for myself, I maintained my vow of detachment from the world. I regarded all men as my sons, which perhaps is why the fate of my real sons caused me so little anguish:

I saw them as two among so many, and from such a distance, as capable of boundless generosity or unlimited cruelty as any other human beings. I prayed for both of them, but most fervently for Benjamin, the most troubled of the two, and I did everything in my power to instil a touch of humanity in him before sending him back into the world. I sometimes feel that I have given birth to him twice.

I was never as interested in making him a seigneur as his father was. I wanted him to improve, for his own sake, certainly, but mostly for the good of those around him. That was my overriding wish. I now see, of course, how wrong one can be, even with the best intentions in the world. Benjamin might wear a powdered wig and silk stockings, but I suspect he is still the same man who took that boy from the village of the Odawas, his allies on the Hudson River. He lured the child away with promises of returning him to his parents, underwent a thousand hardships to bring him to his parents' village, and then stood with the boy across the river, called all the villagers to come and see him, and when they were gathered, he slit the boy's throat with a knife. The next day, he raised his Straw Man not far from the place. When I heard that story, I excised my son from my heart.

And now here he is, wanting to marry one of my Ursulines. What could have put such an idea in his head? If it were a simple matter, I could easily make certain arrangements on his behalf, if I thought that by doing so I could lay his wild, nomadic nature to rest once and for all. There are plenty of young women here who would not turn their noses up at such a husband. But not Sister Souillon. Never Sister Souillon.

The poor young thing was brought here by a man named Boucane, shortly after the American invasion. She, too, had seen the worst that men can do, and the shock left her as numb as it had me. We took her in, and since then she has absolutely refused, as had I before her, to leave us to return to a world in which such things are not only possible but commonplace. Now the letter from Saint-Ours has thrown her into a state of emotional turmoil, understandably enough, and she comes to me for guidance. That, too, is natural, for I have always seen her as my particular protégée, even though in my mind I call her Sister Scullery, as the others do. The Sisters gave her that name when she first arrived here. She had no other skills, poor child, and so she was put to work in the kitchen, washing dishes and scrubbing floors. Now she has charge of the holy relics belonging to our order: relics of Saint Ursula and of Saint Angèle Merici, our venerated founder, of Saint Honorius, Saint Justin, Saint Modeste, Saint Candide, Saint Vital, Saint Francis of Sales, Saint Ignatius Loyola. She even has charge of our splinter from the Holy Cross, and our cutting from the Crown of Thorns. Every morning she kneels before these precious relics and prays to them with a heart-felt fervour: "I greet you in the Sacred Heart of my Divine Husband!" Her position is greatly envied by our other young charges; it is her crowning glory. We are not always as charitable among ourselves as we are with strangers; when I first came here, they called me Sister Savage. Perhaps they still do.

I was more zealous when she arrived here. I was novice mistress in those days, and from the very start I was a kind of mother to her. Perhaps I overprotected her. I suppose I am to blame if the others here are still somewhat ill disposed towards Sister Souillon, jealous as they might be of the extra affection she received from me. Especially those we call the Blue Bloods, who, before coming here, were brought up in noble families and have retained from their worldly lives a propensity for intrigue. They have never accepted her as one of their own. The same must be said of the others, those we secretly call the Pharisees, who aspire to nothing but total beatification, and whose only pleasure is in finding fault in others. The Blue Bloods take to their prayers and lessons, which save them from the rough life they would otherwise have on the farm or in the bush. The Pharisees revel in hysterical adulation and idle mysticism. The worst of them is Sister Ange-Gardien, who is tiresomely fond of saying that when she allows the host to melt on the tip of her tongue, it turns into the blood of Christ. She is the sworn enemy of Sister Souillon. Nothing would please her more than to put a hair shirt on Sister Scullery's back, indeed on all our backs, as though for her own flesh to be elevated to sainthood requires that everyone else's be abased in mortification. It was almost certainly Sister Ange-Gardien, or else one of the other Pharisees, who slid that letter from Benjamin under Sister Souillon's door. "To the most beautiful..." I suppose I have as sharp a tongue as anyone here, but fortunately I keep it to myself. Most of the time.

Sister Souillon is in a tight spot, and I could very well make it worse for her by trying to get her out of it. The Blue Bloods no less than the Pharisees would like nothing better than to find her with that letter in her hands; they will demand her expulsion from the convent. The former will be happy finally to be rid of the little scullery-maid who has dishonoured their habit; the latter will congratulate themselves on having purified a new lamb in the fires of righteousness. Both will be happy to pray for the salvation of her soul without having to put up with her in the flesh.

This is what the letter said: "Will you dare to give up your servitude and embrace the love that you so greatly deserve? I love you, and yet I know not who you are! Imagine how I would love you if I knew you, as I ardently desire to do. But far be it from me to cause you a moment's anxiety. If it is God whom you love, if your cloistered life is indeed the one you have chosen for all time, then tell me now and I will bow to your wishes and desist from imploring you. But do write to me, a gentleman for whom you have cared and to whom the memory of your gentleness has metamorphosed into a delicate and respectful lover, and who has been the first to discover it. Holding you ever in my affections, I remain, your faithful and humble servant, etc...." Reading it over, I cannot help wondering where Benjamin acquired such a pedantic writing style.

Sister Souillon was afraid of being punished, the poor child. She has done nothing to deserve punishment. I am tempted to launch a discreet inquiry; I cannot imagine who could have delivered this letter. Perhaps Benjamin bribed one of the gardeners or, what would be worse, one of the Sisters wanted to get at me by implicating Sister Souillon in a scandalous intrigue. There is no way of knowing; we are dealing with an invisible enemy.

After reassuring her and swearing her to secrecy, I wrote to Saint-Ours on her behalf: "Monsieur, do not write to me again. You are doing me much more harm than good. You could not know it, but your letter has fallen into the hands of the humblest of God's servants here in the convent. I beg of you, do not commit the sails of your love to such unpredictable winds. You seem to be a gentleman, and there is surely in all this country a soul worthier of your attentions than I. Go with God, monsieur, and leave me my peace and tranquillity, which I have worked so hard to attain…" That summer, I sent Sister Souillon to help with the haying on our farm on the St. Charles River.

I thought the affair was settled. But some time later, Sister Souillon forwarded to me a second letter, which read more or less as follows: "Know, mademoiselle, that I would do anything within my power to have you released from your convent. You say you do not love me, but I can not believe that. You would be much less assiduous in your correspondence with me were you not inspired by a reciprocating sentiment. You said in your last letter that you fear to see your scruples changed into regrets. I swear to you that nothing could be further from the case. I will love you forever…" The thing was getting out of hand. It seemed that there had been other letters, some sent and some received. I knew they had nothing to do with Sister Souillon; she would never have written to him without my permission.

Although I have lived between these walls for a very long time, I yet know little of subtlety. I charged like a captain of dragoons. I rented a carry-all and had it take me directly to the

Saint-Ours manor, where I demanded to speak to the seigneur. He received me immediately and introduced me to his household. There was a schoolteacher named Pâtissant, by whose unctuous phrases I immediately recognized the author of those wretched letters; he spoke with the affectations of one who has never lived outside a book. There was also a bailiff and an apothecary, neither of whom inspired a great deal of confidence. And there was the seigneury's curate, a Recollet named Father Barthélemy, who was no more a priest than I am a virgin. Benjamin was the only one in the room who did not seem nervous at the prospect of dealing with me.

I asked to speak to him privately. When the others left the room, I told him that it was I who had taken care of him during his long convalescence (which in itself was something of a falsehood, since a colleague from Trois-Rivières took over my duties early on), and that some charitable soul had just made a generous donation to our convent, and I desired to know if it was him so that I could thank him in person. That was all. He swore that he had made no such donation, and he thanked me for the trouble I had been put to on his behalf during the Siege of Quebec. As he said this, he seemed mystified. As well he might, for he must have been harbouring in his imagination the image of someone much younger than I, a woman of his own age, not a greying old Sister with a wrinkled face, old enough to be his mother.

And yet, I was proud of him. He comportment towards me was that of a seigneur, exactly what his father had wanted. Life seemed to have put some polish on him. He offered me his hospitality for the night, which I of course refused, and while accompanying me back to my carry-all, he asked if I were acquainted with a certain Sister Ange-Gardien. Yes, I replied evenly; we buried her last week. She died peacefully in her eightieth year. His expression never changed. Life seemed also to have taught him the art of dissimulation. Did I regret hardly recognizing my son behind his new façade? Had he changed so much? Or was it his powdered wig that made him look older? It did not matter, either way.

No more letters arrived at the convent. And last week, I read in the Quebec *Gazette* that Claridge of Stillborne has become affianced to the Sieur Pâtissant. Sister Ange-Gardien is no longer among us; she is not dead, merely returned to the affections of her family. I invented that story for Benjamin on the spur of the moment. It is no longer of any importance, but it lent an amusing aspect to our meeting.

The end of all my efforts has been to save little Sister Souillon, and this I have done. I can now assure her that there is nothing more to fear from Saint-Ours; he will not come back. Calm yourself, my dear little Marjolaine.

8

IT has been a full year since I left the Seigneury de la Sapinière, my transitory homeland, and my only regret is that I did not leave it sooner. At the time of this writing, I am wintering at the Moravian mission at Châteaux Bay, on the Labrador coast. The Eskimos here have graciously consented to my prolonged presence, and every day we exchange gestures of open friendship. The Danish brother in charge of this unlikely outpost of God is known as Brother Christian, and I would converse with him willingly would he but speak any language other than New Testament Latin.

Fortunately there are newspapers to read. I have a stack of them from my old secretary Toussaint and another pile given me by the Marquise de Stillborne as a going-away present. Some of them are twenty years old. Reading them affords me the pleasure of remembering things past, and when I have digested them thoroughly, I use them to paper the walls of my little ship.

It amuses me to live surrounded by newspapers. I absorb their contents with a detachment I would have found impossible had I been awake when the events they report actually took place. I enjoy trying to guess how things turned out; when I am wrong, I can smile, and when I am right, I laugh.

Perhaps I ought to have read them before leaving. Reading them now has greatly improved my vocabulary, and the knowledge I have gained might have made up for my poor elocution. I have come to realize that in Canada, this country in which I have lived so long against my will, prestige is a simple matter of how well you control words. This is a pity, because charlatans are much encouraged to profit thereby. But I would do the same were I in their shoes.

Some of the news is fascinating. There is a story, for example, about tea in Boston; the Americans threw tons of it into the harbour, thereby signalling the start of their so-called War of Independence. Such a tempest for a teapot! And I very much enjoyed reading about the American invasion of Quebec. Obviously this was given in the New York papers as a triumphant campaign; in the London gazettes, scorn is heaped upon the invaders. I discovered that while reading these varied accounts, I oscillated between the two points of view; in some ways, I hardly differ from the habitants of Sapinière. Both sides ended with a conqueror and a conquered, but I must confess to feeling indifferent to the outcome. It is not the end of a story that I enjoy, but the telling of it.

Other news is less amusing. The revolt in Corsica has been put down, for example. There were terrible reprisals in Bastia: thousands of rebels racked or hanged in the church forecourts. They seem to have treated the Corsicans as badly as we treat our Indians. Miss Claridge informed me that Juchereau de Saint-Denis, my old compatriot in Quebec, took part in the Corsican massacre. It is worth asking how so gentle a schoolmaster as Pâtissant and his two usual enemies, the bailiff and the apothecary, could be so united in their admiration of France, which has shown itself to be so unimaginably cruel. Perhaps it is because they have never been there. Or perhaps they do not read the newspapers carefully enough. They ought to be more discerning.

Ah, France has a new king, I see: another Louis, the sixteenth to bear that name. Is there so little imagination in kings, one wonders, that they must keep coming up with the same name? No matter....And the Marquis de La Fayette has just landed at Providence. When was that? August 1777. Why could he not have landed at Quebec instead? With his army he could easily have liberated Canada from the English in no time, and all our plottings would have borne fruit. The apothecary and the bailiff, how happy they would have been. Even the schoolmaster went about with a conspiratorial mien; I suspect he would have been far more comfortable as an American than as a Canadian. Of course, they would all have greatly preferred to be French. Anyone with any learning at all has this defect, that they would much rather be mistaken for what they are not than taken for what they are. But let us leave that. A twenty-three-year-old marquis like La Fayette cannot be taken too seriously; besides, the American rebels won, and that, I imagine, is what counts. And now I see they are going to erect a statue of Louis XVI in Philadelphia. Which, when one thinks about it, is not as ludicrous as it seems. A king acquires a certain cachet in a republic.

The French papers say that France is thinking of liberating Ireland. They do not think of liberating Canada, I see; perhaps they think we are free enough as it is. Not exactly free, perhaps, but far enough from Europe that it amounts to the same thing. I wonder if there are any nations in the world contemplating the liberation of France from the French?

Well, well. "Franklin Embraces Voltaire in Paris!" The two are as friendly as fellow Freemasons ought to be, and understandably so. "La Fayette Receives Hero's Welcome in Brest, Crowned with Laurels in Paris!" America admires France, France loves America. And no one ever talks about Canada. No wonder the bailiff and the schoolmaster want to be mistaken for Americans. The apothecary dreams of being mistaken for an Englishman, which is hardly any better.

Scorn is heaped on poor old Bougainville in the popular

presses in France. He is called a coward for having been late to rendezvous with Admiral de Grasse in April 1782, as a result of which the admiral's flagship was utterly destroyed by the British fleet. Well, he never was a stickler for promptness, was he? It was the same at Quebec, when he failed to come to Montcalm's aid. But I like his excuse this time: the cattle he had on board to feed the marines broke out of their enclosures and ran about on the gun deck, to the confusion of the cannoneers. He has a survivor's imagination, does Bougainville; no wonder he writes so well. He would have been better off had he stuck to exploring and discovering; he was better in that role, and it would have brought him greater glory than all his military endeavours. I would have liked to tell this story to Father Barthélemy, he would have laughed heartily. Aha! I see that Captain Cook has finally found Australia. Bougainville missed it by a few hundred leagues, it seems. Now England is sending all its thieves and prostitutes there. No doubt it is worth the cost of discovering a new continent if you can turn it into a penal colony.

All these wars and rumours of wars wear me out. I am much refreshed, however, by the many accounts of our attempts to fly. There are, for example, the Montgolfier brothers, who conceived the idea of launching into the air a flying machine made of cloth and paper. It stayed aloft for seven or eight minutes, it says here, and then crashed to the ground and burst into flames. Is there not here a venture that will improve the lot of humanity? Even better is the story from Versailles, where someone attached a wicker basket to a balloon and sent up a sheep, a duck and a cock. Oh, brave new beasts of the air! How I envy you your borrowed plumes! How I would fly with you!

When I was yet the Seigneur de Saint-Ours, I wanted to repeat the successes of these French balloonists, but my tenant farmers always discouraged me from the attempt. When I spoke of it, they looked at me as though at a madman. Don't do it, sire, they would say. And then, when I persisted: Why are you so keen to get away? What is so wrong with this place? Even

Pâtissant looked at me dubiously. Perhaps he had read the same accounts as I.

The French papers are celebrating the treaty between France and the United States of America. The few journals I have from New York from the year 1783 are also full of the news. Still not a word about Canada. It's as though we don't exist. And, of course, we will cease to exist, except in our own imaginations. Perhaps that is why Monsieur Stillborne dreams of becoming a British nobleman.

It says here that a *Te Deum* has been sung at the Notre-Dame Cathedral in Paris to celebrate the surrender of Lord Cornwallis at Washington and Rochambeau. I wonder if the celebrants have really thought about the words to the *Te Deum?* It is also reported that the first American Loyalists have arrived in Nova Scotia. And there is an interesting article on the cultivation of the potato, which settlers are forbidden to eat for fear that its high food value will render all Canadians lazy and all Indians independent.

And they have buried Harlequin, one of the actors of the Italian Comedy in Paris. I thought the Church had forbidden burial to actors, that Molière himself had had to be buried secretly. One learns something anew every day when you read the newspapers. It seems the proscription applies only to French actors, and Harlequin was an Italian character. A pretty conceit. Father Barthélemy would have enjoyed that one, too, I am sure.

I would also like to have told him about Father Pascal, the priest they burned alive in the Place de Grève for having murdered a little Savoyard boy who spurned his advances. According to the papers, it was the most talked-about execution in Paris since that of Damiens. There must be forty thousand pederasts in Paris; their preferred meeting place is the Jardin des Tuileries. A royal garden, no less....Come to think of it, it is not a bad choice. I would like to see the Tuileries some day. It is one of those places I have seen only in my mind's eye, and for some reason that is becoming less and less satisfying to me.

Ah! Here is another that pleases me. A man has succeeded in flying one of the Montgolfier brothers' inventions. His name is Pilâtre de Rozier, and he took the machine up to three hundred feet above the ground; he might have gone higher, but the machine was tethered to the ground by means of a rope. A month later, at La Muette, before the dauphin and his entire assembled court, de Rozier took the machine up again and flew over Paris for twenty-five minutes. He was accompanied by the Marquis d'Arlandes. It seems the two men's faces were as black as coal miners' when they landed, because of the smoke. I had to laugh, but since reading the account I have felt more than a twinge of jealousy, and I understand now why Pâtissant and the others speak so well of France.

The medical news is also good. Experiments are underway at the Célestine Hospital using electricity for the treatment of certain ailments, under the supervision of the father of electricity himself, Benjamin Franklin. I wonder if, had I had such treatment, it would have cured me of my sleeping sickness. I would also have liked to have had myself hypnotized by Dr. Mesmer, who is making a fortune at it. The Comte de Saint-Germain has died. And Monsieur Diderot. (I do not know who these worthies might be, but I must acquaint myself with them in the event that I end up in France one day. It is like storing up provisions for a voyage.)

More news on the balloon front. Someone has calculated that a balloonist could make a trip around the world in twenty-four hours, but no one is taking him seriously. I do not laugh, however; I know that men are capable of many things that seem impossible. Women, too, for that matter. Here – what did I tell you – here is a newspaper from 1784 that says a woman has flown the montgolfier Marie-Antoinette! No, there is no holding back progress. I also read that actors have been given the right to vote. That is what I call progress.

And another bit of news has caught my eye, more moving than all the rest. My old enemy from Quebec, Captain Cook, who became such a great explorer, has been killed and eaten by savages in Hawaii. They waste nothing there, it seems.

Deputy Pâtissant? Do I read aright? Yes, there he is in black and white: Pâtissant elected to the Legislative Assembly of Lower Canada. What good news! I wonder how he managed it? Perhaps he finally married the marquise, which would have allowed him to use her seigneury as a home riding. I hope that is the case; I always thought they should marry. It would have got her out of my perruque, for one thing, and it would have been the making of him.

I think I managed to convince Claridge that I was in love with the Ursuline. It is perhaps closer to the truth that in those days I loved the idea of being in love, that I required some kind of emotional attachment to cure me of my idleness. I never did find out who the Ursuline was, but her memory filled my dreams and in the end strengthened my resolve to leave Sapinière. Her shadow unknowingly accomplished some good, after all.

And yet I have never solved the mystery of her. Who was she? All I know is that one day I began receiving letters from an Ursuline in Quebec, who felt obliged to tell me that she could never love me. I had simply asked Pâtissant to make some discreet inquiries, to find out who the nun was that I had so briefly seen through my window during my awakening. The letters she sent me were so curious. It was as though she were approaching me in order to flee from me; in the end she even began singing the praises of Miss Stillborne. I became very suspicious when one of the letters came to me signed, the only one that ever bore a name: Sister Ange-Gardien. It meant nothing to me. Once again, I asked Pâtissant to look into it, and he seemed as perplexed as I was. Then another letter arrived, as anonymous as the others had been, asking me to present myself at the convent and to ask for a Sister Souillon. At that point, I realized I understood nothing about anything. I was a poor puppet in someone else's Punch-and-Judy show, I said to myself, and the worst of it was, it was not for the first time.

The next thing I knew, the Mother Superior of the convent turned up at my door, Sister Saint-Exupère. I recognized her as the nun who had saved my life after the Siege of Quebec, but when I thanked her for that kindness, she told me that this Sister Ange-Gardien had just died of old age. It took all my self-control to keep myself from bursting out laughing. The whole story has done me a world of good. I gave up mooning about the seigneury like a love-sick puppy, and encouraged Pâtissant to bestow his letter-writing skills upon Mademoiselle de Stillborne, this time on his own behalf. I said it would help pass the time until he could find some students.

9

WE have erected Monsieur's gravestone. He is not dead yet, but that doesn't matter.

We made it from the best field stones we could find; it would have been highly ungrateful on our part not to somehow mark his passage among us. It would also have been demoralizing for our children's children if they thought Monsieur had not even taken the trouble to die here, as a founder is supposed to do. Look at Maisonneuve, in Montreal. Our young people are sorely tempted by the idea of emigrating; we have to contain the exodus at all costs if we are not to be left alone in this country of frost and mosquitoes. We wouldn't want our future generations to imitate Monsieur's peripatetic ways; we want them to celebrate him as a builder. I have taken that on as my mission.

So we place flowers on his tomb every week when they are available. At Martinmas, the women of the seigneury bring little round loaves of bread marked with the Holy Cross to the manor, even though he no longer lives there. I have also invented a little patriotic holiday, which I call Saint-Ours Day, during which we wax eloquently about his memory. Before I die I will write his biography, and if I have any money to leave behind, I hope it can be used to raise a bronze statue somewhere on the seigneury grounds. One way or another, it is my fondest hope that people in these parts will forget that there is no one lying in the magnificent tomb of Benjamin de Saint-Ours des Illinois.

Although I was only the humble bailiff Grégoire when he knew me, today I am a King's Counsel under the reign of King George, and this cult of Saint-Ours was my idea. When he left, he gratified me with the task of drawing up his will, and I have executed that duty with the greatest possible scrupulosity, following his every wish, and adding a few wishes of my own, as well.

We tried everything to keep him with us. One day, poor old Boucane even hanged himself in his blacksmith shop. He was found by Gaspard, the apothecary, who had come to pay him back some money he owed him. If Gaspard had arrived three minutes later, his debt would have been settled. As it was, he ran out of the shop and fetched Monsieur, who snatched up an axe, ran back to the shop and cut Boucane down with a single swing.

Boucane went around with a strangled voice for a long time, and a scar around his neck. He cried almost constantly. I think he felt as bad about causing Monsieur so much anxiety as he would have if Monsieur had left. "I am an old man," he told Monsieur, "and I could not stand the idea of you going away. I want you to stay here, with us..." Monsieur was deeply moved.

The incident made Monsieur realize just how much he was liked around here. Afterwards, he called all the tenant farmers to a meeting and asked them if it would really mean that much to them if he went away. Everyone said yes, it would, even those who didn't like him all that much. "We want you to stay here so that everything will remain exactly as it is," they said. "We like the way things are. Please, Monsieur, do not leave us." Well, he thought about it for a while; then he did exactly as he wanted, as was his habit.

A short while after the meeting, he called the heads of all the seigneury families to the manor and divided up his cash among them. Then he called upon me to formally make a gift of his possessions to his best friends. Surprisingly, he left nothing to his children. Nicholas and Jeremy I understand; they are no longer here and have their own lives. But the young ones, Josué and Apolline? He did not seem concerned about their welfare at all.

"They do not need anything," he said with a sigh when I questioned him about it, as though their financial independence was a source of sorrow to him. Thanks to some string-pulling by Major Stillborne, Josué had a post in the Royal Navy. He will spend the rest of his days in the arms of a sultry mistress at the other end of the world, or else in those of a pretty English maiden with a cottage somewhere in the Cotswolds. In any case, I wish him happiness of it. As for Apolline, she is still living in Detroit, so far as we know. We never hear from her. "I have only one daughter," Monsieur told me at the end of our conference. "Marjolaine, the daughter of my Valentine. She was so kind to me, I would leave her my house and lands if I knew where she was. But she has disappeared I know not where."

His house and lands? To whom did he wish to leave them, I asked him. "Everything to Father Barthélemy and his house-keeper," he said. "He'll need them, seeing that he is not a priest, and that Virginia is too sick herself to look after anyone else. He is my dearest friend. I am the only one who knows that, but that is of no consequence." It is true that both Barthélemy and Virginia are in dire need.

Barthélemy tried to seduce Monsieur into staying on by the lure of lucre. He opened that brewery of his, which was going to make us all as rich as Croesus. Especially Monsieur. But that idiot apothecary went and denounced him to the bishop as a false priest, and the good Father left us soon afterwards, on a cold, grey day in November, our good, old friend, taking nothing with him but his ragged grey robe, a sack, his begging cup and a walking stick. And Virginia, of course, who walked behind him with her dog – the two poor souls he had welcomed into his church.

The next day, a group of men tied up at the dock. They

marched up to the church and dismantled the shed that had been serving as the brewery, and carried off it and its contents. It took them less than two days. Barthélemy had sold everything to Major Stillborne.

And so the habitants who had planted wheat, barley and hops sold their harvest to the Seigneur du Bec. And when the Sulpician from France arrived to take possession of the church, he found it returned to the condition it had been in before the Recollet had come here: broken windows, porch caving in, the yard littered with human excrement, chickens nesting and roosting in the confessionals and in the rood-loft, feral cats and dogs fighting under the altar. The garden had been ransacked, the presbytery reduced to a few old boards. We were hardly surprised when the Sulpician took a look around and high-tailed it back to Quebec; we are now waiting patiently for the French Revolution to send us another one.

As it turned out, the Recollet and his housekeeper did not go far. As soon as they set foot on the next seigneury, Major Stillborne met them with a cart and horse to take them back to his manor. Barthélemy is now back making beer, and since he believes it is necessary to be a man of God to make good beer, Stillborne has had him made pastor of the seigneury by the Anglican bishop in Quebec. Barthélemy said Mass in a beautiful red-brick church and lived in a grand manse with his wife, Virginia, his former housekeeper and a charlatan.

Such happiness could not last, however. When Stillborne died, his cousin Claridge sold the brewery to the ship's outfitter Molson, from Montreal, and used the money to buy her marquisate. Then she removed Mr. and Mrs. Barthélemy from the premises; she did not find them distinguished enough for her. She also found his sermons incomprehensible. Indeed, to follow them did require a fairly thorough knowledge of French and an ear for dialect. His three parishioners complained that they could not make out a word, and even the sympathetic Stillborne, when he was alive, often had to leave the church so that his laughter would not disturb the service. Once again, the Saint-Ours manor took in the twice-fallen pastor and his ragged wife.

Pâtissant inherited his house on condition that he get some students in it one day. The Marquise de Stillborne got the library, so that, as Monsieur said, she could continue to live her life through books, which were her true country. She'll have enough country now to keep her at home for the next hundred and twenty years. Monsieur also left her his sins, since, he said, she had committed so few of her own.

I would have liked to have been given the newspapers, at least, but he decided to take them with him, which surprised me. "Sorry," he told me, "but these old papers have been indispensable to me ever since I read the Declaration of the Rights of Man in the Quebec *Gazette*, in the same issue that contained a notice offering a reward for the recapture of a runaway slave. The runaway slave turned out to be the same man who turned the presses for the newspaper. It is such delicious idiocies that help me to bear the burden of time." I could hardly insist.

Boucane kept his forge and the shop he lived in. To punish him for having tried to hang himself, Monsieur ordered him to help build the vessel that would take him away from us. At least Boucane insisted on building a ship and not a montgolfier, which is what Monsieur had been dreaming of. He wanted to fly around the world, he said. But in the end he gave up this scheme. It still remains to be done. I am not sanguine about Monsieur's talents as an aeronaut, but I am fairly confident that he can steer a ship.

We convinced Father Barthélemy to make one final attempt to keep Monsieur from sailing out of our lives. He placed himself at the head of a delegation that included Pâtissant, the apothecary and all the tenant farmers. A lot of people. Even the marquise was among them. Monsieur was working on his ship with Boucane when we arrived. Barthélemy presented all the arguments with which we had armed him beforehand, and he spoke eloquently and with sincerity. He spoke mostly about the revolution that was going on in France. All the while he was talking, Monsieur kept working – planing boards, hammering nails – looking up now and then to let Barthélemy know that he was listening. But it took only a few words from Benjamin to win the oratorical jousting match.

"My good friends," he said when Barthélemy had finished, "you all know that I love you dearly, each and every one of you. But you all know, too, that I have no other choice but to leave. I must go to earn what is rightfully mine. The King of France owes me the Cross of Saint-Louis, and I am not coming back here until I have the Girdle of Fire around my waist. I have spoken!" And so saying, he offered us a drink and we all went home satisfied.

Satisfied and relieved. Especially the tenant farmers, who liked Monsieur well enough but who also worried that he would take back the generous gift of cash he had given them. It was the same with the others – Pâtissant, the apothecary, even Boucane. As for me, I inherited nothing from him, but he had paid me more to draw up his will than I could otherwise earn in three years. You can see why no one really insisted after that. Monsieur had thought of everything.

Except that no one really believed his story about the Cross of Saint-Louis. We saw through it right away. Monsieur could be as mischievous as anyone. He knew full well that we do not want people here who cannot put down roots. People like his son, Nicholas, who is an adventurer and so is considered a stranger by us, no matter how much we might envy his success. We refuse to forgive an exile, but we will gladly absolve anyone who wants to return to the Old Country. On the seigneury, we never spoke so well of "Monseigneur de Saint-Ours" as after he had told us that he was coming back.

In the end, we could not resist making one last effort. We on the seigneury have always known that Benjamin de Saint-Ours was awarded the Cross of Saint-Louis on his hospital bed after the Battle of Quebec. It was Bougainville himself who gave it to him. Afterwards, the cross was placed for safe-keeping in the church here on the seigneury; to hide it from the English it had been built into the monstrance. It is still there. All we had to do was tell him, if we wanted to keep him here. If his words to us had been sincere, there would then be no need for him to leave.

We told the story to Barthélemy, but he advised us not to tell our secret to Monsieur. He must be allowed to pursue his own destiny, said the good Father. We suspect he was also afraid of incurring the seigneur's wrath, since he would naturally want to know why we had waited so long to tell him. We could also have told him that the king could not give him the Cross of Saint-Louis anyway, seeing that he had been beheaded by his subjects. Perhaps we ought to have told him that.

Instead, we held a feast for his departure that he will not soon forget. Neither will we. Everyone was there, even the Mother Superior from the Ursuline convent in Quebec, Sister Saint-Exupère. Boucane went all the way to Quebec to bring her here. (Boucane and the Sister had been husband and wife at one time, when they lived up in the bush; everyone here knows that, but no one talks about it.) The party lasted all day, and Monsieur left at sunset. It was an autumn evening.

His tomb sits at the top of a little hill, deep in the seigneury. We took that precaution so that what happened to Major Stillborne's grave would not happen to Monsieur's.

When Monsieur de Stillborne's soul returned to his Maker, his heiress, the marquise of the same name, who is not from these parts but who has had the great good sense to stay here, had his body buried in the little Anglican cemetery down by the river. Pastor Barthélemy performed the ceremony and gave a grand elegy in English. If he understood what he was saying, he was the only one present who did. But the following spring, when the ice melted, the cemetery was flooded and its only tenant, Monsieur de Stillborne, floated off and joined the main stream of the St. Lawrence. We tried to run after him, but

Monsieur de Saint-Ours and his friend Decatte were too quick for us.

They caught up with the coffin, but instead of bringing it back for reburial, they hoisted it into their ship and took it farther out to sea, and then they released it. They wanted it to float all the way to England, the land to which Monsieur de Stillborne had longed to return as a marquis. It was their final tribute to him, they explained when they came back. The marquise was not well pleased; she said now she will have to lie alone for all eternity in the family crypt.

When they returned from their small mission of mercy, the Abenaki turned to Monsieur and asked him, "When do you plan to follow your friend Stillborne?"

"Soon," replied Monsieur. "Before I die, at any rate."

He has kept his word.

10

I AM not dead yet. Far from it: I am more alive than ever. I have been out of what it pleases some to call "my country" now for more than a year, and never have I feared boredom so little. When I left, it was as though I had brought the whole village with me in my head, and I call up their ghosts to keep me company when I realize I am rereading one of my gazettes for the thirtieth time. My memories keep me happy and warm. I know I have often said that nothing ever happens in this country of the damned, but I now see that I was wrong. Everything happens here.

One day, I tried to hang myself. Boucane cut me down just in time; I suppose he owed me that. I was in despair because for the third time I had found a hole in my ship, and I thought someone was going to great lengths to prevent me from leaving. I could not resign myself to accept once and for all that this empty land was to be my permanent home; that I would remain in it forever, stretched out in it as though in my coffin.

I suppose that is what convinced the others that I was serious. From then on, at any rate, they stopped telling me that I was too old, that the king would never give me the Cross of Saint-Louis, and so on. They even pitched in and helped me patch up my boat and fill it with provisions. And then they threw a huge party for me on the day that I left. It was the happiest moment of my life. Village life is all very well, but it is long; each morning is the same, all the seasons are identical. How can anyone mark the passage of time in a village? I can honestly say that I experienced eternity before I experienced death. Now I will live twice as long as I am alive.

It seems funny to me, to be here on a ship that my tenant farmers used to tease me about, saying it looked like a coffin. I knew her for a good, sound ship, but their gibes stuck in my ear; fortunately, I don't think about it anymore. Her hull is stout and round, ideal for navigating among the ice floes we were certain to encounter on our route. She has a solid mast that takes a good sail, and the rest of her is made of heavy wood and thick nails. Boucane knew his job. And I have provisions to last me at least a year.

And so here I am, living on water, as the saying is, for as long as I can. I know I could never take her across the Atlantic to France, but I have made it as far as Newfoundland. And from here, who knows? Maybe Iceland, where I might run into some fishermen who could escort me to Scotland. And from there, Europe...

Not everything has unravelled according to plan, but nothing serious has gone wrong. When push comes to shove, plans are nothing but applied dreams, their primary purpose being to lift us out of our lethargy. At least, that is true of my own plans. For now, I can make new plans, for I see that I have my whole life ahead of me. And I must leave room for chance, which can be even more beautiful than life itself.

I have halted my voyage here at Châteaux Bay in Labrador. The sea was too rough and I was afraid for my ship. Wintering among the Moravian Eskimos has been pleasant, and I have even been tempted to stay on for a while longer. Contrary to what I was told to expect, they have entertained no malice towards me. Far from it, in fact; they have welcomed me as a brother. I have lost no provisions, and they have not so much as touched my ship, although I was warned that they were like magnets to anything made of metal, that they would pull the nails right out of my hull.

Among these people, whose language and customs are so strange to me, I have found a new native country, and it has reawakened my memory. Once again I am a man. I have forever buried Benjamin, adopted name Saint-Ours, called Saint-Ours des Illinois, warrior murderer, also known as the Straw Man, brother of Pascal of Santa Fe who is now a Spanish nobleman and who will soon be an American, son of an unknown fur trader and a stolen, forgotten woman – Monsieur de Saint-Ours, Seigneur de la Sapinière, recipient of the Cross of Saint-Louis.

Oh, yes, I know about that. Father Barthélemy told me about it himself, the night before my departure. He even took me into the church to show it to me, hidden craftily in the monstrance. He thought I would stay if I saw it. "Your voyage is now purposeless," he said, "and even if you took it with you, they would guillotine you the minute you stepped onto French soil, just to get it off your neck." He did not know, the dear man, that the new man who was growing inside me had long ago forsworn such trinkets, had long since ceased to be the dupe of all these well-meaning citizens who only wanted what was good for me. I no longer wanted payment for what the conquerors call exploits and the conquered call crimes. I was no longer tormented by the dream of the Indian woman with her human puppies. I have to search deep in my unconscious to recall that image now, and when I do, it is not terror that I feel, but tenderness.

I did not believe all the stories Barthélemy's compatriots told me about the goings-on in France. To hear them speak, you would think France had become a kind of hell. They had lied to me so often, their accounts were mere fabrications meant to bind me to them; I wanted to see for myself. To see Versailles, to see if the king really was a big ball of grease, and to see if he really would be glad to see me. Borders mean little to me now, as little as when I was a young man. I am that young man, part animal, whom I once knew so well, and who promised himself he would stroll in the Tuileries one day with a former Ursuline nun on his arm. No harm in trying…

And then my new friends the Eskimos and Brother Christian, they, too, wanted to keep me with them. It's as though everywhere I go a village forms around me and then turns into a prison. If I had listened to them I would be married three times over with my feet planted there in solid ground. Brother Christian implored me to at least wait for the next ship to reprovision them in the spring, but I had already been there several months and I could not wait any longer. I left fond memories there, too. They taught me much that was useful, and it is to their knowledge that I owe my life.

I left at the beginning of September, I think it was, time being so vague now. My ship flew south towards Newfoundland, hugging the coastline. When I reached the big island, I spent some time in a rough shelter built on shore and abandoned by fishermen. I needed the time to make some repairs and to kill a caribou and dry its meat. I was then ready to set out again.

A few nights later, however, what I thought had been solid ground under me suddenly shuddered and groaned and slid away from the mainland. I was terrified. It took me some little time to determine that I was on an ice floe – a huge, floating continent of ice. Fortunately I had pulled my ship well up out of the water; climbing into it, I was able to keep dry. In the morning, I ventured outside and built an igloo, partly to give myself a second shelter but mostly for the pleasure of putting something I had learned from the Eskimos to good use. I could not know

where the ice was taking me, what river of winds it would follow. We were floating towards the unknown, and if I was unconcerned, it was because that is exactly where I wanted to go.

Since then I have made a quiet life for myself here on the floe.
I am as happy as a pope. I have plenty to eat, fuel to keep me
warm, and for distraction I catch birds in a net: puffins, mostly
– their dark flesh when lightly cooked is a true delicacy. My floe
could break apart at any moment, of course, and I and my ship
could be plunged back into the ocean. But I am ready for that. I
see the possibility as a promise of new adventures.

I must still be close to the mainland. Last night I lit a fire
because it occurred to me that I might be able to communicate
with the island. I saw several fires roar up in response, and we
had a kind of dialogue between myself and those distant,
unknown fire-tenders. I tried to read words in their flickering
flames. Four days ago, a white bear climbed onto my floe, a powerful beast who must have swum here all the way from
Greenland. He began to shake my boat and woke me up.
Perhaps he smelled the food I had fortunately stored inside.
When he saw me, he immediately threw himself upon me, no
doubt mistaking me for a seal. It was either him or me. It was me.

I fired my flintlock point-blank into his chest. He recoiled,
and I watched him die from a distance. When I went up to him
to assure myself that he was dead, he rose up and threw himself
on me again, fetching my face a powerful blow with his paw. He
merely grazed me, but there was much blood and a deep gash.
If my friends in Sapinière could see me, they would not recognize me under this scarred mask. From time to time the wound
re-opens and fresh blood reddens my beard, which is otherwise
white from old age and rimed with hoarfrost.

I asked the bear's forgiveness for having killed it, as I had
been taught long ago, and then I skinned it and ate the best
parts. I stuck his head on a pike and tied my powdered wig to it
with my black silk seigneur's stockings. At night I cover myself
with his skin and dance about his head to keep warm. I look for-

ward to the day when I can launch my ship in the water again, or meet up with a larger vessel en route to Iceland, or New England, anywhere.

When I have absolutely nothing else to do, I make up stories. I think of Valentine and invent a life for her since she left the manor. I imagine she finds our daughter Marjolaine on a large plantation in Virginia, and sells herself to the planter so she can be near her little girl. Then the planter is made the United States ambassador to Paris, and he gives Marjolaine and Valentine their freedom and takes them with him to France to show them the revolution. Today, Marjolaine is the mistress of a man with a great deal of political influence, a very wealthy man, and he treats Valentine like the queen that she is. All the stories I make up end happily.

My only hardship is that, also like a pope, I am condemned to a life of celibacy. I have enough love within me for a hundred women, at the very least one, if that is my lot. But I must let all that pass for now, and console myself with the thought that I have never been able to love a woman until now because never before have I had so much time to dream her up beforehand. Now that I know how to do it, I am ready.

I think a great deal about the little Ursuline. I dreamed her up, but I was never able to find her in reality. She made me so love-sick, I loved her so solitarily, that I conjure her image now to tell her all the things I was never able to tell her before. I caress her in all her unknown places; I whisper long impassioned speeches that she will never find in any book. We only love those whom we think we love, and I have all the time in the world to think about loving her. On the other hand, I never think about that Sister Ange-Gardien, although she wrote such nice letters, and whom I readily forgive for deceiving me in the matter of her age.

If only my dear friends on the seigneury could see me, draped in a white bearskin, my face a livid scar. I think about them often, and the farther I drift from their neighbourhood, the more I love them. I do not know why that should be, but the merest thought of my tenant farmers is like a nugget of nourishment to me. I see myself among them again, slicing bread and reaching for the jar of molasses or the serviceberry jam. Valentine's jam, which always tasted so good.

One of the memories that keeps recurring is that of the farewell feast they held on my behalf. Old Auguste, my notary-turned-bailiff, who wanted nothing grander than to be a sword-swallower. Boucane, the former Zacharias, the man who could do anything, even make a bear dance if there was one to hand, and who could do magic tricks. Even the good Ursuline, who came all the way from Quebec to say goodbye. I see her now, frail, leaning on Boucane's arm. They would have made a good couple; I hope someone tells them that one day.

And then there was Blaise the Executioner, who became first an apothecary and then a doctor, who loved to tell his lewd stories. And Barnaby, my faithful secretary, now the schoolmaster and the perpetual fiancé of the Marquise de Stillborne, who can still turn a clean somersault and chatter away like anything. Old Pantaloon, who recited *The Imaginary Invalid* to us, who became a king's messenger for a while, until he saw that he was better suited to the role of Father Barthélemy. The rag-and-bone lady Virginia, the executioness, the Queen of Hungary, who can dance like the wind despite her age. Claridge of Stillborne, who stirred our memories as Clémence and sang such rowdy refrains as Colombine, just to make us laugh. I recognized them all, all of them.

Which leaves only Valentine, whom I hope to see again, perhaps in Paris. We shared so much, we two. Especially when all I wanted was to be their little prompter.

This village, the memory of a lifetime. And now the great voyage begins.